Smoked Mullet

Freaky Florida Mystery Adventures, Volume 7

Margaret Lashley

Published by Zazzy Ideas, Inc., 2021.

Copyright

Copyright 2021 Margaret Lashley
MargaretLashley.com
Cover Design by Melinda de Ross

All rights reserved. No part of this book may be used or reproduced by any means, graphic, electronic, or mechanical, including photocopying, recording, taping or by any information storage retrieval system without the written permission of the author except in the case of brief quotations embodied in critical articles and reviews.

The scanning, uploading, and distribution of this book via the Internet or via any other means without the permission of the publisher is illegal and punishable by law. Please purchase only authorized electronic editions, and do not participate in or encourage electronic piracy of copyrighted materials. Your support of the author's rights is appreciated.

For more information, write to: Zazzy Ideas, Inc. P.O. Box 1113, St. Petersburg, FL 33731

This book is a work of fiction. While actual places throughout Florida have been used in this book, any resemblance to persons living or dead are purely coincidental. Unless otherwise noted, the author and the publisher make no explicit guarantees as to the accuracy of the information contained in this book and in some cases, the names of places have been altered.

What Readers are Saying about Freaky Florida Mystery Adventures ...

"I have read Tim Dorsey, Carl Hiaasen, and Randy Wayne White. Those writers are funny but they need to watch out for you."
"Hilarious, weird, and entertaining!"
"I am a mystery reader, but these books made me not care who done it. This Margaret Lashley is a game changer."
"Funny, unpredictable, pure Florida weirdness served up on a hard-to-put-down platter."
"Not too scary or over-the-top paranormal. A truly fun read!"
"The story lines are crazy, and all you want is more!"
"A funny cozy, science fiction, thriller, mystery all rolled into one great story!"
"I read a lot, and Kindle suggested your book. This is laugh out loud funny. Is everyone in Florida crazy?"
"Margaret Lashley has a knack for creating funny, small town strange, off the wall, but so endearing type of characters."
"If you enjoy laugh-out-loud comedy, this book is for you!"

Prologue

Nine months had passed since I first met the odd, yet enigmatic private eye named Nick Grayson. Thanks to him, in the time it takes to gestate a baby, I'd seen enough crazy things to make me question why anyone would ever want to bring a child into this wacko world in the first place.

Don't get me wrong. Even though kids weren't on my agenda, that didn't mean I never wanted to have *sex* again.

Quite the opposite, in fact.

The accident that separated me from my vestigial gonad twin (long story) had also stripped Grayson of his weird fedora and cheesy moustache. (Whichever cosmic entity was responsible for that, thank you on all counts!)

The only problem was, without his shtick disguise, Grayson was actually kind of a *hottie*. And then the guy went and planted a kiss on me earlier this afternoon ...

Mama mia!

For a brief moment, I'd been on cloud nine. But then my distrusting nature had kicked in and I'd fallen back to earth.

Hard.

Grayson had kissed me right after he'd found out my bank account had gone from zero to a million dollars in three seconds flat—thanks to the largess of an unnamed benefactor.

Coincidence? No. Grayson had drilled into me that there was no such thing.

So that left only two possibilities. Either Grayson had romantic feelings for me, or he was after my cold, hard, cash.

For historical accuracy, it was Grayson who'd instigated our odd relationship in the first place. Before I'd had a dime to my name, he'd chosen to mentor me as his P.I. intern. Exactly why, I still wasn't sure. The only things I'd had going for me at the time were my shooting skills and never-ending supply of sass.

I liked to think my aim with both was as deadly as it ever was—but that I was learning new skills every day.

At any rate, thanks to Grayson, I was almost at the midpoint of logging the two years of on-the-job training I needed to become a licensed private investigator in the state of Florida.

And let me tell you, it hasn't been easy. Riding shotgun with Grayson during his crazy investigations into the unknown had almost gotten me killed a couple of times. And, to be honest, I still wasn't convinced I was going to make it out alive for the remaining fifteen months.

The bizarre cryptids, paranormal entities, and freaky happenings I'd experienced since joining Grayson's team had taught me that things were never quite what they seemed. But it was my encounters with all the screwball *humans* along the way that had me constantly questioning not just *my* survival, but that of our entire species.

Chapter One

I could scarcely believe it.
 I, Roberta Drex, was a freakin' millionaire!
Maybe...
Sweat trickled down the base of my neck as I stood outside Securatell Community Bank and stared at my reflection in the glass entry door. I was trying to build up my nerve. But I knew that if I waited much longer, I'd be nothing but a puddle of wet clothes steaming in the midday sun.

I reached for the door, then hesitated a moment longer.

What if...? No!

I hitched up my jeans and adjusted the cheap auburn wig atop my head.

Okay. Here goes nothing...

I took a deep breath, then stormed inside.

I was a woman on a mission. It was time to find out whether the account balance showing on my cellphone was real, or merely a computer glitch—some sadistic joke being pulled on me by the universe.

Hey, it wouldn't be the first time...

I marched up to a middle-aged man sitting behind a desk inside a small cubicle. Oddly enough, both he and the walls of his office appeared to be clad in the same dull, gray-blue fabric.

"I need to verify the funds in my account," I said, then handed him my checkbook.

"Certainly," he said, then smoothed his comb-over with a swipe of his right hand. He pecked a few keys on his computer keyboard. Suddenly, his eyes bugged out of his skull just like a Bugs Bunny choking on a carrot.

"Um ... Ms. Drex? It appears you have slightly over one million dollars in your account," he said, eyeing me with a tad keener interest than before.

"How slightly?" I asked.

"The exact sum is one million, eleven dollars and thirty-nine cents."

I bit my bottom lip. "Could you check it again?"

"Ma'am, I just verified it."

I gave him some side-eye. "Just do it."

The guy flinched. Then he glanced down at his computer screen and clicked a few buttons on the keyboard. "Yes, Ms. Drex. The money's *still* there."

"Uh-huh," I mumbled, my heart pounding in my throat.

Even though I'd spent the better part of a year investigating all sorts of incredibly outrageous and bizarre phenomena with my half-nuts partner, Nick Grayson, the idea of someone giving me a million dollars seemed more implausible than a two-headed Mothman vampire—operating a food truck out of Cincinnati.

"Uh ... can I get that in writing?" I asked.

"Certainly, Ms. Drex."

The manager pressed a few more keys, then swiveled in his chair, grabbed a sheet of paper from a printer tray, and swiveled back to face me. He looked up and shot me a smile he must've held in reserve for VIP customers.

I'd never seen anything like it before.

"Here you go, Ms. Drex," he said, thrusting a piece of paper at me.

"What's this?" I asked.

"A printout of your bank statement."

"Oh. Yeah. Sure."

I should open my mail more often.

"Thanks," I said. Then I cocked my head and waved the statement at him. "You swear on your mother's grave this is for real?"

He blanched and adjusted his tie. "Well ... yes, ma'am. And now that we've triple-verified it, I'd like to inform you that we offer a full range of financial planning—"

"Save it," I said, then turned and ran out of his cubicle and up to the first teller I spotted. She was an older woman holed up inside a tiny Plexiglas booth. She peered at me through cat-eye glasses attached to a chain around her neck, just like the pen lying on the counter.

Geez. They don't trust people with anything *around here!*

"I'd like to withdraw fifty dollars," I blurted to the woman, then drummed my nails on the counter and glanced around, waiting for Ashton Kutcher to pop out from behind a corner and yell, "*Punked!*"

Any other day, a withdrawal of over five dollars would've set off Securatell's insufficient funds alert. But not this time. Kutcher didn't show, either. Instead, I found myself once again on the receiving end of a smile the staff kept locked away in the vault for special occasions.

"Here you go, Ms. Drex," the teller said, grinning as she counted out two crisp new twenties and a ten.

Sweet.

"Anything else I can do for you?" she asked, pushing her pointy glasses further up the bridge of her nose.

"Uh ... yeah."

I smirked and puffed out my chest. I thought about resting the end of a pinkie finger to the corner of my mouth, but managed to contain myself.

"I'd like to withdraw *ten thousand dollars*," I said.

"A cashier's check?" the teller asked, without so much as a blink.

"Nope. Cold. Hard. Cash."

As the teller gathered the money, the branch manager came over and attempted a Southern revival of his marketing spiel.

"Ms. Drex, that kind of money could be earning interest—"

I held my palm out like a stop sign. "Look. Thanks, but I'm in kind of a hurry. Maybe later."

"Very good," he said, then shoved a couple of brochures into my hand. "These outline some of our fine services. You can find out more details online. Or feel free to call us. We're a full service—"

"I'll keep it in mind," I said, already visualizing how the flyers would look spread out in a fan and lit afire.

The manager nodded, his shoulders slumping in defeat. "Very good, ma'am."

I turned back to the teller and watched her count out crisp, new, hundred-dollar bills until she reached one hundred.

"That's ten thousand. Should I count them again?" she asked.

"Nope. I'm good."

The teller stacked the bills tidily, then tucked them inside an envelope and slid it through a slit in the Plexiglas.

"Thanks." I snatched the envelope, then turned and fled out the door, giggling all the way.

As I ran toward my getaway vehicle, I felt giddy. And nervous. And slightly out of control—as if I'd just robbed the place.

And to be honest, I still wasn't a hundred percent sure that I hadn't.

Chapter Two

I sprinted around the corner of Securatell Community Bank and made a beeline for my two accomplices waiting for me in the parking lot.

They weren't hard to spot.

We'd driven there in Bessie, a black monster truck the size of a small freight train. Its tractor-sized tires lifted the bottom of its humongous chassis to just about level with the roofs of the other cars around it.

If that weren't enough to make Bessie stand out in the crowd, she'd recently been equipped with a night-vision periscope. It jutted from atop the cab like a three-foot tall middle finger made of chrome. The ridiculous new accessory had been the brainchild of my cousin, Earl Schankles. He was busy watching me through it as I ran up to the truck.

"Zoom in on *this*!" I yelled at Earl.

I pulled a wad of hundreds from the envelope and fanned them in the air, wiggling my torso like a Vegas showgirl on crack.

Bessie's passenger door flew open. "How much *is* that?" Grayson asked.

"Ten grand!" I squealed, climbing up into the cab.

"Lord a-mighty," Earl said. "We sure gonna eat high on the hog today!"

"Why on earth did you take out so much cash?" Grayson asked as I climbed over him, then plunked myself down in the middle of the bench seat between him and Earl.

"Because I *can*!" I giggled maniacally. "For the first time in my life, I *can*!"

"I hope you have good plans for this money," Grayson said, taking it from me and stuffing it back into the envelope.

I grinned. "Oh, I certainly *do*."

"What?" Earl asked, cranking the ignition.

I laughed. "I'm just gonna *blow* it!"

"Woo-hoo!" Earl hollered. "I heard that!"

Grayson wasn't quite as enthusiastic. "Why would you want to blow ten grand?"

"Because I *can*!" I said, shooting him a sideways look. "What part of that are you not getting?"

Grayson frowned. "Drex, I don't think that's exactly what your benefactors had in mind when they gave you these funds."

I snorted. "*You're* going to give *me* financial advice? That's rich coming from the guy who stored all *his* money inside the paneled walls of a ratty RV."

Grayson stiffened. "I consider that an amygdala anomaly."

"A big dolly lama?" Earl asked, pulling out of the parking lot.

I rolled my eyes at my big bear of a cousin, then I turned and stared at Grayson. "You just made that up, didn't you?"

Grayson's eyebrow did its infamous Spock impersonation. "Amygdala anomaly? I most certainly did not."

I folded my arms across my chest. "I swear. *Men!* They'll blame *anyone* but themsel—"

"I *am* blaming myself," Grayson interjected. "I'm trying to explain *why* I didn't use a bank. You see, based on the research of—"

"Okay!" I blurted, cutting him off. "Let's just say you had your reasons. I *get* it. Now, could you please, just this once, spare us your scientific mumbo jumbo?"

"Fine," Grayson said. "I was only trying to point out the fact that there's an actual physical explanation for why intelligent people sometimes make regrettable decisions."

I glanced over at Earl, then back at Grayson. I slumped into my seat and stared out the windshield.

Holy crap. Regrettable decisions are about the only kind I've ever made! Like now, for instance. Why am I always the one stuck in the middle seat? Wait. No. Like, why am I even with *these guys? Wait! No! Like, I have money now. Why am I not sipping a Mai Tai at a day spa in some luxurious beach resort?*

I frowned at Grayson. "Amygdala anomaly, huh?"

"Yes."

I chewed my bottom lip, then whispered to Grayson, "Let's talk about this some more."

Grayson started to say something, but I pressed a finger to his lips. "I meant *later*."

"Good," Earl said. "'Cause all that talk about llamas is makin' me hungry. What you think they taste like, anyways? Chicken, or what?"

THE SECURATELL BANK branch we'd stopped at was in Naples, Florida. It was about an hour's drive from Plantation, where we'd traveled to pay our respects to one of Grayson's heroes, the recently departed Amazing Randi.

And that's where life as I'd known it had shifted into a new dimension—one with a million bucks in it.

While dropping off a bouquet of flowers at the makeshift memorial set up in front of The Amazing Randi's house, a man had approached and asked who we were. When he'd learned my name, he'd informed me that a benefactor—who wished to remain anonymous—had awarded *me*, Bobbie Drex, a million-dollar grant.

Whether that benefactor had been The Amazing Randi himself, the man either wouldn't or couldn't say. But as far as I was concerned, I didn't give a crap if the money had been pooped out by the Tooth Fairy.

I sure as heck wasn't going to look that gift horse in the mouth. Instead, I planned to ride that pony until its legs were worn down to tiny little nubs.

The cash couldn't have come at a better time, either. Grayson, my mentor, boss, cash cow, and budding love interest, had gone and lost his RV and all the money he'd stashed away inside it.

Whether the old Minnie Winnie motorhome had disappeared into a cosmic wormhole or had been carjacked by a fat man in a white robe high on donut fungus, I couldn't be sure. Life was uncertain that way. Plus, I'd been knocked unconscious at the time.

The point was, when we'd left the hospital in Gainesville this morning to drive down to Plantation to acknowledge the passing of The Amazing Randi, we'd been flat broke. Between the three of us, we'd had eleven dollars and thirty-nine cents to rub together.

Needless to say, after that man told me about the mysterious million-dollar grant, my first order of business had been to make sure it wasn't some kind of scam. (Well, that had actually been my second order of business. The first had been to make an emergency change of underwear.)

As Earl drove Bessie north on I-75, I pinched myself. Then I glanced over at Grayson's shirt pocket. The envelope containing ten-thousand bucks was still there, teasing me like an ice-cold can of beer in the desert.

Only this time, it wasn't a mirage.

The million bucks was real, all right. But was it *legal*?

Considering I had no idea where it had come from, there was no way to be sure. So, to be on the safe side, after securing that ten-grand withdrawal, I'd made the guys hit the gas and get us the heck out of Dodge before Securatell changed its mind.

Earl had joyfully complied, and we were now barreling along the interstate, heading north toward St. Petersburg.

"Y'all, I'm hungry!" Earl complained for the third time. He rubbed his pot belly for emphasis.

"Okay, fine," I said. "Take the next exit and we'll get some lunch."

"I vote for tacos," Grayson said, raising a spidery forefinger.

I smirked at him. "Not this time. In case you don't get it, Grayson, you don't call all the shots anymore. You're no longer the boss of me."

Grayson laughed. "That statement is illogical, Drex."

I blanched. "*Illogical*?"

"Yes." His lips curled slightly on his too-handsome face. "The term 'boss' implies that I was, at some point, able to control your actions."

"Ha! That'd be the day!" Earl hooted, then laughed so hard he snorted like a hog.

I sat back and ground my teeth.

You know what, amygdala anomaly? You totally suck.

Chapter Three

I was the one who'd insisted on stopping for lunch at a hotdog stand. But the whole time I was eating my lousy frankfurter smothered in mustard and relish, I wished I were eating tacos with salsa and guacamole instead.

My amygdala must be a complete idiot.

I wiped mustard from my lips and glanced over at the guys. They were seated across from me at an orange picnic table beside the shabby food truck, packing in tube-steaks like a pair of ravenous apes—one shaggy-haired gorilla in blue mechanic's coveralls, and one tall, wiry spider monkey in black jeans and matching T-shirt.

"I guess we should start looking for a new RV, huh?" I asked, wiping a blob of mustard from my T-shirt.

"Yes, *boss*," Grayson quipped, his green eyes twinkling. "Unless, of course, you prefer to continue to use Earl as your personal taxi driver. He just informed me he's charging by the minute."

"Just a dern quarter a minute," Earl said, then leaned forward and took a loud slurp of Pepsi through a straw.

I glared at my cousin. "Seriously? So, what am I, now? Miss Moneybags?"

"Come on, Bobbie," Earl said. "That only adds up to about fifteen bucks an hour. That's barely minimum wage. And besides, you can't be Miss Moneybags. You're too *old*. You're more like *Ms.* Moneybags."

Grayson laughed, nearly spewing his mouthful of Dr Pepper. As for me, I'd suddenly lost my appetite.

"You know what?" I said. "I'm gonna be Ms. *Outta Here* if you two keep this up. Honestly, I could be lying on a beach somewhere! But *noooo*. Here I am, talking about spending my money on a brand new RV, just so you two jerks can go around chasing imaginary monsters in it."

I shook my head. "I must be nuts."

"You *are*," Grayson said. "Nobody in their right mind would buy a *brand-new* RV, Drex. The depreciation is insane!"

"Mr. G.'s right," Earl said. "You can't go blowin' half a mil on a gussied up gotorhome. If we're gonna keep on investigatin' stuff, we gotta make that money last."

I stared at the pair in disbelief. "Who *are* you guys? All of a sudden you're Morgan and Stanley?"

Earl's brow furrowed. "Is that them two guys on that fishin' show?"

"Face it, Drex," Grayson said. "You're not the greatest when it comes to finances. You should listen to us."

"Fine," I grumbled. "So, what's the plan?"

Grayson turned his laptop around to face me. "Here, take a look at this."

"What is it?" I asked, squinting at the screen.

"The home page for *RV Swapper*," Grayson said, handing me his cheater glasses. "Take a look at the one I highlighted. It's a 1975 Winnebago Brave D18."

I glanced down at the picture. My upper lip snarled. "This hunk of junk looks just like the rattrap we've been rolling around in for the past nine months! The only difference is the pin-striping's yellow and orange, instead of green."

"You mean citrus yellow and sunset orange," Grayson said. "That's because it's from the '70s instead of the '60s. Call me nostalgic, but I think she's a beauty."

"Me, too," Earl said. "And I like me the name 'Brave,' too. It's like that RV's sayin' if we choose it, we'll be ready for anything."

I crinkled my nose at Earl. "I suppose 'brave' is better than 'coward.' But *you're* not the one who has to live in it." I glanced over at Grayson. "Couldn't we get one with more modern amenities?"

"Like what?" Grayson asked.

"You know. Air conditioning? A microwave? Built-in GPS?"

Grayson stared at me like I was insane. "Any model newer than this would come with an electronic ignition, Drex. That would render it powerless in the event of an EMP, remember?"

I rolled my eyes. "Not that stupid electromagnetic pulse thing again!" I turned to Earl. "What about Bessie? If that happened, her electronics would be fried, too."

Earl grinned. "Nope. I got me a work-around."

"What?" I asked.

He tapped his brow with a meaty index finger. "I'll tow her with the RV."

Lord help us all.

Grayson flipped the laptop back around so he could see the screen. "Listen, Drex. It says here that the roof on this one was replaced with heavy sheet metal. That's half our monster trap already built in."

My face puckered. "Awesome. But like I said, what's in it for *me*?"

"Here's something," Grayson said, flipping the computer back so the screen faced me again. "It says it's got a *fantastic* fan in bathroom."

I opened my mouth to make a snide comment, then recalled Earl's frequent guest appearances and switched gears. "Well, that *is* a salient selling point."

"And the price is right, too," Grayson said. "Look."

I glanced down at the screen. "Eleven hundred dollars? Why so cheap?"

"Maybe it's just our lucky day," Earl said.

I shot him a look. "Since when has it *ever* been our lucky day?"

Earl blanched. "Uh, somebody just gave you a million bucks, Bobbie."

I grimaced. "Oh. Right."

"I'll call and make an appointment to see it," Grayson said. "No harm done, correct?"

I frowned. "I guess."

Grayson pulled out his cellphone and started punching in the phone number. As his finger jabbed at the screen, he began barking out orders. "Drex, you get the check. Earl, grab your tool kit. You'll be in charge of checking out the mechanics once we get there."

Earl saluted. "I'm on it, Chief!"

I glared at my cousin. "If we buy this thing, you're going back to Point Paradise, right?"

Earl shrugged. "I wasn't plannin' on it."

I sighed and glanced at the bank envelope poking out of Grayson's pocket.

I wonder how much a decent hitman costs...

Chapter Four

To my surprise, Earl blew past the exit on I-275 that lead to downtown St. Petersburg and St. Pete Beach.

As I watched the lopsided dome of the Tampa Bay Rays baseball stadium disappear behind us, I elbowed my cousin in the ribs. "Hey! I thought we were gonna find a place at the beach for a few days!"

"There's been a slight change in plans," Grayson said. "We're going to check out the RV first."

"Why didn't you tell me?" I grumbled.

"We didn't tell you because we didn't wanna listen to you complain about it all the way here," Earl said.

"Me, complain?" I said. "Why would you think that?"

"Haines Road isn't that far out of the way," Grayson said. "And if the RV checks out, it'll be worth the drive. Besides, if we don't do it right now, someone else might beat us to the deal."

"Ugh. Fine." I crossed my arms and flopped back into my seat. "But if we pass a Walmart on the way, pull in."

"Why?" Grayson asked.

"Because I need a new wig, that's why." I scratched under the right ear of my fake, shoulder-length, auburn hair. "This one from Beth-Ann's emergency wig box is all itchy."

"Aw, I think it's cute," Earl said. "Makes you look like a baby orangutan."

"Ha ha," I hissed, then turned to Grayson. "Thanks to having my head shaved again at the hospital, I'm gonna be wearing a wig again for at least three months. I don't want to be trapped with some cheap-looking polyester hand-me-down. I want the best wig money can buy!"

"Then you don't want a Walmart wig," Grayson said. "You want a Wilshire wig."

I stared at him. "A *Wilshire* wig?"

"Yes. The average one costs about three or four grand."

"Geez!" I gasped. "That's some serious cash. I said I wanted the *best* wig in the world, Grayson. Not the most *expensive*."

"Good," he said. "Because the most expensive wig in the world wouldn't look right on you."

My eyebrow met my wig-line. "I beg your pardon?"

"The most expensive wig in the world belonged to Andy Warhol," Grayson said. "After he died, it sold at Christie's auction for $108,000."

I grimaced. "Seriously? And, uh ... *gross*! Who would want a dead man's used toupee?"

Grayson shrugged. "There's no accounting for human taste."

"You got that right," Earl said. "I bet it's like chicken."

FOLLOWING GRAYSON'S direction, Earl exited I-275 at 38th Avenue. After driving past a couple of blocks of ill-fated historical houses tucked between bland strip centers, Earl was directed to hook a right onto Haines Road.

All of a sudden, it seemed as if we'd driven into another dimension. Gone were all the familiar chain stores and their organized cleanliness. In their stead were sketchy, scabbed-together establishments with names like Scratchy's Smoke Shoppe, Thrift-n-Stuff, Bad Excuses Bar, and Joey's Auto Body & U-Pull-It junkyard.

"What're we looking for, Mr. G.?" Earl asked.

"Flack jackets?" I asked.

"Mullet's Trailer Park," Grayson said, then nodded toward the right side of the road. "There it is, just past Dead Bug pest control."

I followed the trajectory of Grayson's gaze past a giant dead cockroach lying on its back to a battered, hand-lettered, wooden sign that read:

Mullets Trailer's U-Rent bi the Weak

"Oh, goody," I said. "Someplace even more illiterate than Point Paradise. Can we go now?"

"Hold on, princess," Earl said. He turned the wheel and guided Bessie onto the trailer park's main road.

"E Street," Earl said, reading the road sign aloud. He chuckled. "What? They run out a letters after making that sign back there?"

I smirked. "Either that or they finally stuck with something they could spell."

Grayson let out a whistle. "Whoa. Would you look at that."

Earl and I turned to get a gander at what Grayson was talking about. We spotted it and gasped simultaneously.

Apparently, Earl was as dumbstruck as I was. His foot went limp on the gas. Bessie coasted to a crawl. Then, like Baptists at a nudist camp, the three of us craned our necks and gawked as we slowly cruised past the charred remains of a single-wide trailer.

The mobile home had been burned completely in two from the middle, leaving both ends open and half incinerated. Sitting in the scorched yard in front of the bisected trailer was the blackened husk of what appeared to have once been a professional drum set—complete with melted seat and a set of singed, disc-shaped cymbals.

"Lord a-mighty," Earl muttered, then let out a low whistle. "That must a been *some* party."

"Either that, or it was the detonation epicenter of a small nuclear device," Grayson said.

My nose crinkled. "That's not the RV we came to see, is it?"

"No," Grayson said. "It's right over there."

I looked to my left and felt a wave of déjàvu. "That looks almost identical to your old RV, Grayson."

"Indeed," he said, smiling. "But she's nearly ten years younger than the old model."

"Just the way a new girlfriend should be," Earl quipped, earning him the business end of my elbow, yet again.

"Dang it, Bobbie," Earl groused, rubbing his side as he pulled over to the edge of the road.

As we climbed out of the monster truck, a scrawny, middle-aged man missing a banjo and half his front teeth came walking up. He hooked his thumbs inside the shoulder straps of his rangy overalls and said, "How do."

Grayson glanced over at me and whispered, "How do we *what*?"

"We're here about that there RV," Earl said to the man.

"Figured," he said, scratching a feral patch of greasy hair atop his otherwise bald dome. "I'm Danny Daniels."

"Earl Schankles. This here's my cousin Bobbie and her boyfriend, Grayson."

Boyfriend?

My eyes widened. I glanced over at Grayson. He hadn't even so much as blinked at Earl's relationship moniker.

"Nice to meet you," Grayson said. "That's a nice RV you have there. You firm on the price?"

"Well, I might could be up for a swap," Danny said, nodding my way. "Gimme that there beauty and she's yours."

Even though he was repulsive, I smiled coyly at Danny. A girl's got to take a compliment where she can find it.

Earl shook his head. "Bessie? Naw. I couldn't part with her. She's family."

"Not the *woman*," Danny said. "I meant that there truck a your'n."

Earl laughed. "So did I."

Seriously?

Danny walked over and slapped a hand on Bessie's hood and cackled. Then, all three men had a good laugh at my expense while I secretly plotted each of their demises.

Boyfriend, schmoyfriend.

"Hate to break up your little laugh-fest, guys," I said. "But don't you think we should have a look inside that hunk of tin before we decide whether to buy it or not?"

Chapter Five

The interior of the 1975 Winnebago was vintage—in the worst possible meaning of the term. The orange shag carpet contained all of its original decades of grime—as did the propane stove. One quick glance around and I totally understood why lime green and burnt orange had gone out of fashion as interior design elements.

"Woooeee!" Earl hollered as he followed me inside the filthy RV. "Smells like somebody had them a hog boilin' up in here."

"Nah," Danny, said, poking his leathery turtle head in the side door. "She just needs a good airin' out."

"Hey," Grayson said, checking out the dashboard. "Does the ham radio come with it?"

Danny shrugged. "I guess. I ain't got no use for it myself."

"Does it work?" Grayson asked Danny.

"Don't know. Never tried it."

I eyed Danny with suspicion. "How about the 'fantastic' bathroom fan?"

Danny smirked. "Now *that*, little lady, works. I tried it out myself."

And with that visual in my head, my life is now complete.

"So, why are you selling your RV anyway?" I asked.

"Well, little lady, first off, it ain't my RV," Danny said. "Or, at least it wasn't. It belonged to my brother, Mullet Daniels. I'm selling it on account a his recent demise."

"Oh," I said, softening my tone. "I'm sorry for your loss."

"Wait!" Earl gasped. "Was he the Mullet in *Mullets* Trailer Park?"

My cousin, the genius.

"One and the same," Danny said proudly, then sucked on whatever yellowed teeth still clung to his withered gums.

"What happened to him?" Earl asked.

Danny's fuzzy gray eyebrows rose an inch. "You mean to tell me y'all ain't heard about it?"

Earl shook his head. "No, sir."

"Y'all must not be from around here, then."

"We're not," I said.

And boy, am I ever grateful for that.

Danny climbed up into the RV and plopped himself down in the burnt-orange banquette, then settled himself in like this might take a while.

"Well, it was big news 'round here, what happened to my brother Mullet," he said. "Him and Titanic Jones, that is."

"News?" I asked.

"Yep. Y'all notice that burned-up trailer over yonder when y'all first come in?"

"Uh ... yes," I said.

"Well. That's what happened to 'em."

Earl's eyes got as big as boiled eggs. "They partied themselves to death?"

"Uh ... in a matter of speakin', yeah," Danny said. "It happened during the annual Burnin' Mullet Festival two weeks ago. We hold it every year here in the trailerhood. We have us a big ol' time, too. Got us a barbeque, live band, squirrel shootin' competition, and everythin'. Anyways, this year, sump'n real bad happened."

Gee. I can't imagine what could've gone wrong.

"What?" Earl asked, hanging on Danny's every word.

"Well, we ain't quite sure how it all started," Danny said. "We was all dancin' and drinkin' and carryin' on when all of a sudden, Mullet's trailer went up in flames like a two-dollar weddin' ring. I'm here to tell ya, it was a regular fireball. We all run for our lives like roaches from the Orkin man."

"I'll be," Earl said.

Danny shook his head. "Yep. Everybody got out 'cept'n for the drummer, Titanic Jones. Bless his soul. He never had a chance."

"Why not?" Earl asked.

"I'll tell you why," Danny said. "On account of the paradiddle."

"The pair a *what*?" Earl asked, beating me to it.

"Paradiddle," Grayson said, cutting in. "It's a percussion term. One stroke of a drum is a para. Two strokes is a diddle. Therefore, a paradiddle is a drumming rudiment that combines single strokes with precisely placed double strokes."

"That's right, mister," Danny said.

My upper lip snarled. "I don't get it."

"You see, little lady," Danny said, "that fire busted out when the band was playin' *In a Gadda-Da Vida*. Titanic was slap in the middle of that long drum solo, you know?" He shook his head. "Poor feller couldn't stop hisself. It was a matter of paradiddle pride."

"You mean...?" Earl asked.

"Yep." Danny sighed and rested a knobby hand over his heart. "True to his name, Titanic went down with the trailer."

I grimaced, then observed a respectable pause of silence before I spoke. "Uh ... I'm sorry to hear that, Danny. But I thought you said you were selling the RV because your brother *Mullet* passed away."

"Yeah," Danny said, letting his hand fall from his heart and into his lap. "He up and died, too—the very next night. But not in his trailer, a course. It was already burned slap up by then. Nope, we found Mullet's remains right 'cheer inside this very RV. At least, what was left of him, anyways."

I glanced around in horror, wondering what part of burnt orange was actually burnt *Mullet*.

"You said, 'What was left of him.'?" Grayson asked.

"Yep," Danny said.

Earl grimaced. "What happened? 'Coons get him?"

"No, thank the Lord," Danny said. "Mullet was burned up, just like poor ol' Titanic. All 'cept'n one foot. That's how we knowed it was him. You see, Mullet had his name tattooed on it. One letter on each toe."

"But Mullet has *six* letters," I said.

Danny nodded. "That's right, little lady."

While my mouth opened and closed like a fish out of water, Grayson said, "Excuse me, Danny. What was the cause of the fire? Accident? Arson?"

"Neither one," Danny said. "Or maybe both. They never could tell."

Chapter Six

"Did anyone investigate Mullet's or Titanic's deaths?" Grayson asked, sliding his butt into the burnt-orange vinyl bench opposite Danny in the nasty banquette.

"Yep," Danny said, stretching his arms out across the back of the bench. "The cops was here a couple times. A fire investigator, too. But they didn't arrest nobody for it."

"So they weren't homicides?" I asked.

"Nope," Danny said. "Around here, you'd think so, wouldn't you? But them cops ruled out foul play. They talked to everybody around at the time, but they never could figure out who or what killed them boys. The death certificates on both of 'em says the cause of death was due to insufficient means."

"Don't you mean insufficient *evidence*?" Grayson asked.

Danny shrugged. "Whatever."

I glanced around at the filthy kitchen. The cupboards were bare.

Maybe "insufficient means" wasn't that far off the mark…

"Danny, where did it happen?" I asked.

He glanced up at me and scratched a dark spot adjacent to the small island of greasy hair atop head. "Where'd *what* happen?"

"Uh … your brother Mullet's … death," I said. "Where did you find him?"

"Oh. Back yonder in the bedroom. Funny thing. Like I said, he was burnt up to nothin' 'cept his foot and a piece of his skull cap. They was still smokin' when I found him. But it wasn't no total loss."

"It wasn't?" I asked, surprised.

"Nope," Danny said. "The mattress underneath Mullet was still nearly good as new. So I kep' it. Go take a look for yourself."

I grimaced, then took a small, hesitant step toward the bedroom. A second later, I was nearly bowled over by Grayson, who'd hopped up from the banquette and was making a mad dash for the back room.

When I caught up with my partner three seconds later, he'd already whipped off the orange plaid bedspread covering Mullet's bed and was taking pictures of the singed mattress with his cellphone. His expression couldn't have been more captivated if he'd been photographing a *Sports Illustrated* model in a thong bikini.

"Gross," I said, staring at the ashy human outline on the otherwise only slightly stained mattress. "Is that Mullet's body outline?"

"I would presume, Cadet," Grayson said, never pausing from his glamour-shot photoshoot.

"Huh," Earl said, walking into the room. "Looks like that there mattress is one a them good 'uns made outta that memory foam stuff."

"So?" I said, my disgust turning to annoyance. "How is that relevant?"

Earl shrugged. "Well, maybe it remembers what happened."

My eyes closed. My teeth clenched. "I can't believe it," I muttered.

"Me neither," Earl said. "That there mattress is better'n the one I got at home."

"What'd I tell ya?" Danny said, poking his head into the bedroom. "Ain't nothin' a little Windex and a dust-buster can't fix. Am I right?"

"Y'ALL TAKE YOUR TIME," Danny said, leaving us to our inspection of the RV. "I'll let you get a good look at her without me breathin' down y'all's necks. Y'all got any questions, I'll be in my trailer right yonder."

"Thanks," Grayson said.

I waited until Danny was out of earshot, then grabbed Grayson by the elbow. "Don't tell me you're seriously considering buying this hideous thing! Somebody *died* in it!"

"I know. And *mysteriously*, too," Grayson said, his green eyes aglow. "It's almost too good to be true!"

I nearly choked on my own spit. "Too *good* to be true?"

"Yes!" Grayson grabbed me by the arms. "Drex, I believe this RV could be the scene of an incredibly rare phenomenon."

My nose crinkled. "Like what? An upholstery cleaning?"

"No," Grayson said. "Spontaneous human combustion."

"Spontageneous humanoid what?" Earl asked.

"Spontaneous human combustion," Grayson said. "That's when someone bursts into flames for no apparent reason, and is incinerated to ash."

"Oh," Earl said. "I thought that was caused by talkin' to yore mother in law."

I scoffed at Grayson. "Come on. Don't tell me you're back into that crazy stuff again."

"What do you mean, *again*?" Grayson asked. "We haven't even begun looking into the first case of it. Drex, I thought you were on board with this."

I frowned. "I *was*—until I read that bogus report you gave me about the guy in St. Pete Beach who woke up in his car with his arm covered in third-degree burns. Cops on the scene said he'd gotten wasted, then fell asleep with his arm out the window. This is Florida, Grayson. It was just a bad case of sunburn."

"Of course they would say that," Grayson said. "That's what they *want* you to believe. Authorities won't admit to the existence of spontaneous human combustion. That's why I'd like to help prove its existence, once and for all."

"Maybe Mr. G.'s right," Earl said, sniffing the air. "It *does* smell like somebody burnt their biscuits in here."

"Okay," I said. "Suppose this Mullet Daniels guy *did* spontaneously combust in here. Why on *earth* would you want to buy his rolling death trap?"

"For precisely that reason," Grayson said.

"Huh?" I grunted.

"Look," Grayson said. "*Statistically*, this RV is *bullet-proof.* Can't you see? The odds of *two* people bursting into flames in here is infinitesimal!"

My mouth fell open. "I would hope the odds of randomly going up in flames would *already* be infinitesimal. I mean, how many people has that ever happened to, anyway?"

"Between two and four hundred," Grayson replied. "Depending on whose accounts you believe."

My eyes narrowed. "Wait a minute! You planned this whole *thing*, didn't you? Coming here ... to see *this exact RV.*"

"What do you mean?" Grayson asked, looking taken aback.

"You must've heard about the fires and Mullet's mysterious death somehow," I said, "and linked it back to this RV." I shook my head. "You let me believe we were going to St. Pete to have a beach holiday. But the whole while you had your eye on checking out this RV, didn't you? You think Mullet spontaneously combusted in here, and you want to investigate it as part of that *Experiment #5* file you were toying around with before the accident. Admit it!"

"Well, yes," Grayson said. "I'll admit I was indeed intrigued when I received intelligence on the odd circumstances of Mullet's fiery demise."

"I knew it!" I hissed. "Who told you? Operative Garth?"

Grayson stifled a grimace. "Yes. But in an effort at full disclosure, I found the RV during a legitimate search for a replacement vehicle. The possibility that Mullet died in same said vehicle of spontaneous human combustion was only speculation at that point. It wasn't until we got here and were able to get a good look at the mattress that I felt this could become an important leg of our investigation into the phenomenon. So, in all fairness, his mysterious death was just a happy accident."

I sneered. "Not so happy for *Mullet*, was it?"

"True." Grayson cocked his head and braved a look into my eyes. "That brings up another excellent point, Drex. Exploring the cause of spontaneous human combustion could prove dangerous. Therefore, my observation about the RV's statistical immunity to the phenomenon is a valid one. Don't you agree?"

"Whatever," I said begrudgingly. "I suppose the odds of that happening in here again *are* infinitesimal."

Grayson smiled. "So, we're agreed? We should purchase this old Winnebago? For research purposes?"

"Fine," I said. "But then we're going to the beach."

"Suits me," Earl said, scratching his head. "But I still ain't sure what infant testicles has got to do with any of this."

Chapter Seven

Grayson hadn't managed to salvage a dime from his old motorhome before it disappeared. But somehow he'd managed to keep a grip on his research into spontaneous human combustion. He'd kept it all in a mysterious manila file folder he'd labeled *Experiment #5*.

When I'd first spotted the folder a few weeks ago, before the accident, he'd told me it contained pictures of 'hot bodies'. I'd thought the folder had been his porn stash. I'd tried my best to sneak a look at it, but never managed to get my hands on it.

Until today.

After agreeing to buy the RV and help him delve into his latest obsession—spontaneous human combustion—Grayson finally handed over his mysterious folder.

So, while he and Earl took their time combing over Mullet Daniels' slightly singed 1975 Minnie Winnie, I sat myself down in Bessie, cranked the air conditioner on full blast, and cracked open the file labeled *Experiment #5*.

As soon as I did, I wished I hadn't. Because in Grayson's world, 'hot bodies' had a whole other meaning...

Inside the folder, he'd laid out detailed notes on five cases of spontaneous human combustion. I tried to focus on the words, but my eyes kept going back to the gruesome photographs of the victims. Or, should I say, the small bits that were left of them.

If Danny's account was right, Mullet Daniels' case was strikingly similar to the ones in the folder. Each victim had been reduced to a pile of ash, with only a few scraps of body parts left—mainly shards of skull and the odd bit of lower leg or foot remained to tell the tale.

Not exactly the smoldering looks I'd been hoping for from Grayson...

As macabre as the file's contents were, I took some small consolation that this *wasn't* Grayson's porn stash. If it had been, I'd have a whole other kind of weird phenomenon to be worried about.

I closed the folder and glanced out the windshield of the truck. From my raised vantage point, I could see the guys were still busy poking around the old RV.

Disgusted by the photos, but as yet unconvinced by the bizarre reports in Grayson's file, I'd decided to put my own investigative skills to work. But instead of inspecting the RV, I chose a venue that would keep me well out of range of the old motorhome—just in case the hunk of junk decided to beat the infinitesimal odds and spontaneously detonate again.

I WALKED OVER TO DANNY Daniels' trailer, intent on interviewing the old geezer about what he thought had really happened to his brother Mullet. Cautiously, I picked my way through his weedy yard. I climbed two steps, knocked on Danny's door, then stepped back down onto the litter-strewn lawn.

The old man flung open the door, dressed only in his boxer shorts. In comparison, the images in Grayson's file folder didn't seem quite so disturbing.

"Y'all buyin' it or what?" Danny asked, scratching his bare beer belly.

"The guys are still taking a look," I said. "I wanted to talk to you about your brother."

Danny stopped scratching and motioned me to step inside the dark innards of his shabby trailer. "Come on in."

"Uh, I better stay out here," I said. "In case the guys have questions."

"Suit yourself," he said, then took a slug of beer from the can in his hand.

"Do you have a picture of your brother?" I asked, then quickly added, "One taken *before* the accident?"

"Sure." Danny opened his wallet and plucked out a worn photograph of himself that must've been taken decades ago. He was standing next to a portly guy with the thickest, most luxuriant auburn mullet I'd ever seen.

"What did the police say about Mullet's death?" I asked. "Off record, I mean."

"They said it was prolly an accident."

"An accident?"

"Yep. Said it was prolly cause my brother was drunk and fell asleep while he was smokin' weed."

"Do you agree with their conclusion?" I asked.

"I suppose." Danny looked me up and down, then winked at me. "You smoke weed?" He asked. "I got some if you—"

"No, thanks."

"Suit yourself." He nodded at the photo. "The weed. That's why we called him Smoked Mullet, you know."

"Oh." I handed him back the picture. "I thought it was because of his ... uh ... haircut."

"Back in the day, yeah. But me an' old Mullet both suffer from what ya call male-patterned baldness. Me and him both been bald as billiards since we was the tender age of thirty-three. *I* took it like a man. Mullet, well, he took it like a girl."

My shoulders stiffened. "What do you mean, like a *girl*?"

"He took to wearin' cheap wigs. Kinda like the one you got on."

My jaw clamped down like a vice, forcing me to speak between my clenched teeth. "So, you've been bald since you were thirty-three. How many years does that make?"

Eight hundred?

Danny licked his lips, giving me an unwelcomed glimpse inside his mouth. It was as dark and disgusting as his trailer.

"Not *too* many, young lady," he said. "In fact, I still got some spark left in me. You sure you don't wanna come inside? Have a cold one with me?" He wagged his eyebrows. "I could show you my paradiddling skills."

I threw up a little in my mouth. "Uh ... no thanks."

"You sure?"

I've never been so sure of anything in my life. Amygdala, have I told you lately that I love you?

"Tempting offer," I said, backing away from Danny and his aluminum love cave. "But like I said, I've gotta keep an eye out for the guys."

He shrugged. "Your loss."

I smiled.

It most certainly is—not.

"I SEEN WORSE," EARL said, closing the hood on the old motorhome. "But nothin' that can't be fixed with chewin' gum and bailin' wire."

"Think it'll make it to Plant City?" Grayson asked.

"Prolly," Earl said.

"Good. You drive. Drex and I will follow in Bessie."

Earl saluted. "You got it, Chief!"

"Plant City?" I said. "I thought we were going to the—"

"We'll take it," Grayson said over my shoulder.

I whipped around to see Danny walking up behind me.

"All righty, then," the old guy said. "But I don't take no checks."

"Cash okay?" Grayson asked.

Danny gave us another gander at his Jack-o'-lantern grin. "That'll work just fine."

Grayson reached into his shirt pocket and pulled out the envelope with the ten grand, then proceeded to count out eleven bills into Danny's gnarled, leathery hand while I watched my beach vacation funds drain away like oil in a drip pan.

"Where'd y'all get all that cash money?" Danny asked.

"It's *hers*," Earl said, nodding at me.

Danny shot me a lascivious grin that made me want to take a long swim in a pool full of Clorox. "How'd you earn that money, missy? Was you a stripper back in the day?"

Earl hooted, and I suddenly understood how someone could spontaneously combust.

"Why you—" I growled at Danny.

Grayson took one glance at my face and grabbed me by my elbow. "I'm curious, Danny," he said, holding me back from taking a swing at the old letch. "If the fire didn't damage the RV's roof, why'd you replace it?"

"On account a it was plum wore out," Danny answered, pocketing the cash. He looked me up and down. "It's a shame what the ravages of time can do to a body."

Grayson tightened his grip on my arm. "Well, just hand me the title and we'll be on our way."

"Here you go." Danny handed over a tattered piece of paper.

"This looks in order," Grayson said, studying it. "Pleasure doing business with you."

Danny smirked at me. "Pleasure was all mine."

"I bet," I hissed, glaring at Danny as Grayson pulled me toward the truck.

"Give it a rest, Drex," Grayson said under his breath.

But I couldn't. Something about Danny had pushed all my buttons—all except the one labeled "off," that is.

Unable to contain myself, I hollered at Danny as I climbed into the truck.

"You must really miss your brother," I yelled. "It's obvious Mullet left behind a gigantic ash hole!"

Chapter Eight

"What's up with you?" Grayson said as he and I climbed into the monster truck, ready to leave Mullet's Trailer Park and his burned-out abode behind. "I've never seen you so fiery. And that's saying something."

I scowled. "Danny just gives me the creeps."

"He gives you the *creeps*?"

"Yes." I stared at Grayson. "Don't tell me you've never had the creeps before."

He shook his head. "That would be a negative."

I blew out a sigh. "Maybe it's something only a woman can feel about a guy."

Grayson studied me. "The 'creeps' is hardly a term a professional private investigator would use in describing a person."

I frowned. "Well, maybe I don't *feel* like a professional investigator, okay?"

Grayson stopped short of putting the keys in the ignition. "Why not?"

I flipped down the sun visor and stared at myself in the vanity mirror. "Do you think this wig makes me look like a stripper?"

Grayson smirked. "No, but I can't say the same for that outfit."

"What? Since when do jeans and a T-shirt say 'stripper'?"

"Not stripper," Grayson said. "Just shows you've got a hot body."

My eyebrows shot up. I glanced at him sideways. "Are you saying I look like someone who spontaneously combusted?"

"No." He laughed. "The *other* kind of hot body."

I smirked. "So you actually do *know* about the other kind."

"Of course I do." Grayson leaned toward me and gave me a light kiss on the lips.

I gasped. "What'd you do that for?"

"This is the first moment we've had alone since Randi's memorial."

My mouth fell open. "So that first kiss wasn't just one of those amygdala anomaly thingies?"

Grayson shook his head. "Not even close."

I grinned from ear to ear.

Yabba dabba do!

But what Grayson said next erased my grin faster than Mountain Dew on a hillbilly's teeth.

"There's something I should tell you, Drex," he said, locking eyes with me.

I dry gulped. "What?"

"I'm a demi-sexual."

"Demi-sexual?" I asked. "Is it something we can work around?"

He shook his head. "No, I'm afraid not."

Grayson cranked the engine and shifted into drive. I sat back in my seat. A long, slow breath escaped my lips as my hope deflated like a balloon.

Grayson's some kind of pervert.
I knew it.
Why, Universe? Why? Why? Why?

CONVERSATION WAS SCARCE as Grayson and I followed Earl out of Mullet's Trailer Park and past the burned-in-two remains of the deceased owner's unfortunate trailer home.

As I stared at the blackened drum set in the yard, I felt confused, and more than a teensy bit heartbroken. The budding romance between me and Grayson had just been nipped in the bud by some weird sexual preference of his—a preference that, apparently, neither of us could do anything about.

To console myself, I reminded myself of all of Grayson's bad qualities. Hey, a girl had to do what a girl had to do.

But as we followed Earl and the old RV along 38th Avenue toward the onramp to I-275, I remembered something else that was also tragic.

We were headed for Plant City.

Crap!

Fighting the odds, I decided to make one last attempt to reiterate my preference to drink margaritas at the beach rather than hang around a pile of nerdy gearheads in Garth's junkyard wasteland. But as I opened my mouth to speak, up the road ahead Earl did something so unexpected it almost left me speechless.

He and that old RV rolled right past the onramp to I-275.

"Wait," I said. "Why isn't Earl getting on the interstate?"

Grayson glanced my way. "I thought we'd take a quick detour first. To cheer you up."

"Really?" I was so sad I was ready to eat my weight in chocolate. "You think I need cheering up?"

"Or cooling down," Grayson said. "With you, it's hard to tell. Anyway, my compliment didn't seem to do the trick."

"Compliment?" I blanched. "How could you possibly think that telling me you prefer older things like that RV and *me* because age adds character was a *compliment*?"

Grayson grimaced. "My bad. But to be fair, with women you never can tell if you're going to hit the jackpot or a landmine."

Excuse me?

My eyebrows met my hairline. "I beg your pardon?" I hissed.

Grayson kept his eyes glued to the road. "My point exactly."

A horn honked behind us. Grayson switched into the left lane and followed Earl southbound onto 34th Street.

I eyed him with caustic suspicion. "Where are you taking me? To a home for decrepit old ladies?"

"Hang on a minute and I'll show you," Grayson said, avoiding eye contact. "I feel relatively confident that you'll like this."

I scowled. "For your sake, I'd *better*."

I folded my arms and sat stewing in silence as we rolled past a schizophrenic mix of shiny new stores and tired old junk shops along 34th Street. Inside, I felt just as mixed up. On the one hand, I'd been thrilled that Grayson had finally kissed me. On the other hand, he'd totally bummed me out by confessing he was a demi-sexual, whatever the heck *that* was.

And to top it all off, he'd said I was old.

How could this day get any more awesome?

As we tailed Earl and the RV closer and closer to downtown St. Petersburg, a thought popped into my head. "Wait. Are we going to the beach?"

"No," Grayson said. "Even *better*."

"Better than the beach?" I asked. "What could be better—"

Then I saw it.

Lo and behold, on the corner of 34th Street and 1st Avenue North, a Walmart stood glistening in the late afternoon sun like a medium-quality cubic zirconia.

And it was a super center!

"Drop me off out front!" I said.

"Will do."

Grayson followed Earl into the parking lot, then veered to the right and pulled up to the front door of the store to let me out.

"Take your time," he said as I flung open the truck door. "While you're in there, I'll call Garth and Jimmy and let them know we've procured the vehicle."

"Whatever," I said, then hopped out of Bessie and made a beeline for the wig aisle.

Chapter Nine

"Do you have any human-hair wigs?" I asked the posterior of a pair of polyester pants that was protruding from underneath a blue smock. They were clinging to the bulbous bottom of a middle-aged woman who was bent over, stocking the shelves with boxes of hair dye.

"Hold on," she grunted, then slowly stood and turned around.

I nearly gasped. I hadn't seen that much makeup on a woman since Tammy Faye Baker signed off the air. She batted her blue eyelids at me, then glanced at the top of my head and asked, "Is that a Ginger Ultima Bob you got on?"

"A what?" I asked.

"I bet it's the 2018 model," she said.

I frowned. "All I know is that it's itchy. I want a new one."

"Well, you've come to the right Walmart, then."

Beaming with pride, the woman in the blue smock extending her arm like a gameshow model revealing the prize-winning showcase. "We got the best wig selection in the tri-county area." She leaned in and whispered, "I'm wearing one myself."

"I hadn't noticed," I said, trying not to stare at the platinum-blonde bird nest perched atop her head like a prepubescent cockatoo.

The wig sparkled like a vat of spilled glitter as she wagged her eyebrows at me and said, "It's from the Lolita, from the new Diamonette line."

"Wow," I said. "It doesn't look trashy at all."

Her eyes brightened. "I *know*, right? That's because it's made with the latest in polyester technology."

"I can see that. It's really ... *nice*. But I was hoping for real human hair?"

The clerk's smile faded a notch. "We don't carry that in store. But you might be able to special order it online."

"That's okay. I kind of want one *right now*." I gestured toward a red pixie wig sitting slightly askew atop a Styrofoam head. "How about that one?"

She nodded her approval. "That's a pretty popular model."

I wasn't sure if that was a good thing or not. "Lots of buyers?" I asked.

"Don't know about *that*. But those ones seem to disappear pretty fast."

She glanced up and down the aisle, then said, "You wouldn't believe where people stuff things so's they can shoplift 'em. Last week we caught an old man toting out a nine-pack of wieners in his pants, if you catch my drift."

Unfortunately, I did.

I cringed, then plucked the auburn wig off the display head and held it between two pinched fingers as if it were a dead rat. "Uh ... do you have a fresh one of these?"

She shook her head. "'Fraid not. Whatever we got in stock I done put out here on the floor."

"Are you sure? Maybe there's one in the back?"

"Nope. I'm sure. Wig truck only comes on Thursdays. Looks like all's we got's that display model you're holdin'."

I grimaced. "Okay. Then, where's your wig wash?"

"Right over there." She pointed to a pink bottle on a shelf. "But Dawn dishwashing soap'll do the job for half the price."

"Wise words, indeed," a man's voice sounded behind me.

I turned to see Grayson eating Cheetos from a family-sized bag.

"You ready to check out?" he asked.

"Yeah."

I thanked the wig lady, then turned and grabbed Grayson by the arm. He grinned. "So my plan worked. Your new Walmart wig seems to have gotten you in a better mood."

"Not exactly," I said. "When we get back to the truck, I want you to help me look up that Wilshire wig website."

"Okay. But I may be able to do you one better."

I stopped in my tracks. "Better than a *Wilshire* wig?"

Grayson shrugged. "Maybe not *better*. But definitely *faster*. And cheaper. And, I might add, a whole lot *nicer* than that deceased rodent you're carrying."

I glanced down at the mangy wig in my hand. "Okay, Grayson. You're on!"

I flung the tangle of red hair into a bin of pool noodles. A few seconds later, as we headed toward the door, I thought I heard a grown man scream.

Chapter Ten

The anticipation of getting a fancy new wig to replace my itchy one had brightened my mood somewhat, so I decided to cut Grayson some slack.

"Thanks for saving me from another Walmart wig," I said as we left the store and walked back to our vehicle.

"You're welcome. I think you deserve better."

That made me smile. Being Grayson's love interest might not be in the cards for me, but I was still his private eye intern. And, honestly, that's what I'd originally signed on for anyway. I decided to be happy about it, and make the most of that.

As we approached Bessie in the Walmart parking lot, a few spots away I saw Earl. He was bent over the open hood of our newly acquired crap-heap of a Winnebago.

"Okay," I said, turning to Grayson. "So where are we gonna find one of these fabulous wigs you promised me?"

Grayson reached for the driver's door of the truck. "Hold on. I've got it right here."

Stunned, I said, "You already bought one?"

Grayson smirked. "You were in Walmart longer than you think." He reached up and opened the truck's door, pulled out a box, and handed it to me.

The small carton was white, but all I saw was red.

"*Fat Guys' Beauty Wigs*?" I hissed, reading the name on the box lid. "Nick Grayson, you better be glad I had to take my Glock outta my purse to go inside Walmart!"

Grayson blanched. "I didn't *name* the place, Drex. Take a look inside the box. Geez. When are you going to learn to ask questions *before* you start shooting?"

I scowled.

Never, I guess.

"Go on. Open it," Grayson said.

I slipped the lid off the box. Inside, nestled in pink tissue paper, was an absolutely gorgeous auburn bob. Compared to it, the wig currently resting atop my head looked like a glob of dried-up spaghetti.

"It's beautiful," I said. "But how—?"

"I did some research while you were in Walmart," Grayson said. "I found out that Fat Guys' Beauty Wigs carries nearly as good a selection as Wig Villa downtown. But luckily for me, Fat Guys' is located right across the street."

Grayson pointed to his right, but I didn't bother to look. Instead, I leapt into Bessie's driver's seat, commandeered the rearview mirror, and swapped out my hand-me-down wig for my new, first-class coiffure.

"I love it!" I said, tugging it to the right for one final adjustment.

"That's a relief," Grayson said. "Now, can we get going?"

"Yes, sir." I scooted across the bench to make room for Grayson to climb into the driver's seat. Once he was inside, I touched him on the arm. "Thank you."

"You're welcome," he said. "So, off to Plant City?"

I nodded. "Sure. I guess a day or two there won't kill me. But I still don't understand why we can't get the RV worked on at a garage around here."

Grayson stiffened. "There are a few custom modifications I want to make that aren't available at your average mechanic shop."

My face went slack. "Like *what*?"

Grayson glanced up at my wig. "You were happy with that surprise. Can you trust me with another?"

I bit my lip. "I guess so."

"Excellent. I'll inform Earl." Grayson reached for the door handle. "Oh. Here he comes now."

I glanced past Grayson to see Earl shuffling toward us in his blue coveralls. He took one look at me, and shook his head. "Wooeee, Grayson. It was about time you upgraded your girlfriend."

"Har har," I said. "Can we get out of here now?"

"Sure thang, Cuz." Earl wiped his greasy hands on his mechanic coveralls. "Only one small problem."

"What?" I asked.

"The dad-burned RV won't start."

"WE SHOULD CALL DANNY," I said after taking a look at the RV's engine myself. "Everything appears in order. Maybe there's some trick to starting it."

"Good idea," Grayson said. "Call him."

I blanched. "*I'm* not talking to that old letch! Let Earl do it. Those two speak the same language."

"Mechanics?" Grayson asked.

"No. Redneck."

After ten minutes of listening to Earl say, "Uh-huh, uh-huh, uh-huh over the phone, I was ready to hit him over the head with a frying pan.

"Wrap it up," I said. "It's hot as fried asphalt out here."

Earl nodded, then said, "Will do, buddy. Gotta go." He clicked off the phone and locked eyes with me. "You were right, Bobbie. I *was* missing something."

"What?"

"The jiggle factor," he said, smirking at me.

I frowned. "Why are you looking at me like that?"

"Because Danny told me to make google eyes at you when I said 'jiggle factor.'"

Where's a damned skillet when you need one?

"What exactly is this 'jiggle factor' of which you speak?" Grayson asked, walking up to us.

"The secret to startin' the RV when it's cranky," Earl said. "Danny told me the trick was to squinch my left eye and suck my left eye tooth while I'm jigglin' the keys in the ignition."

I shook my head. "Earl, you've been played for a fool."

Earl shot me a sideways look. "Maybe so, Bobbie. But at least I didn't lose at *Old Maid*."

I raised a fist.

"Let's give it a try," Grayson said, stepping between Earl and me. "What have we got to lose?"

"Nothin'," Earl said. "At least, not for the next two days, anyway."

"What do you mean?" I asked.

Earl shrugged. "'Cause that's how long Walmart lets you camp out in the parking lot for free. You ought to know that by now, Bobbie."

I HAD MY DOUBTS AS I watched Earl climb behind the wheel of the RV to try out Danny's 'jiggle factor' routine.

When my big shaggy bear of a cousin squinted his left eye and sucked his left eye tooth—as Danny had instructed—it was all I could do to not wet myself laughing. Earl looked like Sasquatch trying to impersonate *Popeye the Sailor Man*.

I was about to tell Earl he was a hapless victim of Danny Daniels' prank when, to my amazement, the old motorhome cranked on the first try.

"Ha! Told ya!" Earl hollered.

Crap!

Not only had Earl bested me—but now that the RV was running, Plant City was back on the horizon.

"Fine," I admitted. "You were right, Earl. But you were on the phone with Danny for nearly ten minutes. He must've told you something besides 'try jiggling the keys.'"

"Well, yeah," Earl said. "I was talkin' to him about what it would cost me to rent a trailer in Mullet's Trailer Park."

I recoiled at the thought. "What? *Why*?"

"Well, Bobbie, maybe you ain't the only one that wants outta Point Paradise."

"How much does he charge per month?" Grayson asked.

"Seriously?" I said, hitting Grayson on the arm.

Earl shrugged. "Don't know. Danny said he won't know for sure till he has Mullet's old burnt-up trailer hauled away."

"That doesn't make any sense," Grayson said.

I rolled my eyes. "What part of this *does*?"

"Grayson's right," Earl said. "I got the same hinky feeling when Danny told me that. And it got me to thinkin', you know?"

You? Thinking? No, I don't know.

"Thinking what?" Grayson asked.

"About maybe things ain't so kosher up in that trailerhood," Earl said. "So I put on my investigator hat and asked Danny if'n he was slam sure that there fire what burned up the trailer and the one what burned up his brother wasn't related somehow. By locationality and all, you know?"

Crap. That's a valid question. Stupidly put, but valid. And one I failed to ask during my interview with Danny. But then again, Earl, being a guy, is immune to the 'creep' factor...

I bit down hard and swallowed my pride. "So, what did Danny say, Sherlock?"

"Danny said ain't no way them fires could a been related."

"Why not?" Grayson asked.

"On account a locationality, like I said," Earl replied. "You see, when Danny's brother Mullet burned up in the RV, he wasn't at the trailer park. He was out campin' in Fort De Soto Campground."

I glanced over at Grayson. I could almost see the gears turning in his head.

"Intriguing," Grayson said. "Did Danny happen to mention which site Mullet was camping in at the time?"

Chapter Eleven

"My phone battery's almost dead," Grayson said as we stood beside the RV in the Walmart parking lot. "Let me use yours, Drex. I need to inform Garth that we've had a change of plans."

"What are you talking about?" I asked as Earl danced around me, chanting "Jiggle factor," complete with an encore performance of his idiotic Popeye impression.

"I know you'll be greatly disappointed," Grayson said, "but our trip to Plant City is on hold for the moment. We're heading to Fort De Soto Park instead."

My eyebrow shot up. "Seriously? Not that I'm complaining, but why?"

"Isn't it obvious?" Grayson asked.

I stared at Grayson.

Obviously not.

"Can't you see?" he said. "We've been presented with a unique opportunity."

"Opportunity?" I asked.

"Yes. To recreate Mullet Daniels' death, complete with original crime scene and exact geographic location."

I glanced over at Earl. He'd gotten into Grayson's bag of Cheetos and was sporting long, orange vampire fangs.

I shook my head. "If we're gonna use Earl as Mullet's stunt double, I'm in."

"No," Grayson said. "I don't believe that will be necessary. A scientific observation of the environmental conditions should suffice. My plan is to set up the RV in the same campsite where Mullet met his demise. We'll spend the night in the camper, recording any—"

"Excuse me," I cut in. "But if you think I'm staying in that disgusting old dead man's camper, you've got serious brain damage!"

Grayson eyed me carefully. "Did I mention Fort De Soto Park was voted one of the most beautiful beaches in the world? But if you prefer to go to Plant City—"

"Ugh! Fine," I said. "But I call shotgun on sleeping in Bessie. You two can fight it out over Mullet's burning bed. In the meantime, I'm heading back into Walmart for supplies. There's no way I'm sleeping on that dead man's mattress, *or* in Bessie in Earl's stupid Superman sleeping bag."

"Fair enough," Grayson said. "But first, hand me your phone."

I grumbled, but began fishing through my purse. "Why don't you just call Garth on the ham radio, like you usually do?"

"I checked. The radio isn't working."

"Did you try the jiggle factor?" I quipped.

"Not applicable," Grayson said. "It's unfortunate I wasn't able to salvage my radio from my old RV. I guess I'll never see it again, or any of my other investigative tools."

As my fingers encircled the phone in my purse, a thought dawned on me like a golden sunbeam from heaven itself.

All of Grayson's investigative tools are gone—including that blasted EEG machine! No more electrodes! No more paste! No more hideous images scaring the bejeebers out of me!

The revelation almost made up for Grayson being a demi-sexual.

Almost.

I handed Grayson my phone. As I watched him punch the buttons for Operative Garth and begin to speak, I reminisced about how his lips had felt on mine.

So handsomely close, yet so nerdily far.

I shivered, then snatched the bank envelope from Grayson's pocket and marched toward Walmart.

I may not be able to buy Grayson's affections, but I most certainly have enough cash to buy some consolation prizes.

Look out, candy aisle. Here I come.

ON THE DRIVE TO FORT De Soto Park, I barely noticed the view. Instead, my eyes went in and out of focus as I stared at the rear of the ratty RV ahead of us being driven by my annoying cousin, Earl.

So much had happened in one day, my head was spinning.

Someone had given me a million dollars. Grayson had kissed me, then confessed he was a demi-sexual. We'd bought another RV almost identical to Grayson's old one. Grayson had kissed me. I'd gotten a new wig. Grayson had kissed me. We were on our way to relive the fiery death throes of a redneck named Mullet.

Grayson had kissed me.

Thoughts buzzed around in my head like a swarm of hungry mosquitos, yet I'd remained silent. I hadn't know where to start. But since I'd no doubt be bunking alone in the truck for the next untold number of days, I let my amygdala run free. The anomaly it came up with was a doozy.

I turned to Grayson and asked, "Are you just interested in me for my money?"

"What?" Grayson turned and stared at me. "Where did *that* come from?"

"I dunno," I said sullenly. "It's just that, well, you didn't seem interested in me before I had a million bucks in the bank."

"Oh." Grayson let out a sigh. "Look, I already told you why. It's because I'm a demi-sexual."

I frowned. "What does that mean? You like demons, or what?"

Grayson's lips formed half a smile. "No, Drex. But if *that* were true, I fail to see how that would rule you out."

"Ha ha," I said. "You pick *now* to develop a sense of humor? Brilliant."

Grayson's eyes returned to the road. "Drex, being a demi-sexual means that I need to get to know a person pretty well before I can become sexually attracted to them."

"Oh."

I could barely speak, the air knocked out of my lungs by a punch of relief.

"That's weird," I managed to squeak out.

"Why is that weird?" Grayson asked.

"Not *weird* weird," I said. "What I meant is, I'm the exact opposite. Usually, the more I get to know a person, the *less* I like them. What's *that* called?"

"Typical."

Grayson waited a beat, then turned and smiled at me.

I grinned. "So, you're saying your attraction to me and the money are just a coincidence?"

"No. As you know, I don't believe in coincidences. These two factors just happened to have temporally coincided."

My nose crinkled. "What's the difference?"

"About two weeks."

"Huh?"

Grayson glanced over at me. "Right before we lost the old RV, I realized I was feeling something more for you than a business relationship. Then, when you were injured and I thought you might not make it ... well, that was the catalyst that crystalized my feelings."

"Are you saying you underwent some kind of *chemical reaction*?" I crossed my arms. "How romantic."

Grayson sighed. "I'm *trying* to be. Would you quit busting my chops?"

I winced. "Sorry."

"When you were undergoing surgery, I kept wondering what I would do if you died. I realized then that the world wouldn't be the same without you in it."

"Oh, Grayson!" I said.

I leaned over to kiss him. Just as our lips were about to touch, a horn honked. Our eyes darted to the windshield. Bessie had wandered over the line and was straddling two lanes of the interstate.

"Cripes!" Grayson said, pulling the truck back into its lane. "Sorry, Drex. Looks like that kiss will have to wait. Rain check?"

I smiled. "You got it."

I unhooked my seatbelt and slid into the middle seat beside Grayson. I thought he'd hold my hand or something. But he didn't. Instead, he kept glancing out the side window.

"What are you doing?" I asked.

"Looking for cumulonimbi," he said.

"For *what*?"

Grayson glanced over at me. His green eyes flashed. "Cumulonimbi. *Rain* clouds."

"Oh." I grinned getting his joke. "So, tell me. How does it feel to be a demi-sexual?"

Grayson shrugged. "Okay, I guess. How does it feel *not* to be?"

I grinned and kissed him on the cheek. "Typical, I guess."

Chapter Twelve

Finding out that Grayson wasn't a demon worshipper or even a pervert (hopefully) had me feeling all warm and fuzzy inside. So did the scenery out the window of the truck.

Gone were the run-down trailer parks and sketchy, low-rent establishments. They'd been replaced by palm trees, seagulls, and the sparkling Gulf of Mexico.

"That'll be 75 cents," the old guy at the toll booth said, holding out a hand covered in a clear rubber glove.

"Nice shirt," Grayson said, admiring the man's tropical, button-down top. It was emblazoned with colorful palm trees, flamingoes, and other Florida icons.

"It's my official uniform," the man said, beaming. "If you like it, you can get you one online."

"Not my style," Grayson said, handing over three quarters. "But festive."

"Too bad it doesn't come in black," I quipped.

"Hey. Black goes with everything," Grayson said, veering out of the toll lane. "My parents taught me that."

I smirked, then turned to admire the view as we drove across a bridge shaped like a camel hump. It spanned the Intracoastal Waterway, which separated the strip islands from the main coast of Florida.

Crossing over the bridge, I felt like Dorothy in the *Wizard of Oz*. What lay on the other side looked like a whole other planet altogether.

The water itself was a gorgeous shade of cerulean blue. On either side of the road, the land appeared to have been swallowed alive by condo towers in shades of coral pink, sand white, and sunny yellow. Each condo community was protected by its own gated entrance, tucked tastefully amid expensive-looking tropical landscaping.

"Wow, this area looks posh," I said as we drove past a sign announcing our arrival in Tierra Verde.

"Perhaps," Grayson said. "But I prefer to be closer to nature myself. How about you?"

"Depends on the nature," I said.

We drove past the condos, then kept pace with Earl and the RV as he turned left at a streetlight and headed south, following the brown signs for Fort De Soto Park. As we traveled along the flat, low-lying strip of land, on either side of the road more condos with tropical landscaping beckoned, but not quite so exuberantly.

A couple of miles down the road, I spotted a gleaming retail center on the right. It called to me with the promise of tropical island wear and delicious stone crabs.

I wanted to answer both calls.

"Hey, let's stop there," I said, then stared blankly out the window as we blew past the place.

"Can't," Grayson said. "We need to get settled in before sunset."

I glared at Grayson, then noticed the golden tones of the sun on the water. It was late afternoon. He was right, but I still felt cheated out of what *I* wanted to do. After all, I had the money now. Shouldn't I be in charge?

I started to say just that, then stopped and chewed my lip instead. Was I letting the money thing do a power trip on my head?

I glanced over at Grayson. The flip-flopping of our financial circumstances hadn't seemed to affect him. In fact, he hadn't seemed to mind at all.

Suddenly, I realized *I* minded that he *didn't*.

How screwed up am I?

Somehow, in my malformed Southern brain, Grayson's lack of concern over who made the money was causing his masculine allure to shrivel in my eyes. It was crazy, I knew. Why should it matter who brought home the bacon? Was I merely being influenced by the old "the man makes the money" diatribe I'd grown up with? Or had my amygdala gone all anomalous on me again?

Then a thought hit me like a love bug on a windshield.

Without Grayson, I'd have never known about The Amazing Randi or the other people out there who were willing to pay big money for evidence of cryptids and other paranormal stuff. Furthermore, it was Grayson's Mothman scat—or the sample of his own vestigial body part—that had impressed that mystery benefactor enough to give me the money in the first place. All I'd done was just mail the samples in.

So, to be fair, it was actually *Grayson* who deserved the credit for my financial windfall.

I glanced over at him.

But he doesn't have to know that.

He shot me a smile.

Or maybe he already does...

"Are you sure the fact that I have the money now doesn't bother you?" I asked.

"Why should it?" Grayson said. "Money, like time, is just a construct, Drex. A matter of perception."

"Yeah, right." I grabbed the bank envelope from my purse and fanned the remaining bills in Grayson's face. "This looks pretty real to me!"

"Sure. But in and of themselves, what intrinsic value do they possess? You can't eat them or wear them or build a shelter with them."

"Sure you can," I said. "You pay for all that with these." I shoved the dollars at him again.

"Only if the other person shares your perception about their value," Grayson argued. "If capitalism were to capitulate, you'd find yourself in possession of nothing more than a handful of processed and stained wood pulp."

"Huh?"

Grayson turned and locked eyes with me. "If Walmart closed and there were no more places to buy anything, those funny-looking pieces of paper in your hand would be about as valuable as toilet tissue."

I stared at the bills with new eyes. Then I glanced up at Grayson and said, "You've obviously never found yourself stranded in a bathroom staring at an empty roll."

Chapter Thirteen

After reaching our destination, Grayson and I walked into the odd, six-sided building at the entrance to Fort De Soto Campgrounds.

"Sorry, folks. We're all full up for the night," a man clad in a khaki shirt and olive-green cargo pants said. "This time of year, we're usually booked six months ahead."

I shot Grayson a look. "Now what?"

He whispered, "Play along."

Oh, great. Can't wait.

"No problem," Grayson said. "We're only here to visit a friend for a few hours."

The ranger, a clean-cut man in his late thirties, eyed us with suspicion from behind the reception counter that separated the staff from the campers.

"Really," he said. "That's what the guy ahead of you in the RV said, too."

"Interesting," Grayson said.

"We won't stay long," I said, reading the man's nametag. "Okay, Ranger Provost?"

Ranger Provost looked us over, then sighed and wiped a hand across the top of his military buzz cut. "Keep in mind, we only allow two vehicles per camping site. We spot check every couple of hours. You've been warned."

"Excellent," Grayson said. "Could we have a map of the campsites?"

"Here you go." Ranger Provost slid a map across the counter. It looked like a paper placemat from a cheap roadside eatery. "Which site you looking for?"

"Number 113," Grayson said.

"That's in area two. That section allows all rigs, and it's pet friendly. But anything on four legs has to remain on a leash at all times when outdoors. You have any pets with you?"

"No four-legged ones," Grayson said, glancing at a glass case containing a display of local seashells.

"Good," Ranger Provost said. "To get there, take either of the two lefts you come to. The streets make a loop. Enjoy your stay with your friend."

"Thank you," I said, tugging Grayson away from the display case.

"Oh, and one more thing," Ranger Provost said as we left. "The front gate is locked from 9 p.m. to 5:30 a.m., so plan accordingly."

"Duly noted," Grayson said, handing me the map. "Here you go, navigator."

We left the station, climbed back into Bessie, and drove a few yards down the main road. Earl was waiting for us in the parking lot just inside the gate. I rolled down my window and hollered at him, "Follow us!"

"Roger dodger," he yelled back.

I turned my attention to the map of the campsite. "Looks like we've already passed the first left, so take the next one," I said to Grayson. Then I watched in the side mirror as Earl pulled out and followed us in the RV.

Grayson hooked a left and drove slowly down the narrow, two-lane road. It quickly got even narrower, and the slick asphalt pavement turned to a crunchy, white mixture of crushed fossilized shell and limestone.

That wasn't all that had gone native. All around us, the lush, tropical landscaping threatened to take over the roadway. Cabbage palms, vines, long-leaf pines, sea grapes and scrub oaks formed a veritable jungle that leaned in and hugged both sides of the road.

Each campsite appeared to have been individually carved out of the jungle scape. Thick islands of vegetation stood all along the borders of each site, both dividing them and forming privacy barriers between campsites.

"Very nice," Grayson said. "You can barely see the neighbors."

"Hopefully, you can't hear them, either," I said, studying the map. "Site 113, right?"

"Affirmative."

"All right!" I exclaimed.

"What?" Grayson asked.

"It looks like the odd-numbered sites back up to the water. We've got a waterfront site!"

"Excellent," Grayson said. "Now, all we've got to do is hope our happy camper isn't all *that* happy."

"THERE IT IS," I SAID, pointing at a small, wooden sign engraved with the numbers 113.

Grayson stopped in the road directly in front of the campsite and craned his neck to see past me out the passenger window. Parked in number 113 was an old, white Chevy van half eaten up with rust. Sitting at the picnic bench were a couple who appeared to have squandered their entire car- maintenance budget on blue hair dye and tattoos.

I turned to make a snide remark to Grayson, but he was already hopping out of the driver's seat. I whipped back around and watched him make a beeline for the couple. I scrambled out the door and tried to catch up with him.

"Hi there," Grayson said as he got within earshot of the illustrated couple. "Nice day, isn't it?"

The strangers stared at us, then exchanged looks with each other.

"Shhh," I whispered to Grayson. "You sound too smarmy. Let me handle this."

"Hi," I said to the couple. "This may sound weird, but we'd like to pay to camp in your spot."

"What?" the guy said, the bandana rising an inch on his wide, sweaty forehead. "I don't think—"

"Hold on," the woman said, silencing him like a dog. She looked me up and down as she brushed teal bangs away from her heavily-lined eyes. "How much?"

"How long do you have it for?" I asked.

"The next three days," the guy said, his tongue piercing clicking against his front teeth when he said the word "three."

"You're stoned," the woman said to him. "We're paid up for the next week."

"So, what are we talking here?" I asked. "Three hundred bucks?"

"Something like that," she said. "But we're not staying here for our health. A hotel would cost double that."

"So, six hundred and it's ours?" I asked.

"Six hundred bucks!" the guy hooted, as if he'd just won the lottery. "You got it!" He pulled a joint from his shirt pocket and lit it to celebrate.

"Not so fast," the woman said, eyeing me with her suspicious, Egyptian eyes. "What's in it for *us*? We spend that money on a motel, and in a few days, it's a wash for us."

Looks like you could use a wash right now.

"I understand," I said. "I want to be fair, but I'm not made of money."

Behind me, I heard Earl laugh. "Don't listen to her! Somebody just give her a million bucks!"

Arrgghh!

The Queen of Tattoos' lips curled sinisterly. "Ten grand and we're out of here before you can crank your engine."

I glanced over at her boyfriend, then back to her. "Two grand, and I won't call the cops about the weed."

The woman's eyes narrowed, then softened. "Okay. Deal."

Chapter Fourteen

As Grayson and Earl backed the RV into campsite 113, I stared at the registration form I'd just shelled out two thousand dollars for.

Geez. I could be staying at the Don Cesar for this kind of money!

But this was what Grayson had wanted. And this spontaneous human combustion case, no matter how dubious or idiotic it might turn out to be, was part of my official P.I. training.

Huh. I wonder if it's tax deductible...

A camper walked by on the road and waved at me. It suddenly dawned on me I had a little housekeeping to do.

"Okay, we need to get our stories straight," I said, walking over to where the guys were setting up camp. "If a ranger or anybody official-looking comes by and asks our names, Grayson, you're Frank." I looked back down at the registration. "And, believe it or not, I'm *Bessie*."

"What about me?" Earl asked. "Who am I?"

A big, dumb pain in my ass, that's who.

"Earl, you're just Earl," I said.

He pouted. "But I wanna be somebody else, too."

I smirked. "I can't blame you there. But we're only changing our names so they match the ones on the campsite registration."

Earl doubled down on his droopy dog impression.

"Ugh. Fine. Who do you want to be?"

Earl grinned. "I wanna be Bessie."

I blanched. "You want to be the *girl*?"

"The girl *truck*." Earl nodded toward his humongous, black monster truck. "Now that she's got that shiny new periscope, I wouldn't mind."

I shook my head. "So you want to be a hermaphroditic truck."

Earl shrugged. "I guess that'd be all right."

I blew out a sigh. "Earl, the Bessie I'm talking about is the woman who was here in the campsite when we pulled up. *Not* your truck. So could you just do me a favor and stick with being yourself, and let *me* be Bessie?"

"The hermit Frodo-ite?" Earl asked. "Well, with that bald head of your'n, I guess you fit the role better'n me anyways."

I sneered. "Shut your lint trap and get the fire going in the grill while we've still got some daylight, okay?"

He laughed. "Whatever you say, Boss-Man Bessie."

IT WAS BARELY PAST seven o'clock, but the sun was already setting fast on our little rectangular patch of crushed shell in the jungle paradise known as Fort De Soto Campgrounds.

Everything was in place. The old RV was parked at the back end of the campsite, butting up to some low bushes. Beyond the low hedge lay a patch of green grass with a walking path that skirted the water's edge.

To the left of the motorhome stood a government-issued, Army-green picnic table, along with a small, rectangular barbeque grill mounted on a metal pole. Bessie hogged the rest of the site, her tailgate mere inches from the road.

"Hotdogs again?" Grayson asked, coming out of the RV. He joined me and Earl as we stood around the grill watching the tube steaks sizzle.

"Sorry, but tacos don't travel well," I said, plucking a wiener from the grill and wedging it into a bun. "Earl, where's the mustard?"

My cousin shot me a sly grin. "In the cooler—in the RV."

I frowned. "Go get it. I'm not going in there."

"Why not?" Grayson asked.

My teeth clamped together. "Just ... *because*!"

Earl chortled. "'Fraid you gonna spontaneously discombobulate in there, Boss-Man Bessie?"

"No!" I growled.

"Really, Drex," Grayson said. "There's no cause for concern about that."

I pursed my lips. "Why? Because of the infinitesimal statistical probability?"

Grayson shrugged. "Well, *that* and the fact that spontaneous human combustion requires an ignition source."

Earl smirked at me. "Would being hot as blazes under the collar do it, Mr. G.?"

"Hmm," Grayson rubbed his chin. "Probably not. But that's an interesting concept."

"Tell us some more about them poor folks what went up in flames like Mullet did," Earl said, stuffing half a hotdog into his cavernous maw. "Like, who was the first one in history to burn up like a crispy critter?"

"Geezus," I said, shaking my head.

"You could be right," Grayson said.

"Huh?" I grunted.

Grayson set his unbitten hotdog down on the paper plate. "It's a distinct possibility. You see, some researchers believe that the Shroud of Turin could be the first known relic left behind by a victim of spontaneous human combustion."

"What?" I gasped. "Are you saying Jesus burst into flames?"

"Who knows?" Grayson said. "I wasn't there when they put him into that crypt. No one's even certain the Shroud of Turin is his actual burial cloth. All I'm saying is that the shroud—whoever it belonged to—could be actual physical evidence of spontaneous human combustion."

"He's right, Bobbie!" Earl said. "You saw that mattress in the RV. I think I seen Mullet's face in it. It's almost the same exact thing!"

"Ugh!" I groaned. "Gimme a break!"

Earl shot me a look. "Hey. If the sheet *fits*, he must a been *lit*."

I glared at my cousin. "Who died and made you Johnnie Cochran?"

"Look, you two," Grayson said. "Without access to it, we can't be a hundred percent certain about the Shroud of Turin. But Earl could be on to something comparing it to Mullet's mattress."

"How on Earth would that be true?" I said.

"Because Mullet Daniels' case appears to fit within the four formal parameters that define spontaneous human combustion," Grayson said.

"Ha! Told ya!" Earl stuck his tongue out at me.

I folded my arms and stared at Grayson. "Which *are*?"

"I'm glad you asked. First, victims of spontaneous human combustion are presumed to have caught fire from within," Grayson explained, counting out each point on his spidery fingers.

"Two, their bodies are rapidly reduced to ash. Three, they don't appear to have put up any resistance. And four, the immediate area around the victims remains virtually untouched by the fire."

"Wouldn't that rule out Jesus?" I said. "The Bible says he arose three days later."

"Surviving spontaneous human combustion is not without precedence," Grayson said. "Angel did, too."

"Angels and Jesus?" I laughed. "Sorry, Grayson. But so far, your argument sounds more like a sermon than science. I'm surprised at you."

"I didn't mean *heavenly* angels, Drex," Grayson said. "I meant the case of Jack Angel, the traveling salesman."

"Oh. *Jack* Angel," I said sarcastically. "How could I have been so stupid?"

Grayson shrugged. "I don't know. That's beyond my pay grade. Anyway, getting back to Jack, his case began in November of 1974, after he parked his motorhome in a parking lot in Savannah, Georgia."

"Oh! Was it a Walmart parking lot?" Earl asked, grabbing a handful of Cheetos from a family-sized bag as big as a bed pillow.

"I'm not sure," Grayson said. "But I don't think that's relevant to the facts at hand."

Earn nodded studiously and crammed his mouth full of Cheetos.

"Okay," I said. "Then what happened?"

Grayson fiddled with a jar of pickles. "So, Jack Angel parked his RV overnight, with the intention of meeting a customer the next morning."

"That RV. Was it a Winnebago, like ours?" Earl asked, waving a Cheeto like a tiny orange baton.

I glanced over at Grayson and smirked.

"Uh ... not sure," Grayson said. "Anyway, the point is, Mr. Angel woke up *four days later* with his arm severely burned and a large, gaping hole in his chest. It was as if he had *exploded from within*. Nothing else around him was even singed."

"Whoa!" I said, then glanced over at the old RV. "And you guys wonder why I don't want to go inside that death trap?"

Grayson shook his head. "You're missing the point."

"Which is?" I asked.

"In some cases, spontaneous human combustion is survivable."

"What do the survivors say happened to them?" I asked.

"That's unclear. So far, no survivors have been able to provide any helpful details."

"So, Mr. G., what do *you* think causes it?" Earl asked.

Grayson reached for the bag of Cheetos. "As a scientist, I prefer to keep an open mind while we explore the possibilities."

"Then I will, too, chief," Earl said, and bit the head off a club-shaped Cheeto.

Chapter Fifteen

I awoke the next morning curled up inside a truck named Bessie, masquerading as a weed-addicted drifter named Bessie.

Take that, Twilight Zone.

A squeaky sound at the window made me crack open an eye.

I gasped.

Sasquatch was peering in at me through the glass.

"Mornin', Bobbie," Earl said, rubbing his meaty knuckles on the windowpane.

"Rrrumph," I grumbled.

He grinned. "I'm gonna go get us some donuts and coffee, Miss Sunshine."

I sat up and rolled down the window. "Okay. But remember, whenever anybody else is around, you need to call me Bessie. And call Grayson, Frank."

Earl nodded. "Got it. Now get outta the truck. Unless you wanna ride along with me, Boss-Man Bessie."

"Stop calling me that."

"But you just said to—"

"I meant Boss-Man," I snarled as I squirmed out of the sheet I was wrapped up in. I snatched my toothbrush and toothpaste from atop the dashboard. "Don't call me *Boss-Man*. Just call me *Bessie*, plain and simple."

"You got it." Earl opened the driver's door. "This mornin', I'm gonna make your coffee an extra-large."

"Thanks," I said, eyeing him suspiciously as I scooted out of the truck.

"No need to thank me." Earl climbed into the truck. "Right now, I'm just thinkin' of me and Grayson's survival."

"Ha ha." I shook my toothbrush at him like a club. "Very funny."

"You need anything else while I'm out gallivantin'?"

"Not that I can think of."

"Okay." He grinned and waved at me. "See ya later, Bessie Plain and Simple."

As I watched Earl pull out of the campsite and drive off, I couldn't decide whether he was an idiot redneck or an idiot savant. But as I pondered the idea, I took consolation in that fact that, either way, he was still an idiot.

WHEN I RETURNED FROM the campground's community bathroom, Grayson was walking around the campsite, staring up at the sky.

"Looking for UFOs?" I quipped.

"Hmm," Grayson said, still scanning the sky. "No. I was checking for overhead power lines."

"Why?"

"Mullet's camper was parked in this very spot when he burned to death. I'm trying to ascertain whether there were any geographic anomalies that could've served as an external ignition source."

"Huh?" I grunted, flopping onto the picnic table bench. "For crying out loud, Grayson. Speak English. I haven't even had any coffee yet."

"I'm simply trying to figure out why Mullet Daniels caught fire in *this* particular campsite."

I toyed with my toothbrush. "I thought you said it was spontaneous human combustion. Didn't you say it's caused by an internal source of ignition?"

"Yes. That's the general working theory, however improbable. But only by ruling out the probable can one come to the conclusion of the improbable. That's what keeping an open mind is all about."

"Right." I sighed, stuck my elbows on the table, and rested my head in my hands.

"Drex, if you want to be a good investigator, you should practice being more open-minded."

I scowled and looked up at him. "Even before my morning coffee?"

Grayson shot me a look. I sat up and let my arms fall to my sides. "Okay, fine. How do I practice keeping an open mind?"

"By giving consideration to *all* options, even the seemingly improbable."

"Like what? Give me an example."

Grayson locked his green eyes with my brown ones. "How about the existence of alien life forms?"

"Always with the aliens," I sighed. "Couldn't you pick something not so far out there for once? Like I said, I haven't had any coffee yet."

Grayson smirked. "Okay." He leaned down toward me and said, "But first, how about a good-morning ki—"

The crunch of tires on crushed shell made us both look toward the road. A second later, the nose of Bessie's huge black chassis appeared as Earl pulled up into camp.

Great timing, you big oaf.

As I glared at Earl, Grayson said, "Here's a lesson in open-mindedness, Drex. How about considering the idea that your cousin Earl possesses above-average native intelligence?"

"What?" I said.

"Hey, y'all!" Earl yelled, waving at us through the open driver's window. "They didn't have no donuts left at the camp store, so I got us this big ol' bag of candy corn instead!"

I shot Grayson a look. "These alien life forms you mentioned earlier. What galaxy would they happen to be from?"

"SAY CHEESE," I SAID, and snapped a picture of Earl and Grayson drinking coffee and eating microwaved Hot Pockets with a side of candy corn.

"What you takin' pictures for?" Earl asked.

"Vacation memories," I said. "I wouldn't want to forget this breakfast of champions."

Grayson shot me a look. So much for my lesson on open-mindedness.

Oops.

I turned to my cousin and forced a smile. "Earl, I'm trying to keep an open mind about breakfast foods. Can you tell us why you chose candy corn to supplement our well-balanced start to the day?"

Earl shrugged. "I guess cause that's what they had the most of at the camp store. And it was on clearance, too. I got this here big ol' bag for a dollar. I reckon on account of Halloween being over and all."

"Yeah. About six months ago," I said. I glanced over at Grayson. "Well, that certainly makes perfect sense."

Grayson cleared his throat. "These Hot Pockets are quite tasty. Speaking of which, they remind me of a man who burst into flames because of one."

My mouth fell open. "Because of a Hot Pocket?"

Earl, who was about to shove the tail end of his Hot Pocket into his huge maw, froze in place. The half-eaten pastry pocket hovered at the entrance of his mouth like a damaged shuttlecraft caught in a tractor beam.

Possibly sensing our distress, Grayson clarified himself. "Uh, not one of *these* Hot Pockets," he said. "It was the pocket of a pair of pants that overheated."

Earl glanced down at his lap, a horrified look on his face. I shot Grayson a smirk, then pursed my lips to keep from bursting out laughing.

"What I *meant*," Grayson said, "was that the man's pants caught fire due to a malfunctioning lithium battery. It exploded in his pocket like a firework."

"Oh," Earl said, visibly relieved. "Why was he walkin' around with batteries in his pocket anyways?"

"We all do. Every day," Grayson said. "Lithium batteries are in all kinds of devices. Including our cellphones and computers."

Earl cocked his head. "Then why ain't we all blowin' up?"

"Well, sometimes we do," Grayson said. "But it's rare. And in this particular case, the fiery culprit was a cheaply made vape cigarette."

"He put a lit cigarette in his pocket?" I asked.

Grayson looked at me oddly. "No. Vape cigarettes are *electronic*. It was the battery that caught fire."

"Oh. Right," I said, my ears heating up.

"So why did that vape pipe blow up?" Earl asked, then shoved the rest of his Hot Pocket into his mouth.

"Well," Grayson said, "According to the investigator's report, the man had just made a purchase at a convenience store and had put his change in the same pocket as his e-cigarette. A coin lodged between the battery's terminals, causing a short circuit. In a matter of seconds, the battery heated up and exploded like a fireball."

"Geez," Earl said. "You think that's what could be causing all these cases of spontaneous human discombobulation?"

Grayson shook his head. "Not likely. Lithium batteries didn't become commercially available until the 1970s. So that definitely rules out a lot of cases, including The Cinder Woman."

"The Cinder Woman?" I asked.

"Yes. That's the case that initially drew me here to St. Petersburg in the first place. Didn't you see it in the folder? It's the first one in the file."

"Oh. Sure," I lied.

"Who's this Cinder Woman you talkin' about?" Earl mumbled through his mouthful of Hot Pocket.

"One of the most infamous cases of spontaneous human combustion on record," Grayson said. "It involves a widow named Mary Hardy Reeser. One July morning in 1951, she was found burned to cinders in her apartment near downtown St. Petersburg."

I blanched. "Seriously?"

"Yes," Grayson said, appearing slightly annoyed. "It was all in the report. Didn't you read it?"

I winced. "I kind of got distracted by the pictures."

"Understandable," Grayson said, his annoyance fading.

"What happened to the poor old lady?" Earl asked.

"Well, according to the *report*," Grayson said, his eyes darting to mine, "It was Mrs. Reeser's landlady who discovered her. She went to check on her and found that the doorknob to Mrs. Reeser's apartment was hot. So she used her key to open the door and was met by a horrific scene."

"Yikes," Earl said. "How horrific was it?"

"The upholstered chair where Mary usually sat had been burned down to its springs," Grayson said. "However, the rest of the room was barely touched by the blaze. Interestingly, a nearby clock had stopped at 4:20 a.m."

"That don't sound so horrible," Earl said. "If all that was left was a burned-up chair, how did the landlady know Miss Mary was dead?"

"Excellent question," Grayson said. "She knew because lying beside the rubble of Mary's favorite chair was a human foot, neatly burned off at the ankle. It was a left foot, and it was clad in one of Mrs. Reeser's favorite silk slippers."

I cringed, remembering the photo. "I still don't see how that proves Mrs. Reeser was a victim of spontaneous human combustion."

"Those who investigated her death would disagree," Grayson said. "And so would I."

"Me, too," Earl said, wiping his greasy face with a paper napkin. "You know what they say, Bessie Plain and Simple."

"What?" I said.

"If the slipper *fits*, that must be *it*."

Chapter Sixteen

My much-longed-for day at the beach would have to wait. After discussing the mysterious case of Mary Reeser over a breakfast of Hot Pockets and candy corn, Grayson had hustled us into the truck for a field trip. All three of us were on our way to St. Petersburg for a first-hand look at the apartment where the poor Mrs. Reeser was purported to have spontaneously combusted.

Even though Grayson had originally been in a big rush to get going, as soon as a certain opportunity presented itself, we suddenly had all the time in the world to make it to Mary's.

"Slow down for a left-hand turn," Grayson said to Earl as we cruised east along Central Avenue, a main artery that made a straight shot from the beach to the heart of downtown St. Pete.

The city's high-rise buildings were still a haze in the distance up ahead. "What gives?" I asked. "I thought Reeser's apartment was downtown."

"Turn in here," Grayson said, ignoring me. "The online reviews for Casita Taqueria are exceptional."

"Seriously?" I said.

Not only was it just past eleven o'clock, the restaurant looked like an old gas station that had been gussied up with a coat of screaming-orange paint. On the wall above the outdoor patio, a painted mural of a giant pink skull grinned down at us.

Just in case that was too subtle, two words flanked either side of the flowery skull. One word was TACOS. The other was BEER.

Lovely.

I was about to voice my objections when I remembered my pledge to be more open-minded.

"Looks good," I said half-heartedly.

Grayson shot me a sideways glance, but said nothing as Earl pulled into the parking lot. We all climbed out of Bessie and stepped into the former filling station. To my surprise, the place was clean inside, and the staff was friendly. Within a few minutes of our arrival, we'd already been given menus and been served our drink order.

Huh. Maybe there was something to this open-minded stuff...

"Hmm," Grayson said, reading from the menu. "Dehydrated tissues. Vaporized blood. Charred vertebrae."

"Geez," I said. "And I thought candy corn and coffee was a bad combo."

"This isn't the menu," Grayson said, lifting the case file he'd tucked inside the menu. "It's the autopsy notes on Mary Reeser. Did you know that police at the scene of her combustion reported no odor of burning flesh?"

I grimaced. "I do *now*. And might I add my life has *not* been enriched by the knowledge."

Grayson shot me a look, then kept reading the report. "The coroner said Mrs. Reeser's 170 lb. body was reduced to ten pounds of remains, comprised mainly of her unburned foot, a handful of vertebrae, and a skull shrunken to the size of a teacup."

I nearly choked on my Dr Pepper. "Gross. So much for ordering the blackened fish tacos."

"Why?" Earl asked.

"I'm getting to that," Grayson said, misreading Earl's question. "It says here that the level to which Mrs. Reeser's bones had been reduced to ash was greater than is typically achieved by commercial cremation."

"Good for her," I deadpanned. "I hear commercial cremations cost a fortune."

Grayson sighed. "Commercial cremations usually leave behind bone fragments so large they have to be ground up afterward in order to fit into a traditional memorial container."

I groaned. "Honestly, Grayson. Can't this information wait until *after* we eat?"

"I wanna know more about Miss Mary," Earl said. "Mr. G., how could it be that a little old lady was able to perform her own homemade cremation so good?"

Grayson blanched. "Don't ever use that term again."

"What term?" Earl asked.

"Homemade cremation."

Intrigued, I asked, "Why not?"

Grayson grimaced. "It gives me the willies."

I smirked. "So 'the creeps' isn't professional, but 'the willies' is?"

Grayson's eyes shifted back to his report. "To answer your question, Earl, no one's yet been able to fully explain how victims' bodies are so thoroughly turned to ash."

"They can't?" Earl asked.

"No," Grayson said. "That's one of the reasons these cases are so interesting. The level of cremation Mary and other victims like her exhibit would require a minimum of 2500 degrees Fahrenheit. Also, traditional cremation takes hours. Many victims reported to have spontaneously combusted went from flesh and bone to ash in a matter of minutes."

"How many minutes?" Earl asked, sucking up a straw full of Pepsi.

"Now *that's* an interesting question," Grayson said. "The quickest case on record was Helen Conway. She was reduced to ashes in under six minutes."

"Six minutes!" Earl gasped. "Talk about your fast cooker!"

I grimaced. "Earl, nobody was talking about a fast cooker."

"Hey, you all!" a young waitress called out, rushing up to our table. "Sorry for the wait. I got stuck helping out in the kitchen. Our fry cook burned a batch of taco shells down to a pile of blackened crumbs."

She sniffed the air. "I hope you can't smell them."

Well, there goes the remains of my appetite ...

Chapter Seventeen

"*That's* Reeser's apartment?" I asked as we pulled up in front of a nondescript, single-story concrete-block building at the corner of Cherry Street and 12th Avenue. Located seven blocks from downtown St. Petersburg, the place was painted battleship gray with white trim, and looked about as ominous as a kitten playing in a basketful of yarn.

"Yes, this is the address," Grayson said, checking it again in his file. "Let's get out and do a quick inspection. Mrs. Reeser lived in apartment number two."

"Number two," Earl chortled. "Guess that accounts for her crappy luck, huh Bobbie?"

"Sure," I said. "That's some real scientific thinking you got goin' on there, Earl." I turned to Grayson, trying to win Brownie points against my cousin. "I noticed there's a power line running along the side of 12th Avenue."

He nodded. "Yes, but we already ruled that out as an ignition source in Mullet's case."

"Sure," I said. "But that doesn't automatically rule it out in Mrs. Reeser's case, does it?"

Grayson shot me half a smile. "Fair enough, Cadet. What else on the premises could have caused an incendiary spark?"

I looked around. "That large slab of concrete patio out front. Walking over that and the concrete step up to the apartment could cause a buildup of static electricity."

"It certainly could," Grayson said. "One theory being considered in these cases is that a buildup of static electricity inside the body leads to electrolysis."

"To hair removal?" I asked. "How the heck does *that* happen?"

"I'm talking about the electrolysis of *water*, Drex, not hair. In the right conditions, electricity can decompose water into oxygen and hydrogen gas."

"I'm still not following you."

"Me neither," Earl said.

"Okay," Grayson said. "Humans are between 70 and 80 percent water, right?"

"If you say so, Mr. G.," Earl said.

Grayson nodded. "I do. Now, if all the hydrogen and oxygen atoms in your bodily fluids should suddenly separate into their base component atoms, it would render you highly flammable."

"How so?" I asked.

"You'd be full of oxygen and hydrogen gas," Grayson said. "Remember the Hindenburg? It was filled with hydrogen gas. One tiny spark set it off. It burned to ashes in a matter of minutes."

"Interesting," I said. "So my idea about static could be right?"

"Theoretically, perhaps," Grayson said. "But it's highly unlikely." He glanced around the yard in front of Reeser's old apartment. "What other external factors could be at play here? Think."

I chewed my lip. "What about this? I heard Tampa Bay is one of the most active lightning areas in the world. Could that be an ignition source?"

"Excellent notion," Grayson said. "Unfortunately, no lightning was reported on the night Mrs. Reeser died."

My shoulders slumped. "Oh."

"Still, good work," Grayson said. "I think it's time we moved on to the victim herself, Mrs. Reeser."

Grayson sat down on a bench at a concrete table in the front yard of the apartment building. He opened the file folder labeled *Experiment #5*, turned a page, and began reading aloud.

"The profile of the typical victim of spontaneous human combustion is plump, over 70, female, and prone to imbibe in alcohol, drugs, tobacco, or any combination thereof." He looked up at Earl and me. "Mrs. Reeser was described as being 67, rotund, and partial to a nightcap."

"Nightcap!" Earl said. "You think that's what might a shrunk her skull? You know how plastic gets all shrivel-like when you light a match to it."

My mouth fell open. "Earl, how would you—ugh! Forget it. It was the *fire* that shrunk her skull, you dumb lug-nut!"

"You're both wrong," Grayson said, shaking his head. "Shrinkage is not the typical result when bones are exposed to fire. In fact, fire usually *expands* bone, causing it to crack."

"Oh." My brow furrowed. "So how did they explain her shrunken head?"

"I know!" Earl said. "Maybe she was seein' a psychiatrist!"

My eyes darted to Grayson's face. I smirked.

Who's got the open mind now?

Grayson let out a sigh. "To answer *both* of your questions, first, there was no psychiatrist involved. And second, as far as an explanation for the shrunken skull, none was ever proposed. At least, not publicly, anyway. The coroner only said he'd never seen anything like it before."

"Weird," I said.

"Weird indeed," Grayson agreed.

"So who was the last person to talk with Mrs. Reeser before she died?" I asked.

"Her son, Richard. He reported he last saw his mother the Sunday night before she combusted. According to him, he'd left his mother sitting in her favorite easy chair, dressed in a nightie and smoking a cigarette. Right before he left, Mrs. Reeser told him she'd taken two Seconal sleeping pills and planned to go to bed soon."

"So she was pretty drugged up," I said.

"Not necessarily," Grayson said. "Habitual users can build up quite a tolerance for both drugs and alcohol."

"But she smoked," I said.

"I *bet* she did," Earl said. "Especially when her nightcap caught fire."

I squeezed my hands into fists to restrain myself from reaching out and throttling Earl. "My *point* is, could *cigarettes* be the source of external ignition?"

"Probably not," Grayson said. "A cigarette igniting clothing couldn't achieve the 2500 degrees required to reduce Mrs. Reeser to ash. It's true that drinking and smoking do seem to be suspiciously common themes among many of the victims. However, having said that, skinny teetotalers have also been known to burst into flames."

"Mullet Daniels drank and smoked weed," I said.

"True." Grayson flipped another page inside his *Experiment #5* folder. "And John Irving smoked a pipe."

"The poet?" I gasped. "I didn't know he spontaneously combusted, too!"

"He didn't," Grayson said, looking down at his notes. "I meant to say Dr. John Irving *Bentley*. Back in 1966, he was found incinerated to eight pounds of ash and rubble in his bathroom. There was nothing left of him but his charred walker and one lower leg, neatly burnt off at the shin."

"Eww," I said.

Grayson rubbed his chin. "Oddly enough, Dr. Bentley's foot was also clad in a bedroom slipper, just like Mary Reeser's."

"Huh," Earl said, rubbing his chin. "Looks like if there's only one *slipper*, you can bet it ain't the *Ripper*."

Chapter Eighteen

"Too bad we couldn't go inside Miss Mary's apartment while we was here," Earl said, turning the keys in the monster truck's ignition.

"Yeah," I said. "I can't imagine why the lady living there wouldn't let you in. Especially when you explained that you only wanted to see where the woman who used to live there had 'caught fire and burned slap up to a cinder.'"

"I *know*," Earl said, shaking his head. "So much for Southern hospitality."

"Well, we better get going," I said, keeping an eye on the exterior door to a hallway that led to apartment number two. "I heard her say she was calling the cops."

"Where to, Mr. G.?" Earl asked, easing the gearshift out of neutral.

"Take a left and head back up to 4th Street," Grayson said. "There's another location I want to check out."

"What location is that?" Earl asked.

"Who cares?" I said, gasping as the hallway door flew open and the lady from apartment two stepped out. She was on her cellphone, shaking an angry fist at us.

"You heard Grayson," I said, elbowing Earl. "Punch it."

Earl punched it.

We peeled out of there, bouncing like human popcorn as Bessie's huge tires grappled with the dips and swales in the uneven brick street.

At the corner of 13th Avenue and Cherry Street, Earl hooked a left on two tires. Once we were out of sight of the angry tenant, Earl slowed down and we ambled slowly up five or six blocks lined with quaint old houses until we reached the commercial strip called 4th Street.

As Earl turned right onto it, he said, "I was thinkin'. Maybe these human discombobulation folks caught fire on account a they was all stewed up with booze."

"Actually, that used to be the standard theory back in the 1800s," Grayson said. "Folks believed spontaneous human combustion was sent from the heavens as a just reward for the vice of drunkenness."

"Seriously?" I said, laughing.

"Yes. In fact, the idea was so popular back in the day that Charles Dickens himself used spontaneous human combustion as a foil for a nefarious character named Mr. Krook in his novel, *Bleak House*."

"Was it aluminum foil?" Earl asked.

I shot Grayson a smirk.

"No," Grayson said. "But the theory that alcohol alone could cause spontaneous human combustion was disproved in 1851 by Baron J. von Liebig."

"How'd he do that?" Earl asked.

"Pretty straightforward," Grayson said. "He injected alcohol into the bodies of rats and set them on fire."

"Geez!" I hissed.

Grayson shrugged. "As it turns out, they didn't burn any better than non-alcoholic rats."

My nose crinkled. "So if it isn't the alcohol *inside* the victims, what about outside accelerants, like gasoline?"

"That was one of the first possibilities explored," Grayson said. "In Mrs. Reeser's case, the FBI pathologist reported no evidence of oxidizing chemicals or accelerants."

My eyebrows shot up. "The FBI got involved in her case?"

Grayson nodded. "Yes. That's another interesting aspect of the Reeser case. It caught the attention of the FBI. In fact, J. Edgar Hoover himself signed off on Mrs. Reeser's case file."

"What did the FBI investigation conclude?" I asked.

"They attributed Reeser's death to falling asleep with a cigarette in her hand—even though tests trying to recreate the same effect had failed, proving that couldn't have been the cause. Interestingly, the official lab reports remain confidential to this day."

My brow furrowed. "Why would the lab reports remain confidential—unless there was something to hide?"

Grayson shot me a knowing look. "Exactly."

"I DON'T GET IT," EARL said as we cruised north on 4th Street. "If lightning and cigarettes and candle wax can't burn a person to smithereens, what can?"

"Good question," Grayson said. "Ruling out *external* forces, what's left?"

"Martians?" Earl asked.

"I was going for *internal* forces," Grayson said.

My eyebrows rose. "So it's electrolysis after all?"

Grayson shook his head. "No."

I blanched. "You're telling me there are *other* ways a person can accidently cremate themselves?"

"Yes."

"Geez," I said. "How many ways can a body become a walking hydrogen bomb?"

"A few more," Grayson said.

I grimaced. "Like what?"

"Actually, a fellow named Paul Rolli set out to answer that question back in 1745," Grayson said. "In fact, he was the first to suggest the possibility of internal combustion as the source of spontaneous human combustion."

"What made him think that?" Earl asked.

"Scientific observation of the facts, just like we're doing now," Grayson said. "Earl, take a left just past the Taco Bell."

"You got it, chief."

"What facts are you talking about?" I asked Grayson.

"Well, for one, Rolli noticed that victims didn't appear to have put up any sort of resistance. And often, such as in the Reeser and Dr. Bentley cases, portions of their limbs didn't burn—as if the main, internal source of ignition ran out of fuel before it could finish the job. So he theorized that it must happen instantaneously within the torso."

"I mean, that's interesting and all," I said. "But besides electrolysis separating our oxygen and hydrogen molecules, what else could make someone's guts suddenly catch on fire?"

Earl let out a big belch.

I smirked. "Besides the diablo sauce at that taco place, I mean."

"Actually, Earl just made a good point," Grayson said. "Rude, but on point."

"How's that?" I asked.

"One theory is that spontaneous human combustion is caused by an overproduction of methane in the intestines. Methane is highly combustible."

"Ha! I know that's right," Earl said. "Remember old Roy Campbell? He used to set his farts on fire in gym class."

I shook my head. "If farts made you spontaneously combust, Earl, you'd have been a goner a long time ago."

"It's not just methane that's required," Grayson said. "Human intestines can also produce phosphine, a gas that ignites spontaneously upon contact with air. A chance combination of phosphine and methane could prove deadly."

"Actually, I beg to differ," I said.

"On what grounds?" Grayson asked.

"I can personally attest to the fact that Earl's methane alone has almost killed me a couple of times."

Grayson shook his head. "Take the next right, Earl."

"Yes sir, Mr. G."

I glanced out the window. "Wait a minute. This is Haines Road. We're not going back to Mullet's Trailer Park, are we?"

"Yes," Grayson said. "I want to take another look at that burned out trailer. It just might be that Titanic Jones *also* spontaneously combusted."

"But ...," I stammered, not looking forward to another redneck rendezvous with Danny Daniels. "Grayson, you just said that that chances are victims ignite from some source within their own bodies."

"Correct."

"So why do we have to go back to look at the scene?" I argued. "Shouldn't you be calling the coroner's office or something and getting a report from them?"

"I'm working on that," Grayson said. "In the meantime, we're going to inspect the location for the same reason we went to Mary Reeser's apartment. *To rule out the conventional.* Then what we're left with is the unconventional."

I frowned. "I just don't—"

"We're almost there," Grayson said. "I don't see what the big deal is."

I scowled. "The big deal is, I don't want to see that human cesspool again!"

"Titanic?" Earl asked, pulling onto E Street.

"No," I hissed. "Danny Daniels."

Grayson shook his head. "Grow up, Drex. If you want to become a private investigator, you're going to need to learn how to deal with unsavory characters."

"Unsavory?" I hissed. "You make him sound like a stale graham cracker. That guy's a lecherous pervert!"

Grayson blanched. "How do you know that?"

"I just do!"

Grayson shot me a dubious look. "Not 'the creeps' rationale again."

I was going to argue, but it was too late. I'd spotted my nemesis. "Ugh. There he is."

Danny Daniels was standing by the side of the burned out trailer clad in nothing but a pair of cutoff jeans. In all his half-naked glory, he was busy hosing down a huge metal garbage dumpster.

"Looks like we're getting here just in time," Grayson said. "I want to snap some pictures before they start tossing all the debris into the garbage container."

Earl pulled up to the side of the road. Danny dropped his garden hose and ambled over.

"Howdy, Danny," Earl said. "You fixin' to clean out that trailer?"

"Huh?" Danny grunted.

"I see you done went and got yourself a dumpster."

"Oh," Danny said. "Yeah. That's for the pool party we got comin' up."

"Gross," I muttered under my breath.

Danny peered into the cab and shot me a lascivious leer. He stuck his nasty tongue out between his rotten teeth, licked his disgusting lips and said, "You should come to the party, little lady. I just might be the man who can make all your wishes come true."

"Ugh," I hissed. "The only wish I'd like *you* to make come true is to one day be identified by your dental records."

"Drex!" Grayson scolded.

"Oh, sorry," I said. "What was I thinking? There obviously wouldn't *be* any dental records."

"Well, there goes that bridge," Grayson said. "I can feel the flames all the way over here. Let's roll."

I elbowed my cousin. "You heard the man."

Earl reached for the gear shift. "I know," he said. "Punch it."

Chapter Nineteen

"Well, so much for investigating the scene of Titanic Jones' unresolved death," Grayson said, giving me a hard look.

"Yeah," Earl said. "Good thing Danny had to run back to his trailer for his shotgun, or we'd all be goners."

I straightened my shoulders against the back of Bessie's bench seat and held my head up high. "If that means we can never go back to Mullet's Trailer Park, I consider that *mission accomplished*."

Earl let out a huge sigh. "I might as well not even bother to check on livin' there no more. Thanks, Bobbie. There went my future, up in smoke."

My upper lip snarled. "Come on, Earl. You've got to have better hopes for your future than Mullet's disgusting trailer park!"

"You forget what it's like livin' in Point Paradise," Earl said. "You done been away too long."

I winced. Earl had a point. "Beth-Ann's there," I said, trying to cheer him up.

Earl shrugged. "Yeah. And your point is?"

Seriously?

"Ugh! Nothing." I rolled my eyes. Last time I'd seen my best friend Beth-Ann she'd confessed she had a thing for Earl. Apparently (but not surprisingly) my cousin had been too dumb to notice.

What a bonehead. What does Beth-Ann see in him, anyway?

"So, where to now?" Earl asked as we cruised past the junk shops and tattoo parlors lining Haines Road.

"I think we should follow Danny's example," Grayson said.

"*What?*" I gasped.

"Yes," Grayson nodded. "Let's have a party at the campground."

"A party?" I asked. "Why?"

"Field reconnaissance," Grayson said. "Let's pick up some refreshments and something to cook on the grill. Then we'll invite our camping neighbors over for informal interviews. Perhaps some of them saw something the night Mullet died."

I didn't take much stock in Grayson's idea. "Danny told us Mullet died two weeks ago. I doubt any of the same campers would still be around."

"Perhaps not," Grayson said, locking eyes with me. "But given we *no longer* have any other leads, I'm keeping an open mind to the possibility. I suggest you do the same."

STILL SMARTING FROM being called on the carpet by Grayson, I stayed behind in Bessie and let the guys go it alone in the grocery store—but not before giving them strict orders to bring me back some Hot Pockets and a case of Dr Pepper.

I was in desperate need of emergency junk food and a few moments to myself. But even more than that, I needed to talk to another human being. And by that, I meant another *girl*.

I fished my phone from my purse and called Beth-Ann. She answered on the first ring.

"Hey, you!" she said. "How goes it with that sexy detectsy?"

I sighed. "Mixed bag."

"Hmm. You don't sound too happy. What's going on?"

"Grayson told me he's a demi-sexual."

"Oh," she said. "Is it … uh … *curable*? You know how slim the pickings are when it comes to men around here."

"Actually, it's nothing that bad," I said. "Grayson says it means he needs to take it slow. You know, that he needs to know someone before he can have feelings for them."

"Dang, Bobbie. That actually sounds *good*. So what's your problem?"

"I dunno, Beth-Ann. It's just that ... aw, never mind."

"Bobbie Drex! You tell me right now, or I'm gonna drive over there and throttle it out of you!"

"Okay!" I said, a smile cracking my face. "It's just that, well, it took Grayson nearly a year to get up the nerve to kiss me. How long will it take for him to—"

"Stop right there!" Beth-Ann yelled. "Grayson *kissed* you?"

"Uh, yeah. A couple of times, now."

Beth-Ann's voice raised an octave. "And you're just now getting around to telling me?"

"It just happened today! And I've been kind of preoccupied with—"

"So?" she said, cutting me off. "When are you two going to seal the deal?"

I cringed. "That's just it. I don't know. At this pace, I'm not sure my lifespan is long enough to make it to that point. I'm not related to Betty White, you know."

Beth-Ann laughed. "It'll happen. Be patient."

"I'm not so sure. With Earl hanging around, it's virtually impossible. Every time Grayson and I have a moment alone together, *bam*! Earl shows up. I'm beginning to think his middle name is cock-blocker."

"Aw, come on, Bobbie!"

"I'm serious, Beth-Ann! If we didn't need him for transportation—"

"Wait. I thought you already got a new vehicle. That old RV."

"How'd you know about that?"

"Earl texted me a picture of it," she said. "Captioned it with three words. 'Bobbie's new ride'. The big oaf didn't even add 'hello', 'how are you', or 'kiss my foot' to go with it."

"Mr. Romance, Earl isn't," I said. "And neither is Grayson. At least not with Earl around. Maybe it's contagious."

"So send Earl back here," Beth-Ann said. "Then you and Grayson can get cozy in the RV."

My nose crinkled. "The problem is, I don't even want to go inside that creepy RV."

"Why not?"

"You saw the outside. The inside's even worse."

"How is that possible?" Beth-Ann asked.

"Because someone *died* in it, that's how."

"Geez, Bobbie. This is *Florida* we're talking about here. If we didn't go anywhere someone had kicked the bucket, all we'd be left with is a canoe in the middle of Lake Okeechobee!"

I winced. "I guess you're right. But that's not all that's bothering me."

"There's more?"

"Yeah. I think Earl is *competing* with me."

"What? He wants to jump Grayson's bones, too?"

"No. He wants to be a private investigator. At least, that's what it seems like. He keeps poking his nose into everything we're doing, pretending he's an intern right along beside me."

"What's so bad about that?" Beth-Ann's voice sounded defensive. "Earl doesn't mean any harm. He's a good guy."

"I know he is. I just wish he'd be a good guy somewhere else. Look, you like him. Couldn't you do me a favor and call him? Let Earl know how you feel about him?"

"I don't know, Bobbie. Some men don't like it when a woman comes on too strong."

"That's exactly my problem, too. I don't want to turn Grayson off by trying to turn him on."

Beth-Ann laughed. "Sheesh, Bobbie. I don't know if that's profound or psychotic."

I sighed. "Who says it can't be both? Anyway, will you at least *think* about calling Earl?"

"Okay. But *you* think about something, too."

"What?"

"You don't get different results by doing the same old thing."

"Geez, Beth-Ann. Now you're starting to sound like Grayson."

"Is that so bad?"

I smiled. "No, I guess not."

Chapter Twenty

"Yes, sir-eee," I quipped, staring at the guys' Winn Dixie party banquet they'd spread out on the picnic table back at the campsite. "Nothing lures the folks in like Cheetos, kosher dill pickles, and pigs in a blanket."

"Thanks," Grayson said. "I thought the symbolism was a nice touch."

"Symbolism?" I asked.

"Yes." Grayson gave me an odd look. "You know. The *pigs* in a *blanket*?"

My upper lip hooked skyward. "What's symbolic about cocktail wieners wrapped in crescent roll dough? Other than epitomizing bad taste, I mean."

"I think they taste mighty good, myself," Earl said.

I smirked. "That's not the kind of 'taste' I was talking about."

Grayson picked up one of the pigs in a blanket. "Drex, these tube-steak treats are *symbolic* because they remind me of one of the tests used to try to replicate spontaneous human combustion."

"Geez, Grayson," I said, my appetite fading. "In another life, were you some kind of reverse-psychology diet coach or something?"

"This has nothing to do with dieting," Grayson said. "I'm talking about the Wick Effect. Didn't you read any of the background information in the file I gave you?"

I cringed. "Uh ... I guess I didn't get to that part yet."

"What's the Wick Effect?" Earl asked.

I flopped onto the picnic bench and braced myself.

Dear lord, here it comes.

"It's a theory that attempts to explain spontaneous human combustion," Grayson said. "It purports that once a person's clothes catch fire, the fabric acts in a similar way to a candle wick."

"You mean what them FBI fellers thought happened to Miss Mary?" Earl asked.

"Yes. Proponents of the Wick Effect believe that a victim's clothing wicks up the person's body fat as it melts, keeping the flame alive as the person slowly incinerates."

"Gee, that sounds yummy," I said, eyeing the dough-wrapped sausage in Grayson's hand. "But I still don't get the pigs in a blanket connection."

"I'm getting to that," Grayson said. "The researchers attempting to prove the Wick Effect couldn't exactly test the theory on human subjects. So they simulated it by wrapping dead pigs in blankets, dousing them with an accelerant, then lighting them afire and monitoring how they burned."

And with that, Grayson took a savage bite of his pig in a blanket and my stomach did a belly flop.

"Whoa!" Earl said. "What did them scientist fellers end up with when they torched them hogs, Mr. G.?"

"Barbequed pork, mostly," Grayson said. "Their experiments failed to replicate spontaneous human combustion. Even though they let the fires burn on for hours and hours, the pigs remained un-cremated."

My brow furrowed. "That doesn't fit with the evidence," I said. "Some cases took mere minutes to burn their victims to ash."

"Exactly," Grayson said. "Therefore, the Wick Effect, in my and many other scientists' opinions, can be ruled out as a possible cause. People—and pigs—simply can't be reduced to ash merely because their clothes catch fire."

"That's interesting," I said. "But take my advice, Grayson."

"What?" he said, grabbing a handful of Cheetos.

"Don't repeat any portion of what you just said to anyone you might lure here with your free junk-food buffet."

Grayson's head cocked to one side. "Why not?"

I winced. "Just trust me on this one."

"Hey, Bobbie, you want one?" Earl asked, shoving a pig in a blanket at me with a tong.

I held up my palm. "No thanks. I think I've reached my frankfurter quotient for the week. I'll have a Hot Pocket instead."

"Uh-oh," Grayson said.

"What?" I asked.

He shrugged. "We forgot to get the Hot Pockets."

"Seriously?" I said.

Men!

ONE BY ONE, LIKE HUNGRY raccoons, our neighboring campers caught the scent of roasting wieners and crept by for a peek, disguising their craven interest as merely a leisurely afternoon walk that just happened to pass by our campsite.

The mission at hand was to elicit any information we could from our fellow campers about Mullet Daniels' stay in the park a few weeks ago. To that end, we all had our roles to play.

Earl's job was to stand at the corner where our campsite met the road and invite people in for a sample.

Grayson's job was to interrogate our hapless fellow campers.

As for me, my job was to dole out the free treats—and keep Grayson from working spontaneous human combustion into the conversation.

Over the next few hours, partakers to our impromptu feast were many. However, people with any useful information were nil. By a quarter to seven, we were down to our last two pigs in a blanket and a handful of Cheetos.

"It's time to call it," I said, standing up from the picnic bench. "My butt is killing me."

"Okay, fine," Grayson said.

I yelled over to Earl. "We're done here!"

"Okay by me," he hollered back.

"Well, that was a bust," I said to Grayson.

"Not completely," he said. "I forgot how much I really enjoy a nice pig in a blanket."

"Where is everybody?" Earl hollered, walking back from his post by the road. "It ain't even seven o'clock yet!"

"Just as well," I said, watching Grayson eat his twelfth pig in a blanket. "We're out of food and I'm out of patience. If I have to hear another story about how bad the mosquitos are around here, I think I'll go ballistic."

"You're just hangry," Grayson said. "Eat something."

Eh, maybe he's right. What the hell...

I reached for the last mini frankfurter wrapped in dough.

"Hey, wait!" Earl said. "Here comes somebody!"

Grayson slapped my hand away from the lone pig in a blanket. "We might need it," he said.

Little did we know, we were about to hit pay-dirt.

Chapter Twenty-One

I turned my eyes away from the platter holding one last pig in a blanket and glanced toward the road. Earl was escorting a tiny little old lady our way. He must've snagged her as she was tottering back to her camper from the community bathroom. At least, I hoped that's where she'd been coming from, considering she was wearing a bathrobe and slippers.

As they slowly inched toward us, I noticed that atop the woman's head was an old-fashioned sleeping kerchief. Poking from underneath its elastic edges were what could possibly have been the last remaining set of pink plastic curlers still in use on the planet.

"Well, aren't you a pleasant young man," she said to Earl as he ushered her arm-in-arm toward our picnic table as if she were strolling the red carpet at the Emmy Awards.

"Thanky," Earl said.

"I'm Doris Halafacker," I heard her say as they got closer to us. "Nice to meet you."

"I'm Earl," my cousin said. "Like I tole ya, we're havin' us a little party. Would you care to partake?"

Doris stopped in her tracks. Her pasty face puckered. "I'll have you know that I don't do drugs, young man. Like the First Lady said, 'Just say no!'"

"Oh," Earl said. "We ain't got no drugs, ma'am! All we got is cocktail wieners and Cheetos."

"Oh." The old woman smiled and gripped Earl's arm again. "In that case, maybe I'll drop in for a minute."

The slow-walking senior glanced down at a crook in her arm. That's when I noticed there was something living in it. It appeared to be a skinned rat with a tuft of blond hair sticking straight up on its bug-eyed skull.

"Would you like a late-night bite, snookums?" Doris asked the creature. It whined. She glanced up at Earl. "That means yes!"

Earl reached over to pet the critter. It growled and snapped at him like a piranha with a Mohawk. "Yow!" he yelled, pulling his hand back.

"Oh, don't mind him," Doris said. "He's an ornery little cuss."

"Welcome," I said as Doris and Earl finally made it to the picnic table. "Nice to meet you. I'm Bob—*Bessie*."

Crap! I almost blew my cover!

"Well, hi there, Bob-Bessie," she said. "Name's Doris. Mighty neighborly of you all to invite me over."

"Our pleasure," I said.

As Earl helped her sit down at the bench, I noticed something bulging from her robe's side pocket. It appeared to be a mason jar half full of a golden yellow liquid. I tried not to think what it might be.

"Hello," Grayson said to Doris. "That's an interesting animal you have there."

"Sweetie pie?" She petted its ratty little head. "He's my constant companion."

"How constant?" Earl asked.

"Doris!" I said. "You seem to be the only night owl in the place." I glanced at my phone. It was 6:38 p.m.

"Oh, well, yes," she said. "Most everybody around here goes to bed with the chickens."

"There are chickens in the campground?" Grayson asked.

"Oh, no," Doris said. "That's just an old country expression."

"Interesting," Grayson said. "So, when exactly do chickens go to bed?"

"At sundown," Doris replied. "Right now, that's about seven-fifteen. But usually, you barely see a soul around here after six forty-five."

"Why's that?" I asked.

"Well, they've got to get ready for *Wheel of Fortune*. It comes on at seven."

"You're a Wheel watcher?" Earl asked.

"You bet!" Doris showed us her expensive-looking set of dentures. "It's hard to beat that cutie pie Pat Sajak. He gets better looking every year. I bet he's got buns of steel from working that wheel!"

"Right," I said. "How long have you been camping here in Fort De Soto Park?"

"Going on three weeks now," Doris said, munching on a handful of Cheetos. "People come and go like flies around here. You all are the third ones to use this campsite since I set up next door."

"You're right next door?" I asked. "Which site?"

"Number one-eleven. Why?"

Grayson cleared his throat. "We're investi—"

"We're looking to invest in the area," I said. "We're curious. Did you happen to meet the man who was here a few weeks ago? He went by the name of Mullet."

"Oh. Mullet." She smacked the name as if it tasted bad on her orange tongue. "I met him, all right. That man was a total burnout."

You don't know how right you are...

"Why do you say that?" Grayson asked.

"He was loud," Doris said. "Rude and inconsiderate. Always making too much noise."

"Noise?" I asked. "What kind of noise?"

"That ne'er-do-well brought a *drum set* with him," she said, shaking her head. "To a community campground! Can you believe that? Played it all the time, too." She let out a sigh. "A body comes out here for some peace and quiet, and that malcontent idiot is beating on the drums day and night. What's this world coming to?"

"I'm sorry that happened," I said.

"Thanks," Doris said. "I was pretty upset about it. And I wasn't the only one, by golly. Enough of us finally got fed up enough to ask Ranger Provost to do something about it."

"Did he?"

"Yes. That nice young ranger told me he brokered a compromise. Mullet could still play the drums, but had to quit by 7 p.m., so folks around here could watch the *Wheel* in peace."

"And Mullet stuck to the agreement?" Grayson asked.

She shrugged. "We never found out. He left the next day."

"Did you happen to notice what time he left?" I asked.

Doris shook her head. "No. I went off for my regular weekly wash and set at Peggy's beauty parlor in Tierra Verde. When I came back, Mullet and his old RV were gone. Funny, now that I think about it, his rig looked a lot like the one you all have there."

"That's because it's the—" Grayson began.

I poked an elbow in his ribs. "It's a very popular model. At least it was back in the 1970s."

Doris smiled. "Honey, so was I, back then. But I wouldn't want to be out on the road anymore myself. People have gotten so ill mannered. Well, I better call it a night."

As I helped her up, I said, "One more question. What day do you get your hair done?"

"Every Wednesday, ten o'clock on the dot. You want the name of my hairdresser? She's really good."

"That's okay," I said. "I wear a wig."

"Thought so," Doris said, making my smile fade. "Well, you all enjoy your evening." She turned to go, then turned back. "You all watch out for the bugs. They're huge around here!"

"Yes, ma'am," I said. "We heard all about the mosquitos."

"Mosquitos?" Doris asked. "No, I meant the lightning bugs."

"Lightning bugs?" I asked.

"Yes. Big, white ones. I saw them coming back from the bathroom the other night. Out in that direction. She pointed a gnarled finger toward the east. "They're way bigger than the ones we have out in Sacramento."

"Are you sure you didn't see a plane or something?" Grayson asked.

"Sonny, I know a plane when I see one. I'm not mental. The lights I saw were white only. And they seemed to follow my flashlight beam. I've seen them half a dozen times on my way back from the showers."

"What time of night do you shower?" I asked.

Doris looked at me oddly. "Why? You aren't one of those funny girls, are you? I don't swing that way."

"Uh ... no, ma'am. I only asked because I'd like to see the lightning bugs for myself."

"Oh." Her face brightened. "Well, just keep your eyes open. I'm sure you'll see them around."

Doris patted the tufted little head poking up from the crook in her arm. "Come on, honey. It's sexy Sajak time!"

"Thanks for stopping by," I said. "Are you sure you won't have a—"

"Oh, all right. One for the road," she said, then grabbed the last pig in a blanket and tottered off toward her campsite.

"Well, that was certainly interesting," Grayson said.

"It sure was," Earl said. "What was that thing stuck up in her arm? A mangy rat?"

"A Chihuahua, I think," I said.

"There's something weird about that old lady," Earl said.

"Why do you say that?" Grayson asked.

"Well," he said, "it's been a long time since I seen somebody totin' around a pee jar like old Uncle Otis used to. How do you explain that?"

I sighed. "I dunno, Earl. Old people do weird things."

Chapter Twenty-Two

"Well, I'm gonna hit the hay," Earl said, getting up from the picnic table where we'd all sat for a while, eating Cheetos and watching the stars. He wagged his eyebrows at me.

"What?" I said, not catching his drift.

"Nothin." He grabbed the bag of Cheetos from the picnic table and ambled toward the RV. "Y'all don't stay up too late, now. You hear?"

I watched Earl close the RV door behind him, then asked Grayson, "Speaking of weird sightings, those strange lights Doris mentioned. Could they have been a meteor shower?"

"Let's see." Grayson clicked an app on his cellphone. "No. It shows none on the schedule for the past three weeks."

"Huh. What about fireflies?"

"Unlikely," he said, slipping his phone into his shirt pocket.

"Why not?" I asked.

"In North America, dusk-active fireflies emit yellow bioluminescence. Dark-active ones emit green light. So I'm afraid white bioluminescence is off the table, unless some new species is out there yet to be catalogued."

I chewed my lip. "Then what else could the lights be?"

"Good question. According to Rolli—"

"Rolli?" I asked. "Who is he again?"

"The man who first proposed that spontaneous human combustion started from an *internal* source, remember?"

"Oh. Yeah, sure."

"At the time of his investigations, Rolli noted that people had been reporting sightings of luminous humans—people who seemed to glow and spark under certain circumstances."

My eyebrows shot up. "What *kind* of circumstances? Like when they grabbed ahold of a live electrical wire?"

"Doubtful, as electricity didn't make its public debut until 150 years later at the Chicago World's Fair in 1893."

I chewed my lip. "Seriously, Grayson. Glowing humans?"

Grayson shrugged. "That's what the historical records say."

"Either way, I don't think that's what's going on here," I said. "Doris may be a bit nutty, but I think she'd be able to tell if the light she saw was emanating from a person or not."

Grayson rubbed his chin. "You're probably right. The correlation between strange lights and spontaneous human combustion is tenuous at best."

I yawned and stood up. "I think that's enough investigative discussion for me for one day. I'm packing it in."

"I'm going to watch the stars a little longer," Grayson said, looking up at the sky.

"Suit yourself." I walked around the table and lingered a moment, wondering if I should try and kiss him goodnight. I reached out to touch his shoulder...

"Oh!" I heard Earl yell. I looked over to see his big fat head poking out the side door of the RV. "I just thought a something Danny told me."

"*What*?" I grumbled.

"Danny said that the night Mullet died, he'd been talking on the phone with him," Earl said.

"Fascinating," I said. "That kind of information certainly couldn't have waited until morning."

"That ain't the information," Earl said. "Them lights Doris was talkin' about. Danny said Mullet tole him he'd seen some kinda weird lights in the sky, too."

"What kind of lights?" Grayson asked.

Earl scratched his head. "Danny asked him, but didn't get no reply. Right after he said it, Mullet's phone cut out."

"That's odd," Grayson said.

"Maybe his battery died," I said. "Or, unlike *me*, he had a hot pocket."

"Don't know," Earl said. "Danny tried calling Mullet back, but he says he didn't answer. So he figured his brother was just wasted and had passed out."

"Probably," I said.

"Anyhoo, when Mullet didn't answer his phone the next mornin', Danny got to worryin' about him. That's when he come out here to check on him and found Mullet all … you know. Burnt slap up and everything."

"An intriguing anecdote," Grayson said. "Perhaps whatever sparked Mullet's incineration also short-circuited his Wi-Fi signal."

"Yep," Earl said. "That's what I was thinkin. Anyhoo, y'all sleep tight!" He winked, then ducked back inside the RV and closed the door.

"Strange lights?" I said. "Glowing people? Where do we go from here? Should we try to find more witnesses tomorrow?"

Grayson shook his head. "It's probably a moot point. The other campers would be of no use."

I blanched "Really? Why not?"

"Because everyone around here is in bed by seven o'clock."

I cocked my head. "So?"

"It's hard to see lights in the sky while the sun is still up."

"Oh. Sure," I said sheepishly. "Well, what about possible witnesses to flames or smoke coming from Mullet's RV?"

Grayson glanced up at the stars. "Statistically, that's another improbability."

"Why?"

"Because the vast majority of spontaneous human combustions occur between midnight and 6 a.m."

My nose crinkled. "That's weird. Why would that be?"

Grayson shrugged. "Who knows? I don't make up the rules. I just follow the clues."

I reached over and touched Grayson's hand, hoping he'd follow *that* clue.

He did. He smiled and leaned in for a kiss.

Yes!

I made a silent wish that Earl wouldn't pop out of the RV and foil our moment again. But I should've wished for something else.

Just as our lips were about to touch, my gut gurgled like an unclogged drain. Done in by Cheetos and Dr Pepper, my sphincter puckered. It was either let loose a fart and pray it was silent, or suffer my own spontaneous human explosion.

I farted discreetly. Well, as discreetly as I could...

"Did you hear that?" Grayson asked.

"Uh ... no," I blurted. "I didn't hear anything."

"It came from close by."

I winced. "Okay. It was—"

"Shh!" Grayson said, putting a finger to my lips. "There it is again."

This time, I heard it, too. A low, faint, pulsing sound.

"It's probably just Earl sawing logs in the RV," I said.

Grayson locked eyes with me. "Perhaps a paradiddle?"

Really? Grayson finally gets around to seducing me, and I'm ready to blow like the Hindenburg? Great timing, Universe...

"Uh ... hold that thought," I said. "I'm just gonna run to the ladies'—"

"Shh!" Grayson said. "Listen."

He held tightly to my hand, foiling my escape. I winced against the pressure boiling up in my gut, and stood beside him as he sat at the picnic table and listened into the night.

"Aha!" Grayson said. "There it is again."

I heard it. A rhythmic beating, like Poe's telltale heart. It was surreal—but not nearly as disturbing as the thought of releasing another telltale *fart*...

"I think it's spirit drums," Grayson said.

"Huh?" I grunted, wincing from gas pains.

"Spirit drums," Grayson repeated, letting go of my hand.

Suddenly, the door to the RV burst open again. Earl popped his shaggy head out. "Hey, y'all hear that drumming sound?"

"Yes," Grayson said.

"Good," Earl said. "After all them piggies in blankets, I was thinkin' maybe my aorta was about to blow. What you think it is, Mr. G.?"

"I was just telling Bobbie that it could be Mullet Daniels playing the spirit drums."

"What?" I said, backing my butt up to the tropical hedgerow and loosening my relief valve.

"Why would Mullet's ghost be out here beating drums?" Earl asked.

"It could be a serenading solo," Grayson said. "One in honor of his paradiddling partner, Titanic Jones."

"What?" I gasped. "Mullet and Titanic were *lovers*?"

"Not that I know of," Grayson said. "What gave you that idea?"

My face sagged. "So, you're not using *paradiddling* as a euphemism?"

"A euphemism for what?" Grayson asked.

I farted. Grayson turned toward me. "Did you hear that?"

"Hear what?" I asked.

"Oh!" Earl said. "I got a *question*, Mr. G."

"What's that?" Grayson asked.

Earl's brow furrowed. "That's what you ask when you want to know somethin'."

I shook my head. "He meant, what's *your* question, Earl, not what's *a* question."

"Oh." Earl scratched his head. "Well, I was wondering. If a drummer like Titanic Jones comes back to life, is that what they call a repercussion?"

Grayson's face sagged. "I don't believe so, no."

"Too bad," Earl said.

"Yeah," I said.

Too bad whoever was paradiddling out there didn't drum some sense into your gigantic, Neanderthal noggin.

Chapter Twenty-Three

"Stupid Earl," I muttered, yanking at my twisted sheet. Relegated to another night of lying prone and alone in the front seat of the monster truck, I could've spit nails. My cousin had thwarted my romantic plans with Grayson once again, and I was so livid I couldn't sleep.

I turned onto my side for the millionth time, scrunched my eyes closed, and willed myself to fall asleep.

Then I heard it.

The thump of the spirit drums again.

Only this time, they sounded closer.

A *whole lot* closer.

Holy crap!

I un-scrunched one eye, glanced up at the driver's window, and nearly swallowed my tonsils.

In the moonlight, the ghostly visage of a ragged-looking man stared back at me through the glass.

Scared breathless, I gasped for air and floundered to extricate myself from my Walmart-sheet mummy wrapper.

As I did, the dark figure rapped its knuckles on the window again. Harder this time.

"Hey!" he said. "You got any weed?"

What?

The breath of life reentered my lungs with a vengeance.

"Are you kidding?" I yelled, bolting up to sitting.

"You're Bessie, right?" he said. "I heard I can get weed here."

"What the—" I hissed. Then I remembered I was illegally camping with somebody else's permit.

"Oh. Right," I said. "Sorry, Frank and I are fresh out."

"It's cool," the guy said. "Peace out." He shot me a victory sign and disappeared into the darkness.

Great.

Pumped up with adrenaline, I sat there listening to my own spirit drums as blood thumped through the veins in both temples. No way I was going back to sleep any time soon.

I lay back down, pulled the sheet over my head, and prayed for a bit of unconsciousness. A moment later, I heard another rap on the window pane.

I jerked the sheet from my face and hissed, "What now?"

Someone new was staring back at me through the window. But this time, they didn't say a word.

And they weren't human.

At least, not *anymore*.

Chapter Twenty-Four

"Aaarrghh!" I screamed at the grotesque face leering at me through the window of the truck.

In the darkness, I made out the form of a human skull. Its cheekbones glowed in the moonlight. Atop its exposed cranium, something red flickered like flames.

Holy crap! It's the ghost of Mullet Daniels!

I screamed again, then kicked my way out of the sheet and up to sitting. In a panic, I scooted across the seat toward the steering wheel, not daring to look at the creature on the other side of the thin plate of glass.

Trembling, my fingers fumbled with the bundle of keys hanging from the ignition. Flashbacks of every horror movie I'd ever seen played in my brain.

Start, Bessie! Please start!

I cranked the engine. It caught.

My heart pulsing in my throat, I slowly turned my head and took another glance at the driver's side window, just to make sure that I wasn't hallucinating from whatever gut bacteria had caused my earlier gastric distress...

No such luck.

Through the quarter-inch pane of glass dividing us, a hideous human skull grinned at me, eyeball to empty eye socket.

As I stared, frozen with shock, fire shot from the skull's cranium. Then it raised a skeletal fist full of bones and banged it against the window.

I came unglued.

"Aaarrgh!" I screeched, shifting Bessie into reverse.

I stomped on the gas and peeled backward out of the campsite, spewing twin waterfalls of white gravel. Glancing back through the windshield, I realized I wasn't safe yet.

That damned skeleton was running after me!

I shifted again and burned rubber, Bessie's tractor tires spinning out on the shell road. They caught, and Bessie lurched forward like a carnival ride. Even so, I mashed the gas pedal to the floor, taking the next curve on two wheels.

On my mad dash for the campground's back exit, I caught a glimpse of a huge, white light in the sky. It was hovering above the trees, about 70 feet off the ground.

"What now?" I screamed as I blew past the eerie orb.

At the exit gate, I slammed on the brakes and waited for it to open. Then my addled brain kicked in. I realized I had to push a button to activate it!

"Come on!" I said, mashing Bessie's window button with all my might. As the pane of glass slowly disappeared into the door, I glanced into the rearview mirror.

Emerging from the jungle was the skeleton of Mullet Daniels. Then it took off, racing straight for me.

My heart was trying to escape out my throat as I reached out and palm slapped the button to open the gate.

"Hurry up!" I screamed as the creaky gate began to leisurely swing its lazy ass open.

I stuck my head out the driver's window and took another glance behind me. The skeleton was closer now. I could see the flame shooting from its head as it zoomed toward me in the night.

"Aargh!"

I mashed Bessie's window button for all I was worth, praying the pane would get its butt back up before it was too late.

"Please, Universe!" I begged aloud. "Get me out of this and I'll never make fun of a mullet again!"

I glanced in the rearview mirror. The flaming skeleton was mere yards from my back bumper. Another few seconds and I was a goner!

"Come on!" I screamed.

The gate finally squeaked opened wide enough to squeeze Bessie's huge chassis through. I stomped the gas pedal, blew past the gate, and hooked a left onto the main road.

Where I was headed, I didn't care.

And as for that skeleton? Who knows?

I never dared look back again.

Chapter Twenty-Five

I pulled into the parking lot of that posh strip mall we'd passed on the way to the park, shaking so badly the steering wheel felt like a jackhammer in my hands.

Under the glow of a street lamp, I glanced around the lot, worried Mullet's freaking spirit skeleton had followed me somehow. With no sign of him in any direction, I reached for my purse to call Grayson.

I fished around inside every pocket, but my fingers felt numb and my hands were still trembling. I dumped my purse out on the seat beside me and rifled through the receipts, lipsticks, and assorted candy wrappers.

My Glock was there, but no phone.

Then I remembered. Grayson had borrowed it again after I called Beth-Ann, and hadn't given it back.

Crap! What am I gonna do now?

I couldn't go back to the park. That flaming Mullet freak might be waiting for me. Besides, the gates wouldn't open again until 5:30 in the morning.

I thought about trying to find some stranger and borrow their phone, but that would've required me to be able to remember Earl's or Grayson's phone numbers. That would've been challenging enough under normal circumstances. But at the moment, my brain was so scrambled I could barely remember my own name.

So I stuffed the junk back into my purse and resigned myself to calling the strip mall parking lot my home for the night. I grabbed the wadded bedsheet from the floorboard, leaned against the side of the passenger door, and pulled the sheet up to my neck. Then I laid my trusty Glock in the seat by my thigh.

I didn't know if you could kill an already dead skeleton with bullets, but one thing was for sure.

I wouldn't sleep a wink that night.

I WOKE UP WITH MY LEFT cheek plastered to the driver's side window. I peeled it off as a man in an oversized Boy Scout uniform gave me the once-over.

"Hey, lady, you okay?"

"Uh, yes, officer," I said, sitting up and rubbing my sore neck. "I just fell asleep."

"I'm not a cop," he said. "I'm a park ranger. I noticed you slumped over in your vehicle and wanted to make sure everything was all right. You aren't in any trouble, are you?"

"No sir. I'm fine, thanks."

"Wait, you're that woman from yesterday," he said.

I glanced at his tag. Just my luck. The guy was Ranger Provost.

"Yes," I said.

"Why are you out here?" he asked.

"Uh..." I fumbled, scrambling to think of an excuse as to why I would be sleeping in a truck I didn't own, in a town I didn't live in. With a gun by my side.

Shit!

I shot the ranger my best early-morning, no-caffeine smile. "I'm just waiting for the shop to open so I can get some coffee."

His eyebrow ticked up a notch. "Is that right? Well, I'm afraid you've got a long wait. It's six-thirty, and they don't open until nine. Plus, you're parked in front of a dry cleaners."

"Oh," I said. "Uh ... it was dark when I pulled up here."

Ranger Provost shot me a look that let me know he didn't believe my story. I tried to hitch up my smile. "Could you tell me where to find a good coffee place?"

He shot me a weird look. "Uh ... right across the street."

He pointed to a coffee shop across the road. I tried to giggle, but it came out as a maniacal cackle.

"Oops!" I said. "I'm not from around here."

Provost's brow furrowed. "Maybe we should call someone to come get you."

"No need," I said, cranking the engine. "Besides, I left my phone at home. Thanks for the info. Have a great day!"

As I pulled away, the ranger kept his eye on me until I'd pulled out of the lot, crossed the street, and parked at the coffee shop. Only when I got out and waved at him did he finally get in a green Jeep Cherokee and take off.

I walked into the coffee shop feeling like a fool.

A ghost skeleton with its hair on fire? Get real, Bobbie!

What I thought I'd seen last night couldn't have been real. It had to be something else. My eyes must've been playing tricks on me.

Then a thought made me gasp.

Maybe I've got brain damage!

Barely three weeks had passed since I'd had the vestigial twin removed from my brain. Maybe the surgeon screwed up and left a pair of tongs in my head or something.

"What'll it be?" the coffee shop clerk asked as I stepped up to the counter.

"Three coffees and a dozen donuts," I said.

"What kind?" she asked.

"Black," I said. "The kind made with coffee beans?"

"I meant the donuts," she said.

"Oh. Sorry," I said. "I just had a bad night."

"I understand," she said, giving me a look that only hardened retail workers can master. "I'm having a bad day."

Chapter Twenty-Six

As I drove through the front entrance to Fort De Soto Campgrounds, my ears began to burn. I was mortified to see Ranger Provost's green Jeep Cherokee parked in the lot.

He was on duty again today.

I slunk down in my seat and turned my face the other way. All I needed was another run-in with the guy. He must've thought I was a complete idiot.

With my eyes off the road, I didn't see the speedbump just past the ranger's station. I hit it doing at least 30 mph. The three coffees popped up in the seat, but, thankfully, remained snug in their cardboard carrying container.

The donuts, however, weren't quite so lucky. The paper bag flew forward and hit the dashboard. Donuts exploded out of the bag, zipping around like frosted flying saucers.

Crap!

I had a mess on my hands, but I wasn't about to stop on the main street and have Ranger Provost witness the scene. So I took the first left turn toward the campsite and pulled into the community bathroom parking lot.

There, I wiped as much dirt as I could from the donuts and stuck them back in the bag. Then I got back on the road and made my way to campsite 113.

I hoped Earl and Grayson were still asleep and hadn't noticed I'd run off like a crazy woman in the night.

But, apparently, they had.

When I pulled into the campsite, Grayson was sitting at the picnic table, talking on the phone. He saw me, stood up, and began making a "What's going on?" gesture with his free hand.

Not wanting to complicate an already awkward story with having to explain away a dozen dirty donuts, I left them in the car and climbed out, toting the coffees.

As I got up to the table, Grayson clicked off the cellphone. No sooner had he hung up than it rang again.

"No, Earl, I'm still not Bobbie," Grayson said. "Yes, I still have Drex's phone. Yes, it's still me."

Grayson glanced at me and shook his head, then said into the phone, "Yes. Correct. Hold that thought, Earl. I've got some good news. Drex just came back."

I heard Earl holler, "Woohoo!" through the phone. I stifled a smile.

"What's that?" Grayson said into the receiver. "Yes, Bessie appears to be unharmed."

My smile evaporated.

Grayson put his hand over the receiver and glanced at me. "Earl wants to know if you've already partaken of your first cup of coffee this morning."

My eyes narrowed. Two could play at this game. "Yes. And tell him I brought some special donuts, just for him."

Grayson removed his hand from the receiver and spoke to Earl. "Yes. The coast is clear. And she brought donuts."

Earl let out another "Woohoo!"

Grayson clicked off the phone and turned to me. "What happened last night? Where'd you go? I tried to call you, but then realized I still had your phone."

"I took off," I said.

"Obviously," Grayson said. "But why?"

I glanced around. "Is Earl in the RV?"

"No. He walked up to the camp store. Why?"

"I don't want him to hear what I'm about to tell you."

Grayson's shoulders straightened. "Are you in some kind of trouble?"

"No. I mean, I don't know."

"What?" Grayson asked.

I grimaced. "I saw him last night."

"The weed guy? He's harmless. He came by the RV, too."

"No, not the weed guy."

"Then who?"

"Mul—"

"There you are!" Earl yelled, running in my direction with his arms outstretched, a plastic bag in one of them. "I was worried to death about you!"

I smiled and took a step toward him.

Earl swerved and ran over to Bessie's front end and gave the grille of his monster truck a big hug.

What a jerk!

Earl grinned and said, "Look what I got to go with the donuts!" He pulled out another huge bag of candy corn from the plastic tote. "It's a breakfast vegetable!"

And that, ladies and gentlemen, was when I lost it.

"Arrgh!" I screamed. "Earl Schankles, you are the biggest, dumbest idiot in the whole universe!"

My cousin stopped dead in his tracks.

He stared at me for a moment, then said, "Fine, Bobbie. You don't want me and my candy corn around, you got it."

Then he climbed into Bessie and peeled out.

Chapter Twenty-Seven

For days, (well, technically, *months*) I'd wanted my cousin Earl to get out of my hair and give me some alone time with Grayson. I'd finally gotten my wish.

But it hadn't been worth it.

As I watched Earl peel out of the campsite in Bessie, I didn't feel victorious. I felt terrible. Not only had I lost my cousin—I'd also lost my toothbrush, toothpaste, and my bed for the night.

On the verge of angry tears, I turned to Grayson, who was opening his coffee lid. "Why did I say that to Earl? Why do I keep doing such stupid stuff?"

"I've been wondering that myself," Grayson said, which I found astoundingly unhelpful.

"Drex, you've always been feisty," he said, adding a touch of salt to his coffee. "But for the past few days, you've been bordering on the edge of the B-word."

I gasped. "The B-word?"

"Yes. Barbaric."

I sighed and picked up my coffee. "I know. I guess it's just that I've been—"

"It's a shame my EEG machine was lost in the accident," Grayson said, rubbing his chin. "I would love to test your alpha waves right now."

Seriously? My alpha male is only interested in my alpha waves. Geez, Universe. You sure know how to karma a girl's ass.

After hallucinating a flaming skeleton last night and roasting my cousin alive with my tongue this morning, I decided to share my darkest fear with Grayson. I mean, at this point, what else did I have to lose?

I chewed my lip. "Do you think my brain might be going haywire? You know, because of the surgery I had?"

"You mean brain damage?" Grayson said, putting the lid back on his coffee. "I suppose it's possible. But I examined your post-op MRI scans myself. They looked clean. And they showed you were healing nicely. But then again, anything is possible, I suppose."

Nick Grayson. The only man with no bedside and *no bedside manner.*

"What about that amygdala anomaly stuff you mentioned yesterday?" I said. "You blamed it for why you stored your money in your RV. Could it also be the reason I'm so cranky?"

"Cranky?" Grayson snorted. "I would categorize your behavior as a great deal more than—"

I shot Grayson a death stare. To his credit, the man was smart enough to realize it was time to switch gears.

"Hmm," he said. "It's possible. But a true amygdala anomaly is typically triggered by situations involving either high anxiety or huge reward."

"What do you mean?"

"Well, I kept my money in the RV because I was concerned about a worldwide economic collapse."

My nose crinkled. "Seriously? I'd never do anything *that* dumb."

"No?" Grayson said, setting his coffee on the table. "Okay, what would you do if Operative Garth asked you to send him nude pics of yourself? Would you do it?"

I nearly spewed my sip of coffee. "No way! Not in a million lifetimes!"

Grayson nodded. "Okay. What if Brad Pitt asked you to?"

I hesitated.

Grayson smiled. "You're thinking about it."

I frowned. "Well, a little. So what?"

"You just told me there was no way in the world you'd send nude pics. But then a mere two seconds later, here you are considering doing that very thing—even if only for a moment. Tell me, what changed?"

I shook my head. "I dunno."

"The size of the reward, that's what," Grayson said. "You weighed the value of the reward, and found it worth contemplating doing something you normally would 'never in a million years' consider. That's an amygdala anomaly in action. It's the reason politicians take bribes. It's why so many health professionals smoke. It's why otherwise sane people watch reality TV."

I shook my head in disbelief. "But *why*? Why do we do it?"

Grayson shrugged. "According to one study, under the right circumstances, a subconscious neurobiological sequence in our brains causes us to perceive the world around us in ways that contradict objective reality, distorting what we see and hear. The authors of the study called it 'brainshift.' They reported it can happen to anyone, regardless of morals, intelligence, or past behaviors."

I grimaced. "How do we stop it?

"We can't. In fact, we're never even aware it's happening. But the good news is, like I said, it usually only occurs in situations of high anxiety or huge reward. Under those conditions, with enough pressure, we're likely to do anything, no matter how regrettable."

"So you think that's why I'm making bad decisions?" I asked. "Because I got a million dollars? It's a huge reward, like you said."

"Yes, but I doubt that's the root cause. The behaviors you enacted to obtain that reward were completed weeks ago. Therefore, I don't think the money is related to your current situation."

"So I guess that leaves high anxiety to blame," I said.

Grayson nodded. "It would appear so. Are you fearful of losing the money?"

I blanched. "Well, I *wasn't*—until you just mentioned it."

"Oh. My bad. What else might be causing you high anxiety?"

Uh, let's see. Setting Earl off on a rampage. Possible post-op brain damage. The fear of never having sex again. Or perhaps it has something to do with being attacked by a freaking flaming ghost skeleton last night...

"I dunno," I said.

Grayson nodded. "Well, don't be too hard on yourself. For the most part, human beings don't consciously decide to act foolishly. But when our perceptions become distorted, we can act in ways that make sense to *us*, but not to anyone else around us."

I smiled sourly. "So when in doubt, blame it on your amygdala."

Grayson grinned. "Precisely."

We laughed, then Grayson's eyebrow suddenly arched into a triangle like Spock's.

"Now tell me," he said, "What made you take off last night like a Chiroptera out of Hades?"

Dang. I was kind of hoping he'd kind of forgotten about that...

Chapter Twenty-Eight

I glanced across the picnic table at Grayson and shrugged. "It was nothing, really."

He locked eyes with me. I could tell he wasn't buying my bull.

"I'm serious," he said. "Why'd you take off in the truck last night?"

I tapped a fingernail on my empty coffee cup. After learning about amygdala anomalies, I wondered if somehow the flaming skeleton could've been caused by that. But no. Not unless it was a bad decision on my part to *see* it. So that excuse wasn't going to fly.

"I guess after all that talk about ghostly lights last night, I just got spooked," I said. "Either that, or the fumes emitting from Earl's truck seat had me hallucinating."

"Spooked?" Grayson said. "Hallucinating? What did you think you saw? The white lights Doris mentioned?"

"Uh ... yeah," I said, which, technically, wasn't a lie. It just wasn't the whole truth ...

Grayson cocked his head and studied me. "Intriguing. Were you able to ascertain whether they were fireflies, as Doris suspected?"

"Yeah. And the answer's a big fat no. Not a chance. The light I saw was too big."

"How big was it?"

"I'm not sure. I only saw it for a second as I sped by."

"Sped by?" Grayson's eyes narrowed.

"Uh ... yeah."

"So the *light* wasn't what originally caused you to take off in the truck, was it?"

I grimaced. "No."

Grayson aimed his green eyes at me like a double-barreled shotgun. "Then *what* did?"

I winced. For better or worse—brain damage or not—I'd seen what I'd seen. And I had to own up to it.

"You won't believe it," I said. "I barely believe it myself."

Grayson's face shifted from curiosity to concern. "What was it? Tell me, Drex!"

"Mullet Daniels!" I blurted. "Or, more like ... maybe his spirit skeleton?"

"What?" Grayson said. "How did you know it was Mullet? Did you see the tattoos on his toes?"

"Huh?" I blanched. "No. He didn't have any *skin*, Grayson. He was a *skeleton*."

"Then how—"

"It was his *hair*. Okay? I recognized his *hair*!"

Grayson's back stiffened. "Drex, if you're going to be technical about it, skeletons don't have *hair*, either."

My jaw clenched. "Well, *this one* did. It was a mullet. And it was on fire!"

"Are you sure?"

My mouth fell open. "Are you saying you don't believe me?"

Grayson's face shifted back to his scientist-examining-a-lab-rat look. "It's just that you've been so fiery lately, I'm not sure what to believe."

"Do you really think I'd make up a story about seeing a skeleton with flaming mullet hair?"

"To be fair, you just told me you barely believed it yourself."

My shoulders slumped. "I know." My frustration shifted into confusion. "But it really *happened*, Grayson. I swear. I didn't make it up."

"Perhaps not intentionally," Grayson said. "But humans are an odd species. They make up things all the time, then choose to believe them as fact."

My eyes narrowed. "Grayson, that thing—whatever it was—chased me all the way to the campground exit!"

"Fair enough," he said. "Then there ought to be tracks."

I PICKED UP A STICK and poked at a tire-tread impression in the crushed limestone road. "Maybe ghost skeletons don't make tracks."

"Or maybe they wear hiking sandals," Grayson said, examining a shoe print.

"You don't have to get sarcastic about it," I said.

"Who's being sarcastic? I'm merely pointing out plausible possibilities."

We'd spent the last half an hour looking for imprints in the unpaved road and the grass alongside it, all the way from our campsite to the back exit of the campgrounds.

"I think we're done here," Grayson said. "There's nothing to point the finger at a skeletal perpetrator."

"Okay," I said. "It's just that—"

A horn sounded behind us. We stepped out of the road and let a huge, black, Ford F-150 drive by. As it passed, I thought about Earl alone out there somewhere, with nothing to sustain him but a giant bag of candy corn and a dozen assorted brain cells.

"I hope Earl's cooled down by now," I said, following Grayson back toward our campsite.

He shrugged. "Maybe he found the donuts you bought and took them as a peace offering."

Or as another dirty trick. Oh, crap!

I chewed my lip. "Maybe."

As we reached site 113, I said, "You know, Earl may not come back today. We need to call a cab or something."

"Why?" Grayson asked.

"So we can get a motel room for tonight."

"Why?"

"Because I'm not sleeping in that nasty RV, that's why."

Grayson laughed. "Come on. It's not *that* bad."

"Seriously? I'm surprised at you, Grayson. You're usually such an OCD clean freak."

Grayson stifled a smile. "You know me pretty well. But you haven't even given the old RV a chance. Go on. Check it out."

My nose crinkled. "I'd rather not."

"What if I told you I spent all last night cleaning it from top to bottom?"

My eyebrows rose an inch. "You did?"

Grayson nodded. "I did. With you gone, I couldn't sleep. So it was either clean the RV or carry on a conversation with Earl about the nutritional value of candy corn versus jelly beans."

I locked eyes with Grayson. "So you and he didn't talk about the case we're working on?"

"No. Why would we?"

My heart pinged. "So ... you're not grooming Earl to replace me as your intern?"

Grayson nearly choked. "Good grief, Drex. No. What gave you that idea?"

I winced. "Uh ... I'm going to blame this one on my amygdala, if you don't mind."

Grayson smirked. "Be my guest."

WHEN I STEPPED INSIDE of the old RV I nearly passed out. But not from the filth, this time. The inside gleamed from top to bottom, and reeked of citrus-fresh cleanser.

"This is amazing," I said. "How'd you get the stains out of the—*everything*."

"Ancient Chinese secret," Grayson quipped.

"Ha ha."

"I used my old standby, Mr. Clean." He handed me an empty bottle. The guy on the container looked like Earl—if my cousin was bald as a billiard ball.

"Wait," I said. "You used the whole bottle on this place?"

"Don't be ridiculous," Grayson said. "I used fourteen of those babies."

I laughed. "Why only fourteen?"

"Because, after careful calculation, they contained exactly the fluid ounces required to clean the RV, based on square footage. That, plus they only had fourteen bottles at the camp store."

"But what about your theory that Mullet spontaneously combusted in here? Didn't cleaning the place destroy all the evidence?"

"No. Besides the mattress, whatever evidence that might have been in here had already been compromised by the police, EMTs and fire investigators."

"Oh." I took a peek inside the bathroom. "Well, I have to say, I'm impressed."

"So you'll stay the night in here with me?" Grayson asked.

I turned, looked him in the eye, and said, "Not on your life."

Chapter Twenty-Nine

As amazingly clean as the RV now was, there was no way I was going to spend the night inside it with Grayson. What if things got romantic? I didn't want the first time we sealed the deal to be on a dead man's mattress!

No amount of Mr. Clean could dissolve *that* apprehension. But I couldn't tell Grayson that was my reason. It would've been too presumptuous.

Or maybe too preposterous.

"I'm sorry, but I still can't sleep in here," I said, sliding into the squeaky-clean banquette opposite Grayson.

"Why not?" he asked.

"Uh ... I don't have a toothbrush."

Grayson eyed me carefully. "We can get one at the camp store. But I have a feeling that's not what's bothering you."

I frowned. "Why can't we just get a motel on the beach?"

"Two reasons," Grayson said. "One, I want to stay here and investigate the lights and the skeletal apparition you saw last night. We can't do that if we go to a motel."

I sighed. He was right. "And the second reason?"

"The RV won't start."

"What? Again?"

"When Earl and I heard you peel out in Bessie last night, we tried to go after you. But no matter how much we jiggled the keys and made the requisite jiggle face, it was Operation No-Go."

An image popped into my mind of the two of them making Popeye faces. I had to purse my lips to keep from laughing.

I cleared my throat. "So we're stuck here."

Grayson shrugged. "I wouldn't call it *stuck*."

"What *would* you call it?"

"I prefer the term 'temporarily landlocked.'"

I gave him some side-eye. "So what are we going to do?"

"I say let's worry about the RV later. Perhaps Earl took off to get parts for it."

I let out a sigh. "Maybe you're right."

"Anyway, we should get going," Grayson said, scooting out of the booth. "Right now we've got bigger fish to fry."

"What do you mean?"

He stood and said, "*Carpe diem McGyverem.*"

My upper lip snarled. "Did you just say 'Seize the day like McGyver' in *Latin*?"

"Yes." Grayson grabbed my hand and tugged me out of the booth. "Come on. We better get to it while we've got the chance."

I was about to say "Get to *what*?" when a thought made me nearly gasp.

Was Grayson taking me to do the nasty on that nasty mattress?

I yanked my hand away. "Where are we going?"

"To the camp store," Grayson said. "We need to find out what they have on hand we can use to construct a ghost trap."

My face collapsed. "Oh."

Maybe while we're there I can find something to beat you senseless with, too.

AS WE WALKED TO THE camp store, I focused on the tropical trees and blue sky, trying to eradicate visions of Grayson lying barechested in the RV bed, a rose between his teeth, patting Mullet's ashy mattress as an invitation for me to join him ...

"What are you thinking about?" Grayson asked, startling me. "How to catch the apparition?"

"Uh ... sure."

Snatched from my daydream, I scrambled to think of a question related to the case. "Uh ... do you think that skeleton and the white light I saw last night could really be connected somehow to Mullet's death?"

Grayson stopped to pick a fossilized shell from the road material. "It's not outside the realm of possibility, considering anecdotal evidence of lights being seen around the time of victims' spontaneous combustion events."

My nose crinkled. "Who was the last person to go up in flames around here, anyway?"

"Besides Mullet and Titanic?"

"Yeah."

He tossed the shell back onto the road. "That would be Danny."

"Danny?" I gasped, stopping dead in my tracks. "Mullet's brother got roasted to cinders, too?"

"Not Danny Daniels. I'm talking about Danny *Vanzandt*. From Tulsa, Oklahoma. His was the last reported death in the US to be suspected of being caused by spontaneous human combustion."

"When was that?"

"In February of 2013. Vanzandt's neighbors called the fire department because they saw smoke coming from his house. The firefighters rushed in and attempted to put out a pile of burning trash on the kitchen floor, only to realize it was human remains."

I grimaced. "Unbelievable!"

"Indeed," Grayson said. "Who would burn their garbage inside the house?"

I shook my head. "I don't think that's the point."

Grayson shot me a look. "No. The point is, you haven't read the case files at all."

Oops...

"Why was Vanzandt's death suspected to be spontaneous human combustion?" I asked, trying to be a better intern.

"Officially, it wasn't." Grayson turned his eyes back to the road. "The coroner's office said that Vanzandt likely died of a heart attack while smoking. Then he fell to the floor atop his burning cigarette, causing his clothes to catch fire and his body to be slowly consumed by the Wick Effect."

"But you said the Wick Effect isn't a plausible theory."

"Exactly. And Mr. Vanzandt fits the criteria for spontaneous human combustion to a T."

"How so?"

"He was sixty-five, and a heavy smoker and drinker. Even though his body was extinguished while still aflame, it had already been reduced to forty pounds of remains. There was no evidence of an accelerant, and no indication of a struggle. In addition, the floor underneath Vanzandt's body was undamaged. No other objects or furniture showed signs of fire damage, either."

"Whoa," I said. "That seems to fit the criteria, all right. But if the coroner didn't label his death spontaneous human combustion, who did?"

"The arson investigator on the scene. He said he'd never seen anything like it in his twenty years on the job."

I chewed my lip. "Did anyone ever report seeing Vanzandt's flaming ghost skeleton afterward?"

Grayson shook his head. "Not to my knowledge. In fact, as far as my research indicates, your observation of Mullet's incorporeal visage is unique to all known cases of spontaneous human combustion."

Lucky me.

"This may be a dumb question, Grayson, but how are we going to catch a ghost without the electromagnetic monster trap in the old RV?"

He stopped and turned to me. "I'm not sure. Like I said, it'll depend on what kind of materials are available in the camp store."

Chapter Thirty

The small general store at Fort De Soto Campgrounds reminded me a lot of the Stop & Shoppe drive-thru back in my home town of Point Paradise—except instead of being stuck in an overgrown lot in a crumbling, dead-end town, the camp store sat at the edge of a beautiful waterway, and was perched up in the air on fifteen-foot-tall stilts.

A set of wooden stairs led up to the rustic store's entry door. And for folks who couldn't climb those, a small elevator had been tacked onto the right side of the building. Made of white metal and glass and about the size of an extra-large phone booth, the elevator looked as out of place against the old wooden building as a space suit on caveman.

We took the stairs.

As Grayson and I walked into the store, we were greeted by the clerk running the place. He put down a sandwich, brushed his palm on his shirt, and waved.

"Hey, folks," he said. "Just wanted to let you know, we got candy corn for a dollar a bag."

"WHAT ARE WE GONNA DO with a dozen wiener roasting sticks and a badminton set?" I asked as we walked back from the camp store.

"You'll see," Grayson said, tapping a long, skinny finger against his temple.

Grateful the camp store was fresh out of frankfurters, I shook my head and ripped open a bag of marshmallows. If I was going to have to partake in whatever idiotic plan Grayson was concocting in that strange brain of his, I might as well be buzzing on high-fructose corn syrup.

Once we made it back to the campsite, we hauled the groceries into the RV. While Grayson fiddled around with the badminton set, I tucked the rest of our purchases into the cabinets and mini-fridge.

All except for Grayson's new souvenir gator socks, that is. They were black, of course, and dotted with green gator heads, their mouths agape and full of sharp, white teeth.

It was an odd purchase for Grayson. But he'd been acting a bit strange of late. I wondered if sleeping on Mullet's death bed had anything to do with it.

I picked up the socks, contemplating what to do with them. There was no way I was going into that back bedroom to put them away. Grayson may have cleaned the room to within an inch of its life, but that dead guy's mattress was still in there. And I don't care what Grayson said, it gave me a bona fide case of the creeps.

Just the thought of that singed mattress made the hair on the back of my neck tingle. So I left the socks on the sofa-bed in the living room, and washed a couple of potatoes to put in the microwave. Then I went outside to get the grill going for some sirloin steaks.

"So, what's the plan?" I asked, pouring lighter fluid on a pile of charcoal briquettes.

"I'll let you know when I've thought it through," Grayson said, testing the tensile strength of the net by stretching a section of it between his hands.

"Can't wait," I said, then tossed a match into the briquettes.

Suddenly, I heard a *whoosh*, then smelled the acrid odor of burning plastic. I gasped. In a split second, a huge flame had leapt up from the grill and singed the bangs off my wig.

Crap!

I glanced over at Grayson. Caught up in his project, he hadn't noticed my close brush with spontaneous human combustion. Instead, he and the badminton net were rolling around on the ground together in what appeared to be a wrestling match to the death.

"Uh, Grayson," I said, still a bit stunned from my close brush with death. "You said spontaneous combustion only happens to *old* people, right?"

"No," he said, grunting and kicking his left foot free of the net. "I said the *typical* case involves older people."

"Oh." I patted the remains of my charred bangs, just to make sure the flame was completely out. "What's the youngest case on record?"

Grayson extricated his right foot from the net and sat up on the ground. An oak twig, tangled in his hair, stuck out from his crown like a crooked antenna.

"Tragically, it was an infant only six weeks old," he said.

"Gee," I muttered, glancing at the flaming briquettes. "So *anybody* can burst into flames at any moment?"

Grayson freed his left arm. "With the right set of circumstances and an ignition source, yes."

I took a cautious step back from the grill and watched the flames licking the charcoal, turning the edges of the briquettes to ashy embers.

I grimaced. "What makes *older* people more susceptible, you think?"

"I suspect drugs may have something to do with it."

Surprised, I whipped around to face Grayson. "Drugs?"

"Exactly." Grayson stood up and brushed himself off. "The compounds in prescription drugs could initiate changes to the chemical composition of a body, making it more flammable. Also, as we age, the body's natural digestive system is no longer at its prime. Poor digestion can lead to a higher production of methane."

Uh ... you aren't kidding there.

"That makes sense," I said. I removed the steaks from their plastic package and seasoned them with salt and pepper. I noticed both sirloins nicely marbled.

"What about fat?" I asked. "You said most victims were overweight. How's that related to spontaneous human combustion?"

"Well, that's more complicated," Grayson said, walking over to me. He was still sporting his oak-twig antenna. I smirked and decided not to mention it. "Fat brings up several contributing factors—the major one being potassium."

"Potassium?" I asked, laying the steaks on the grill.

"Yes. The amount of potassium contained in the average person produces 41 million gamma rays a day."

"Seriously?"

"Deadly seriously," Grayson said, eyeing the steaks. "If just two of those potassium atoms collided with a deuterium atom, it would generate a small nuclear reaction that may be enough to ignite the body internally."

"Huh?" I said, nearly dropping my grill tongs. "Deuterium? What's that?"

"It's H-2-O without the O," Grayson said. "Also referred to as heavy water."

My brow furrowed. "So, heavy people have more heavy water in them?"

"Precisely."

"Why?"

"Because the bulk of deuterium is stored in fat and liver cells," Grayson explained, taking a seat at the picnic table. "Therefore, it's logical to theorize that the more fat a person has, the more deuterium—aka hydrogen—they can store. And the more hydrogen, well, now we're back to the Hindenburg example."

I cringed. "Oh, the humanity."

"Exactly. Interestingly, this theory would also help explain why the torso is the predominant portion of the victim that is consumed by fire."

I flipped over the steaks. "So, let me get this straight. You're saying the ignition source for human combustion could be some kind of internal nuclear meltdown?"

Grayson nodded. "That's precisely what I'm saying."

My nose crinkled. "If that's true, how could we possibly prove it?"

"If deuterium is the seed cause, there should be remnants of neutron radiation in the surrounding environment. It passes through paper and cloth, but traces of neutron radiation linger in water, plastic, wax, and fats."

"So you want to test Mullet's mattress for neutron radiation?"

"Exactly." Grayson rubbed his chin. "Too bad the camp store didn't carry Geiger counters. I thought about ordering a detector online, but we haven't had a stable address to have it shipped to."

I shook my head. "So, in a way, I guess Earl was right."

Grayson's eyebrow rose like Spock's. "How so?

"That dumb remark he made about the mattress remembering what happened to Mullet. In a way, he was right. If Mullet spontaneously combusted due to an internal nuclear event, the plastic in his memory foam mattress could actually 'remember' the neutron radiation blast by recording it."

"Absolutely." Grayson looked up at me and smirked, causing his alien oak-twig antenna to fall to the ground behind his back.

"Still think your cousin is the biggest idiot in the whole world?" he asked.

I shook my head. "No."

Maybe that honor should go to me.

Chapter Thirty-One

"The steaks are ready!" I called out over my shoulder as I took them off the grill.

"Uh ... I could use your assistance over here," Grayson called back.

I set the plate of steaks on the picnic table and turned around. Over in the thicket of palmettos, Grayson was once again caught up in the badminton net like a hapless nitwit in a low-budget spider movie.

"Good grief," I said, letting out a laugh as I rushed over to detangle him. "What are you doing, anyway?" I detangled his ear from a piece of the net. It felt oddly inflexible.

"Why is this net so stiff?" I asked.

"I ran copper wiring through it," Grayson said, freeing his right arm from the net.

"Uh ... *why*?"

"I'm converting it to an improvised electromagnetic field trap."

My nose crinkled. "To catch the flaming ghost skeleton?"

Grayson shot me a dubious look, which was pretty hypocritical considering he'd just got caught in his own Venus fly trap—*again*.

"Drex, I would think you would know that nets are useless for capturing incorporeal entities," he said. "They simply dematerialize and slip through the holes. I'm fashioning this trap to hopefully ensnare whatever's causing the mysterious white lights."

"Oh."

I bit my lip. I guess I should've mentioned that the light I saw last night was as big as a house. But there's no point in spoiling his fun with a little fact like that, was there?

Grayson disentangled his last appendage from the net and handed me one end of it. "Take this and help me stretch it out between these two stands of palmettos."

"Aye aye, captain," I deadpanned, grabbing the net. Thanks to its new copper inserts it was as stiff as chicken-wire.

Grayson grabbed a roll of copper wiring and fastened one end of the net to a young pine tree. That finished, he tied the other end to a palm. After testing the tensile strength of the outstretched net, he showed me a cache of three nine-volt batteries he'd hidden on the ground amid the leaf litter.

"What are those for?" I asked.

"I'm going to electrify the net with this battery bank," he said. "Hopefully, the electromagnetic frequency they send out will appeal to our prey."

My nose crinkled with doubt. "Okay. So, what's the light bulb hanging above the net for?"

"I repurposed a lamp cord from the RV into a visual lure."

"Uh-huh," I grunted skeptically.

Why do I suddenly feel as if I'm on an episode of Gilligan's Island *that's about to go horribly awry?*

"So, Professor," I said, "What happens to whatever gets caught in the net?"

"It will be stunned by the 27-volt electrical charge of the battery bank."

"Ah." I nodded thoughtfully. "So, what you've got there is basically a homemade bug zapper."

Grayson's chin rose an inch. "Well, I suppose that's a simplified way to look at it, yes."

"Great, Grayson. But what if whatever's causing the lights aren't bugs?"

Grayson shrugged and headed for the steak dinner laid out on the picnic table. "I guess we'll cross that leg when we stand on it."

"THAT OUGHT TO DO IT," Grayson said, placing a plastic laundry basket beside his badminton-net bug-zapper contraption.

I stifled a smirk and tried to put on a studious intern face. "So your plan is, if something gets caught in the net, you're going to catch it in a laundry basket?"

"If the option presents itself," Grayson said. "Regardless of whether our quarry becomes ensnared in the net, if it touches the wiring, the electrical discharge should stun it for a few seconds."

Sensing it may be time to come clean about overlooked details of my sighting, I asked, "What if whatever's causing the lights is bigger than the laundry basket?"

Grayson shrugged. "Either way, our quarry should be momentarily stunned by the shock. That would give me time enough to photograph it, even if capture isn't possible."

"I guess a photo's better than nothing," I quipped.

"Photographic evidence can prove quite valuable," Grayson said. "I've gotten good money for intriguing photographs."

"Seriously? From who?"

Grayson shot me a haughty look. "There's quite a collection of cryptid connoisseurs on eBay. And, not to brag, but I've got a reputation for delivering photographs with provenance."

I stifled a smirk. "You don't say."

"I *do* say." Grayson eyed me a moment, then said. "Provenance is—"

"I know what provenance is," I said, cutting him off. "I'm not dumb. It's the story that goes along with the object. Provenance is what gives an object most of its value. You'd have to pay to have Andy Warhol's used toupee taken away if it belonged to Joe Blow. I used to sell antiques with Carl Blanchard, remember?"

"Fair enough," Grayson said. "I only wanted to make sure you understood."

"I'm not a dingbat like Earl," I grumbled. "So, what do we do now?"

Grayson cocked his head. "We wait until dark, of course."

"I *know* that," I said a little too defensively. "But it's only like, two o'clock. Can't we do something fun this afternoon? I'm supposed to be on vacation, or have you forgotten that?"

"Are you two bored?" a woman's voice called out from the road. I turned to see our little-old-lady neighbor Doris, driving a pink golf cart.

"Kind of," I said, walking over to her.

"Why don't you two go see the Skyway Bridge?" she said. "Or take a tour of the fort?"

I shrugged. "That sounds nice, but we don't have a vehicle."

Doris hopped out of her golf cart. "Take my cart. It's time for my afternoon nap, anyway."

"Really?" I said. "That would be great, thanks!"

"While you're out, keep an eye out for Daulton, would you? That little jerk got off his leash again."

"Sure thing," I said. "So, how do we get to the fort?"

Doris showed me her dentures. "Easy. You know where the back exit of the campground is?"

Do I ever!

"Uh ... yeah," I said.

"Good. Just take a right out on the main road and keep going. You'll come to the toll gate into the park. Past that, in a mile or so the road ends in a T. If you want to see the Skyway Bridge, go left all the way to the end. There's a little circle where you can park. It's the best place to view the bridge in the whole county."

"Cool," I said. "And the fort?"

"Same thing. Only take a right where the road comes to the T. Keep going and you'll see signs that'll lead you right to it. You can't miss it."

"Gee, thanks, Doris!"

"Glad to return the favor," she said, licking her lips. "That was the best little piggy in a blanket I've had in a long time."

I grinned. "Well, I'm glad you enjoyed it. Have a nice nap!"

Doris smiled and waved at me until she disappeared behind the thicket separating our campsites. I sprinted back to Grayson, who was fiddling with some electronic-looking gizmo.

"Leave that stuff for now," I said. "Let's go do some sightseeing!"

"I've got work to do if this thing is going to be ready by nightfall," Grayson said, not looking up.

I scowled. "Look, I've been helping you do your stuff since we got here. Can't you take an hour off and do this one thing for me?"

Grayson glanced up at me. "If I do, will you agree to sleep with me in the RV?"

I almost swallowed my tonsils.

Had Grayson just propositioned me? Or was he merely trying to get out of going to a motel? I had no clue. But I didn't want to blow my chances by actually *asking*. So I crossed my fingers and hoped he'd meant the former.

Then I said, "Okay."

Chapter Thirty-Two

"I didn't know there was such a big market for photographs of cryptids," I said to Grayson as I mashed the gas on Doris' pink golf cart. "I thought it was only scat or body parts that were worth something."

I was driving the cart along the two-lane asphalt road leading to Fort De Soto Park, trying to strike up a subject with Grayson that didn't involve charred human remains.

"You'd be surprised," Grayson said, taking a picture of the scenery with his freshly charged cellphone.

I glanced around, took a deep breath of sunshine-filled sky, and smiled. "Isn't it beautiful?"

To the right of us lay the same tangled jungle of palms, pines, sea oats and scrub oaks that hid our campsites from the road. On the left side of the road, a wide ribbon of concrete snaked its way through a beltway of green grass. The paved path served as a wander-way for pedestrians and folks on bicycles and rollerblades.

We came to the T at the end of the road where the park's official welcome station stood. Following Doris' instructions, I took a left to head toward the bridge.

"People will pay a lot for items of true rarity or oddity," Grayson said.

"I guess you proved that point with Warhol's wig," I said, shaking my head. "A hundred and eight grand for a used toupee. Geez."

"Exactly. It's the provenance they pay for. The exclusivity of ownership of something with unique historical significance. So you can only imagine what some collectors would pay for an authenticated chupacabra hide or a vampire fang."

My eyebrows ticked up a notch. "You've sold such things?"

"Not personally, no," Grayson said, snapping another picture with his cellphone. "But I've heard of such deals taking place."

"You know, it's a beautiful day," I said, glancing around. "Could we just take a few minutes to enjoy *reality* for a change?"

Grayson shrugged. "Sure. If you want to believe what you see here is reality."

I sighed. "I do."

I so desperately do.

"WE'RE HERE," I SAID, pulling into a parking circle. I climbed out of the golf cart, spotted a small trail amid the sandspurs and scrub palms, and headed for it.

"Come on," I yelled at Grayson. He was lagging behind, staring at his cellphone. Frustrated at his fixation with technology, I turned and walked on without him.

The short trail led up to the water's edge. There, soaring over Tampa Bay, was an amazing feat of construction named the Sunshine Skyway Bridge.

"Whoa," I muttered to myself. From this vantage point, the long span seemed to have appeared from beyond, with no beginning or end in sight. The whole imagery reminded me of a giant gray snake slithering atop a crystal-blue sea.

The center of the Sunshine Skyway Bridge rose dramatically, as if the man-made serpent of concrete and metal had swallowed an ostrich egg, which was now lodged in its middle. The dramatic hump rose sharply, pushing the apex of the bridge nearly 200 feet above Tampa Bay.

Adding to its awesomeness, the huge arch was topped by two triangular sets of yellow cables that supported it. The pyramid-shaped spans above the arch nearly doubled the bridge's already impressive silhouette against the blue sky.

"Wow, that's amazing," I said as Grayson came up behind me. "Looking at the bridge from the ground gives you a whole different perspective than driving across it. It's so tall!"

"Hmm," Grayson grunted.

I glanced over at him. He still had his nose stuck in his cellphone.

"Geez, Grayson, take a minute to enjoy the view, would you?"

"I'm just reading about the bridge," he said. "You're not interested in knowing anything about it?"

"Well, yeah. What does it say?"

"Apparently, the span was a modern marvel when it opened in 1954. But what you're looking at there is not the original bridge."

"It's not?"

"No."

Grayson peered at his phone and read from the screen. "The original one was less than half as tall as this one. It was struck by a freighter on May 10, 1980, causing the central span to collapse. They say 36 people died as a result—including a Greyhound bus loaded with college students going home for summer break."

"Geez. That's tragic," I said. A worrying thought popped into my head. "You don't think that ghost skeleton could be someone who died on the bridge, do you?"

Grayson's eyebrow arched. "It's possible. It says here that exactly a decade to the day of the tragedy, a spectral bus was reported to have been seen crossing the bridge."

"Spectral bus?" I asked.

"Yes. Onlookers reported that all the people on board were facing forward, looks of terror on their faces. A witness said that as the bus passed by, one person in the back turned around and waved."

Despite the bright sun and the warm breeze, the hair on the back of my neck stood up. "That's totally creepy. But it's just a story. It couldn't really be true, right?"

"There appears to be substantiating anecdotal evidence," Grayson said, staring at his phone. "Rumor has it that the bus company used parts salvaged from the bridge disaster in other busses—and that busses receiving those parts allegedly burst into flames."

"Flames?" I gasped. "That could explain why the skeleton's hair was on fire, couldn't it?"

Grayson nodded. "That's what I was thinking, too. You know, this reminds me of a similar story I read about years ago, regarding Eastern Flight 401."

"What do you mean?"

"Flight 401 crashed in the Everglades, killing over a hundred people on aboard, including the pilots, flight engineer, and two flight attendants. Its salvaged parts were used in other planes. Ever since, sightings of the dead pilot and flight engineer have been reported on aircraft that received the spare parts."

I stood frozen in the heat, my mouth hanging open like a dead clam shell.

Grayson gave me the once-over and asked, "Are you having some kind of existential crisis, Drex?"

Really? You're just noticing?

I grimaced. "After hearing all *that*, I just might be." I shot Grayson a pleading look. "Listen. Can we change the subject? I'd like to try and enjoy the sun, the fresh air, the beach. You know?"

"Certainly," Grayson said. "Request for subject change approved. What do you want to talk about?"

I shrugged. "How about those yellow string things supporting the bridge. They're pretty."

"Those are called cable stays, or sails," Grayson said.

I smiled. "They kind of look like sailboat sails, now that you mention it."

"Some people believe that since their installation, those sails have been adopted by aliens, who use them to call home."

I shot him a look. "Again with the aliens?"

"What?" Grayson said. "Aliens are a different topic than ghosts."

I laughed and shook my head. "Right. So, you're saying the bridge here is doubling as some kind of ET telegraph machine?"

"Something like that." Grayson rubbed his chin. "Perhaps the white lights are alien spacecraft—"

"In search of a cosmic Wi-Fi signal," I said.

"Precisely." Grayson glanced back down at his phone. "It says here that the Skyway Bridge is also a famous spot for suicide jumpers. There've been over 200 reported so far."

My shoulders slumped. I turned away from the bridge. "So much for trying to enjoy the view."

Grayson glanced up, a funny look on his face. "Drex, your ghost skeleton. Was it a man or a woman?"

"Huh? If it's not Mullet, then I don't know. Why?"

"It says here that drivers on the bridge have reported seeing a tall, slender, blonde hitchhiker wearing a hooded shirt. Those who pick her up say she begins to cry as the vehicle nears the top of the span. When they turn around to ask what's wrong, they discover she's vanished."

"Good grief." I grimaced. "How can a place that looks so sunny and natural and unspoiled be so clouded with tragedy and high strangeness?"

"Here's one explanation," Grayson said, reading from his phone. "Some believe the bridge is cursed because it was built on several Native American mounds, which were reputedly destroyed during its construction."

I shook my head. Despite the fresh salt air and squawking seagulls overhead, I couldn't shake a growing feeling of dread.

"Let's get out of here," I said, turning back to the trail that led to the parking lot. "Let's go see the fort. Maybe it's not so spooky."

"Good idea," Grayson said. "Did I mention that after the bridge accident in 1980, they used the old fort as a temporary morgue?"

I groaned. "No, Grayson. No you did not."

Chapter Thirty-Three

"Geez. This place looks more like an underground bunker in an old war movie than a *fort*," I said, staring at the squat, boxy concrete structures sunk halfway into the sand.

"What were you expecting?" Grayson asked. "A moat and turrets?"

Well, maybe. Is that so wrong?

I patted one of the dense, bulgy walls. "It sure ain't pretty, but it looks like it was built to last."

"You're right about that." Grayson glanced down at his phone and read from it. "According to this, the fort was constructed hastily by the Army using whatever materials were available back in 1898. That wall you're leaning against is made of a mixture of sand, seashells and concrete. The fort walls range from between eight and twenty feet thick."

"Whoa," I said. "That's a bit of overkill, don't you think?"

"It was designed like this for a reason, Drex. See those mortars over there?"

Grayson pointed to two lonely old cannons loitering in an open courtyard formed by the fort's thick walls. Flanked by weeds and sand, one pit-marked cannon was pointed at the sky. The other stared blankly down into a corner of the fort. For some reason, the pair reminded me of a couple of derelict teenagers doomed to never-ending, detention-hall purgatory.

"Yeah," I said. "I see the cannons. So?"

"Weapons like those are why the walls were built so thick," Grayson explained. "Fort De Soto was originally built to defend Tampa Bay from the Spanish during the Spanish-American War."

My eyebrow ticked up. "That's interesting. Did it work?"

"Perhaps. As a bluff," Grayson said.

"What do you mean?"

"The war was over in less than a year. The soldiers stationed here never got to fire a shot."

"Good," I said.

"Good?"

"Yes. That means if nobody died here, then the fort can't be haunted, right?"

"Wrong," Grayson said. "The heat, mosquitos, and disease did in quite a few of the soldiers. Drowning, as well."

I shook my head. "Geez."

Now I know why Grayson picked Fort De Soto. Not so I could have my beach vacation, but so he could futz around with a bunch of ghouls!

I glared at Grayson, but my death ray found no purchase. His eyes were glued to his phone again.

"Listen to this," he said, not bothering to look up. "They say that as the sun begins to set on the fort, hushed voices can be heard echoing off the stone walls of the southernmost bunker."

I closed my eyes and clenched my jaw. "Come on, Grayson. Stop with the ghost stories, already!"

Ignoring me, he kept on reading. "Phantom footsteps can be heard. And then the apparition of a dripping-wet, fully clothed man appears."

"Gimme that!"

I grabbed Grayson's phone from his hand. "Well, at least we can rule out *that* ghost as the flaming skeleton."

"On what basis do you draw that conclusion?" Grayson asked, taking back his phone.

"On the basis that my flaming skeleton pal wasn't wearing any clothes. Plus, it's pretty hard to catch fire when you're dripping wet."

Grayson nodded. "Logical conclusion. I think you're on the right track about the identity of your spectral visitor."

I am?

"What do you mean?" I asked.

"With the plethora of paranormal activity reported in this park, one of the local spectral entities is most likely to be your perpetrator."

I shook my head at my crazy bad luck. "Grayson, I don't get it. Why on earth would a ghost zero in on *me* to torture?"

Grayson's eyebrow did its Spock impersonation. "Actually, I think I know the answer to that."

I blanched. "You *do*?"

"Perhaps. But mind you, it's just a working theory."

"Well? What is it?"

"Let's take a drive over to the causeway, past the campground entrance. I'll show you what I mean."

"OKAY, SLOW DOWN," GRAYSON said as we approached the toll plaza for Fort De Soto Park. "Look over there."

"What?" I asked, tapping the brakes on the pink golf cart. "All I see is a patch of swampy-looking grass flats."

"Exactly. That's the purported hangout of the romantic trout fisherman."

I frowned. "Wait. Don't tell me demi-sexuals are into three-ways."

Grayson shot me an odd look. "The fisherman I'm talking about is an apparition."

I sighed.

Apparently, so is my love life.

Grayson handed me a pair of binoculars Doris had left wedged between the seats. "Take a look. Do you see anyone?"

I snatched the binoculars from Grayson and begrudgingly peered through them. "What's this creep supposed to look like?"

"He's purported to be a lean, muscular man in his early forties. He has tousled, black hair, and wears dark sunglasses, a navy-blue T-shirt, and dark shorts."

Huh. This guy doesn't sound too bad. Maybe I've still got a ghost of a chance of getting laid...

I squinted into the binoculars, studying the grass flats for any sign of the ghostly Romeo. "Where should I look?"

"It says here he's always spotted wading in the water," Grayson said.

"Well, I don't see anything." I lowered the binoculars. "And anyway, what's this fisherman ghost got to do with why I'm being targeted by a flaming skeleton ghost?"

"Because this particular specter loves to fish—and to flirt with *women*, Drex. You're a woman."

"Last time I checked, yeah. So what's this ghost's M.O.? Once he finds a woman to flirt with, he bursts into a flaming skeleton?"

"Hardly," Grayson said. "According to this article, when a woman speaks to him, he smiles. But when she looks away for a second, he vanishes."

"Huh," I said sourly. "Maybe that's where the dating term 'being ghosted' came from."

"What?" Grayson asked.

"Never mind."

Grayson glanced back down at his phone. "Observers speculate the apparition may be the spirit of Daulton Gray. He was shot to death out here in 1994."

"Fabulous," I said. "Can we go now?"

"Hmm," Grayson said, ignoring me. "Daulton may also be the ghost people sometimes see jogging along the causeway. Whenever he's acknowledged by someone, he actually speaks back."

"Really?" I said, surprised. "I didn't know ghosts could do that. What does he say?"

"According to reports, he says, 'Don't do it.' Then he disappears."

I sighed. "Don't do it, huh?"
I know exactly how he feels.

Chapter Thirty-Four

"Thanks for letting us use your golf cart," I said to Doris as she poked her head out the side door of her deluxe RV.

"My pleasure, honey. Just let me know if you need it again."

"Thanks."

As I handed Doris back the keys, I noticed her hand trembling as she reached for them. The old woman may have been feisty, but she was also fragile. I thought about all the creepy lost souls roaming the park, and got worried for her.

"You don't mind camping out here alone?" I asked.

Doris gave me a denture crème grin. "Not at all. This rig's got the latest security." She glanced down at the little dog in her arms. "Besides, we're not alone, are we snookums?"

I smiled. "Okay. Well, thanks again for loaning us the golf cart. We're kind of busy tonight, but maybe we could get together tomorrow for lunch?"

Doris beamed. "That sounds peachy, honey! I look forward to it!"

I walked back to the campsite to find Grayson on all fours, digging in the hedges like a deranged possum.

"What are you doing?" I asked, shuffling over to him.

"Finishing the trap," he said. "Take a look."

Grayson sat back on his haunches, revealing a hole in the ground he'd been digging. Jutting up from the bottom of the foot-square pit were the business ends of the dozen wiener roasting sticks we'd bought at the camp store that morning.

"You couldn't save me *one* stick to roast marshmallows with?" I grumbled.

"What?" Grayson asked.

"Nothing. What's that supposed to be, anyway?"

"It's a low-tech booby trap," Grayson said. "They used something similar in the Korean and Vietnam wars."

I rolled my eyes and mumbled, "I didn't know those nations liked roasted wienies."

"I don't follow," Grayson said, cocking his head.

"Never mind. So, what's the plan? You think the lights in the sky are going to land here, and some big-footed aliens are going to step on your wiener sticks and surrender?"

"Don't be ridiculous," Grayson said. "This is for the skeletal apparition. And don't discount this primitive booby trap's merit. An enemy with an injured foot is no enemy at all. He's disabled."

"Really?" I said, smirking. "How can you disable something that's already dead?"

Grayson stood and dusted off his hands. "Look. I'm doing the best I can with the meager supplies at hand. I'd appreciate some support here. Now, what can I use to cover the hole?"

"How about a plastic grocery bag?" I offered.

"It won't support the weight of the leaf litter I need to disguise the pit."

"It might, if you open the bag and put it over the sticks like a car cover," I said. "Then sprinkle a light layer of leaves over it. That shouldn't weigh it down enough to make the sticks poke through the plastic."

"Hmm," Grayson said. "Thank you. That was actually helpful of you."

As Grayson turned to fetch a plastic bag from the RV, I stood silent, waiting for him to finish his sentence with "for a change."

But to his credit, he didn't.

And that, ironically, made me feel even worse about my lazy attempt at being his intern.

I'D BEEN BEHAVING BADLY—BOTH as a P.I. intern and as a potential girlfriend. I hadn't bothered to read Grayson's case reports on spontaneous human combustion. And instead of helping him make his field trap, I'd mostly just sat around complaining about not being on vacation.

I needed to do something to prove myself to Grayson. So while he was on the phone with Garth, I put away my pride and called Earl—both to display an attempt at open-mindedness, and to make amends.

Unfortunately, my cousin didn't answer. So I called Beth-Ann instead.

"Hey," I said. "Have you talked to Earl lately?"

"No. Why?"

"We had kind of a blowout. He left this morning in a huff."

"I haven't seen him," she said. "But don't worry too much about Earl. He's probably at some u-pull-it junkyard heaven, throttling a carburetor or something."

I blew out a small laugh. "You're probably right."

"Wait!" Beth-Ann gasped. "That means you and Grayson are alone now! How's your plan for a romantic rendezvous going?"

I grimaced. "Not so great. Beth-Ann, would you do it—"

"With Grayson?" she cut in. "In a hot minute!"

"Let me finish!" I said. "What I meant was, would you do it with Grayson on a dead man's mattress?"

"Sheesh, Bobbie. I gotta say, you do come up with some crazy shit."

"I know. But I'm serious. Would you?"

"Uh ... how'd the guy die?"

"Spontaneous combustion. Maybe."

"Hmm..."

"Come on, Beth-Ann!"

"I'm thinking! Good grief, Bobbie. You sure are picky for a woman who can't shut her mouth about not getting any. You got rid of Earl, and now's your big chance. But what do you do? Instead of jumping Grayson's bones, you call me and complain about the quality of a mattress you have to boink him on!"

"This isn't about the quality of a mattress!" I argued. "It's about ... the memories it holds."

"What?"

"Beth-Ann, I don't want the first time that Grayson and I do it to be on a dead man's mattress!"

"Oh," she said. "I get that."

"So, do you have any advice for me?"

"Yes. Alcohol. Lots and lots of alcohol."

I WAS SITTING OUT AT the picnic table checking on how much a taxi to the beach would be when that weird, ghostly thumping started up again. I ran into the RV.

"Grayson, I hear the spirit drums again!"

He came out of the bathroom, naked save for a towel wrapped around his waist.

"Where?" he asked.

"I uh ... I don't know," I said, unable to stop staring at his killer abs. "Uh ... they sounded nearby."

"And so it begins," he said, brushing past me.

I followed him outside, but the odd drumming had stopped.

"I don't hear it anymore," I said.

"Maybe it was just a warmup," he said, adjusting his towel kilt. "Let's take that as a good omen that the spirits will be active tonight."

"Right."

Grayson took a step toward the RV. "I better go get ready."

"Uh ... look," I said, following him into the old motorhome. My brain was mush. The sight of Grayson's rippling shoulders and arms were about to make me drool.

"What?" Grayson asked, turning around to face me.

"Uh ... I'm sorry I've been crabby the last couple of days. I think I'm just ... *anxious*, you know?"

"Don't worry about it," he said, locking eyes with me. He took my hand in his. "I think I know what's causing it."

I gulped. "You do?"

He nodded. "Neutron radiation. But we can't be sure until Garth gets here with his neutron detector."

I nearly fainted from relief *and* frustration. How was that even possible? I swallowed hard and avoided staring at Grayson's abs as I gathered my wits. "Uh ... so, when is Garth coming?"

"Tomorrow." Grayson turned and headed down the hall.

"So I guess it's now or never," I said.

"What is?" Grayson asked, turning back to face me.

I gulped. I hadn't meant to say those words out loud. "Uh ... to catch these white light things."

"Hmm. So, which position do you prefer?" Grayson asked, then turned and walked toward the bedroom.

I gasped. "Position?"

"Yes. Would you prefer to do it in the bushes or behind the RV?"

From the open bedroom door, I saw the towel fling onto the bedspread.

"I ... uh ..." My knees began to knock. "What do *you* prefer?"

"I vote to take cover behind the palmettos," Grayson called out. "I think it affords us a closer look at anything approaching the field trap from the road."

My gut dropped four inches. "Right. The palmettos. Roger that. I'll meet you there."

"Good," Grayson said. "But be sure to take the spray with you. You don't want to get bitten."

I sighed with disappointment.

Oh, really? Says who?

Chapter Thirty-Five

Mere minutes ago, the sun had disappeared beneath the Gulf of Mexico. The warm, pinkish sky was rapidly fading to gray. Amid the thicket of scrub oaks, vines and palmettos separating our campsite from our neighbors, Grayson and I crouched side by side, each of us armed with a cheap badminton racket.

While we waited in the growing darkness, I argued with Grayson about his decision to leave our guns in the RV.

"We aren't supposed to have weapons in the park," he said. "Besides, bullets have proven ineffective against spectral beings in the past."

"How many ghosts have you actually shot at?" I asked, swatting at a mosquito buzzing around my face.

"A few."

"What do you mean, *a few*?" I said.

Grayson's eyes remained fixed on the improvised field trap stretched across the back end of our campsite. The net was positioned roughly twenty feet away, near the bushes separating our campsite from Doris'. The bare bulb above it gave off a weird, unearthly glow.

"Shh," he said. "No more talking."

"Fine." I glanced to my left. A sudden movement by the road startled me. It was Doris toddling by in her bathrobe and curlers.

"Looks like Sajak's about to start," I whispered.

"It's show time," Grayson whispered back.

I wasn't certain if he was commenting on our stakeout or making a joke. All I knew for sure was that my feet were going numb.

I tried to shift from my squatting position, but my circulation had been cut off at the knees. Unable to feel the earth beneath me, I lost my balance and fell over on top of Grayson.

"You okay," he asked, setting me back up. Then, to my utter shock and surprise, he kissed me.

I blanched. "Are you kidding?" I gasped. "You're going to start this *now*?"

Grayson locked his green eyes with my brown ones. "I realize the timing is not ideal. But sitting here in the bushes with you reminded me of our last investigation. Your life could have been terminated. I don't want—"

"But it wasn't," I said, taking his hand in mine. "I'm still here, by your side."

Grayson sighed. "Look, Drex. I don't know what we're going to face tonight. We could be abducted by aliens. Or propelled into some parallel universe. In case this does turn out to be our last moment together, I just wanted you to know that it's been my pleasure and honor to spend time with you."

My chin hit my neck. Then I dropped my badminton racquet and lunged at Grayson like a hungry panther on a hapless possum.

I kissed him hard on the mouth. He resisted for a second, then kissed me back with equal fervor. Before I knew what was happening, we were rolling around in the dirt like a couple of love-sick otters.

OMG! This is actually going to happen!

I wasn't about to let this moment be thwarted by anyone or anything. Employing my tomboy wrestling moves, I flipped Grayson on his back and straddled him at the waist. As I began to unbutton my blouse, I glanced up—then let out a high-pitched squeak normally only achievable by dolphins.

"What was that?" Grayson asked. "Some kind of hillbilly mating call?"

"Ack!" I stuttered. "Skak!"

Grayson's eyebrow arched. "Not exactly the pillow talk I was expecting, but I'm game."

Speechless, I jabbed my finger in the direction of the palmetto fronds. "Skuh ... skull!" I stammered. "Buh ... back!"

"What?"

With me still straddling him, Grayson sat up and twisted his torso around for a look. "Mother of all Klingons!" he yelled, scrambling to extricate himself from underneath me.

Over by the net, peering at us from between the palmettos, was the same hideous skeletal specter from last night. Its skull was ablaze like a burning marshmallow.

Grayson grabbed his badminton racquet and sprang to his feet.

"What are you doing?" I squealed.

"Stay here," he said. "I'm going after it."

I clattered to my knees, then watched Grayson march toward the skeleton, wielding his badminton racquet like a sword.

In that moment, I'd never been more proud to be his P.I. intern—or his girlfriend.

But as Grayson got to within swatting range of the skeleton, it yelled out, "Don't do it!"

I froze.

The ghost of Daulton Gray!

Grayson must've thought the same thing, because he paused for a second. It was just long enough for the glowing skeletal apparition to rear back a fistful of finger bones and punch him square in the face.

I watched in horror as Grayson's head twisted around sharply. He appeared to hang suspended in that odd position for a second, then he fell face-first on the ground like a drunken sailor.

"Grayson!" I screamed.

I grabbed my badminton racquet and sprung to my feet, prepared to turn that hideous skeleton into a bag of burnt spare ribs. But as I raced toward it, the boney apparition disappeared before my eyes.

Grayson, however, remained in place. As I stumbled in the dark, I stepped right on him.

"Ouch," he groaned.

"I'm sorry!" I said, wincing. "Are you hurt?"

"I am *now*." He pushed himself up to sitting. "But nothing serious, I don't think."

I knelt down beside him, barely able to see him in the dark. "Where does it hurt?"

"My nose and my left kidney. But I'll live."

"Thank goodness!"

He shook his head as if to clear it. "Drex, did I suffer a concussion, or did that skeleton actually say something?"

"It spoke," I said. "In a male voice. He said, 'Don't do it.'"

"I thought so," Grayson said. "That's the same thing Daulton Gray is purported to say when sighted."

"I know." I tried to get a look at Grayson's face. "You think the skeleton could belong to that fisherman ghost?"

"Quite possible," he said, rubbing his right cheek. "He's got one hell of a right hook."

I reached over to touch Grayson's swelling cheek. Suddenly, something darted by in the space between us.

I gasped and jerked back. "What was that?"

The object jetted by us and slammed into the wired-up badminton net trap. Small sparks of electricity danced in the dark like a firework sparkler. Then, whatever it was bounced off the net like a boomerang and fell into Grayson's lap.

"What the?" he said.

Suddenly, a streak of lightning lit up the sky. In that brief flash of light, I saw what had landed on Grayson.

It was a bat. One the size of a full-grown squirrel.

Grayson must've seen it, too. He let out his own dolphin squeal, then scrambled to his feet and made a madman's dash for the RV. To his credit, he only fell twice before he made it inside and slammed the door.

As I turned to follow him into the motorhome, another streak of lightning crossed the sky. At my feet, the bat, stunned but apparently uninjured, took off into the night with almost as much grace as Grayson had.

I stared up into the night sky and shook my head in wonder.

I'd forgotten my superhero boyfriend was afraid of bats.

Then I suddenly remembered that the flaming skeleton ghost was still out there somewhere in the bushes—and I was standing out there alone in the dark!

Before my mind could even wrap itself around the thought, my feet were beating a path for the old motorhome.

Chapter Thirty-Six

I hesitated at the door to the RV's bedroom. Grayson had fled there a few minutes earlier, after encountering the only thing I'd ever seen him lose it over—a bat.

Everybody had chinks in their armor. Even Grayson. But if I was going to be a good partner for him, I'd have to overcome a few of my own.

I cracked open the door and whispered into the room, "Are you okay?"

It was so dark inside the bedroom I could barely make out Grayson's black-clad form sprawled across the bed. My stomach recoiled in disgust at the thought of him lying on the hideous mattress Mullet Daniels had burned to death on. But putting things into perspective, the revulsion I felt was normal—not to be compared to the ingrained childhood trauma of Grayson's fear of bats.

In other words, I knew it was *my* turn to be the grownup in the room.

I drew in a breath, straightened my shoulders, and hitched up my courage.

If Earl's mom could change his dirty diapers and survive, I can withstand a few minutes inside Mullet's homemade crematorium.

I opened the bedroom door a bit wider. "Grayson? Are you okay?" I repeated.

He turned onto his side. "I don't think my nose is broken," he said, "but I can't say the same for my bravado."

"Hey, we've all got our kryptonite," I said softly.

Grayson sighed and propped himself up on one elbow. "I suppose you're right. But the timing couldn't have been worse."

"What do you mean? Do you think we could've captured that skeleton thing if the bat hadn't ... uh ... gotten in the way?"

"Possibly," he said. "But what I meant was, it was bad timing for *us*."

Not wanting to misread his intentions again, I made Grayson spell it out this time. "What do you mean, *us*?"

Grayson sat up and swung his legs over the edge of the bed. His green eyes stared into mine. "Drex, when I met you, I knew I'd need to spend some time rearranging my mind to create a place in it where you could stay."

My heart pinged. As unusual as his words were, they struck me as the most romantic thing any man—scratch that—any *human* had ever said to me.

I smiled softly. "Right back at you, Grayson."

He smiled and reached a hand toward me. "Come here."

My gut lurched. My flesh was most definitely weak. But my mind wasn't willing. So, like an idiot, I stood there in the dark, waffling between "Just say no," and "Just do it."

My love-life had come down to dueling TV commercials.

I've always known this day would come.

I cringed. "Lay down with you on a dead man's mattress? Grayson, I—"

He leaned over and flipped on a small bedside lamp. "This is an air mattress, Drex." He pulled back a corner of the fitted sheet. I stared in disbelief. It totally *was* an air mattress!

"But how—" I fumbled.

"I had Earl buy it at Walmart while you were checking out the wigs. Like I told you before, you were in there a long time."

"So ... you haven't been sleeping on Mullet's creepy death mattress?"

Grayson blanched. "No! Why would you think I'd do *that*?"

Seriously? How much time have you got?

I cringed. "I dunno."

"Sleeping on Mullet's mattress would've damaged crucial evidence," Grayson said, putting the corner of the sheet back into place. "Not to mention reducing its street value."

"Oh, sure," I said, rolling my eyes. "What was I thinking?"

Grayson cocked his head. "I don't know."

My eyes darted around the room. "So ... what'd you do with Mullet's mattress?"

"I put it on eBay."

My eyebrows rose an inch. "On eBay? What idiot—"

"The bid's already up to $13,067.48."

My eyebrows rose *another* inch. "For a dead guy's filthy mattress?"

Grayson smiled. "For a dead guy's filthy mattress *with provenance*."

I laughed. "Touché. Now let me have a look at that swollen nose of yours."

"Sure," Grayson said. He scooted over and patted the mattress next to his thigh. "This is actually quite comfortable. You should give it a try."

So I did.

Chapter Thirty-Seven

In my book, there was nothing cozier than snuggling with someone during a rainstorm—on a mattress that nobody had died on.

After tending to Grayson's bloody nose, I'd insisted he take his black T-shirt off because it had blood on it. It was only a few drops, but hey, a girl had to do what a girl had to do. If I had to take it slow with him, half naked was better than no naked at all.

The rain had just begun to plink on the metal roof when I told Grayson to lie back down in bed. He complied without resistance. I kicked my shoes off and laid down beside him. After such a harrowing run-in with huge bats and glowing skeletons, it was good to feel safe and warm next to him.

I laid my head on his bare chest and breathed in his scent. I wasn't sure what the sweet, musky aroma was, but with Grayson's cabinet of mystery potions missing in action along with the old RV, I was fairly certain it wasn't *eau de Alien Parasite Remover*.

"Nice to know you're a fellow pluviophile," Grayson said.

"Excuse me?" I said, pushing up off his chest. "I've never even *been* to Pluto!"

"A lover of rain," he said. "A pluviophile finds peace and comfort in rainy days."

"Oh," I said, relieved it wasn't yet another perverse hurdle to overcome that night. I snuggled back into Grayson's side and asked, "So, what'd you do with Mullet's old mattress?"

"Nothing." He wrapped his arms around me. "It's right here."

"*What*?" I jerked free of his arms and sat bolt upright. "Where? Please don't say it's under this air mattress!"

"No, of course not." Grayson studied me, an amused grin forming on his lips. "Earl and I sealed it in plastic and secured it to the top of the roof."

"Oh." My body relaxed again as my flare of disgust faded. "So there's nothing left of Mullet in this room?"

"No."

"You promise?"

"Yes. Now lie down."

I let Grayson pull me toward him. I laughed softly, and was about to kiss him when I was overcome with curiosity. "Why'd you put the mattress on the roof?"

Grayson shrugged. "There weren't a lot of options. The roof was supposed to be temporary. I originally planned to take the mattress to a storage unit, but you ticked off Earl before he had a chance to load it into the truck yesterday."

I grimaced. "Sorry." I ran my hand over Grayson's bare chest. "Hey, how about we change the subject?"

"Absolutely. With pleasure."

Grayson's voice sounded smooth and sexy. I smiled up at him. "You know, I really loved what you said—"

Suddenly, a drop of liquid hit me right between the eyes.

"What the?" I said. I wiped the drop off, but it wasn't water. The liquid on my fingers was dark—like blood! Before I could utter a single word, another drop hit me on the nose. I looked up. It was coming from the ceiling!

"Aaargh!" I screeched, scrambling out of bed.

"What's the matter now?" Grayson asked.

"Mullet's fried guts!" I yelled. "They're dripping through the ceiling!"

Grayson glanced up. A dark drop hit him on the forearm. He stared down at it. "How is that possible?"

"How should I know?" I hissed, then made a beeline to the bathroom as the scary scenes of a dozen horror movies flashed a mad montage through my mind. I had to wash that disgusting mystery goo off my face before I turned into some kind of monster, too!

Grayson followed me down the hall and stood in the bathroom doorway, watching me. "The wind is really picking up out there," he said. "I better go check the tie downs on the mattress."

"In a lightning storm?" I said, scrubbing my face like a rabid chipmunk with a washcloth soaked in Mr. Clean.

"I have to," he said. "If the mattress gets damaged, my eBay bids will go down the drain."

"*That's* what you're worried about?" I said, exasperated. "Fine! Go! Have fun."

Grayson put his hands on my waist. "You know, it may be better if *you* checked the tie-downs."

Excuse me?

I whipped around to face him. "Why? Are you afraid of *lightning*, too?"

"Everyone should be afraid of lightning, Drex. But that's not the point. Earl and I may have damaged the roof putting the mattress up there. I want you to go because you weigh a lot less than we do."

"Oh."

Apparently, flattery really *could* get you somewhere. At least in Grayson's case. Out of nowhere, I heard myself say, "Okay."

Grayson slapped a flashlight in my hand. "We better hurry. The rain's beginning to pick up."

RAIN PELTED MY SCRUBBED-raw face as I climbed the little ladder attached to the RV that led to its roof. When I was about halfway up, I felt Grayson's hands gently pushing on my bottom. I didn't know if he was being helpful or copping a feel. But, all things considered, I was okay with either scenario.

As I reached waist level with the top of the RV, I waved the flashlight beam across the motorhome's rectangular roof. The mattress was still there. But it was no longer secure.

The plastic covering it had been wrapped in was ripped open in the middle. The tattered plastic was flapping in the wind like ragged clothes on a line.

"Can you see anything?" Grayson called out. "Is the mattress okay?"

I leaned forward and shone the flashlight directly on the center of the mattress. My breath caught in my throat. The queen-sized hunk of memory foam appeared to have exploded from within!

All of a sudden, a giant gust of wind sent the shredded plastic fluttering at me like white flames from a ghostly fire. As they danced and whipped around, I spied something that made me nearly swallow my tonsils.

From the center of the mattress, a charred, blackened arm reached toward me, grabbing at me like a half-incinerated mummy from an open sarcophagus.

"Aaargh!" I screamed, then fell backward off the ladder.

Grayson caught me in his arms. "What's the matter?" he asked. "Are you hurt?"

"Mullet," I stammered. "He's escaped!"

"What?" Grayson locked eyes with me. Rainwater ran in rivulets from his swollen nose and bare shoulders.

"Mullet's ghost!" I said. "It got out of the mattress!"

The tendons along Grayson's jawline flexed. He set me down, then clattered up the ladder himself.

He shone the flashlight onto the roof and yelled, "Unbelievable!"

Just then, lightning streaked across the sky, illuminating his silhouette against the darkness. As the light faded out on the horizon, I saw that huge, white light again. It was hovering above the treetops on the other side of the road, in the opposite direction of Doris' campsite.

Grayson must've seen it, too.

His face was frozen in the best Spock impression I'd ever seen.

Chapter Thirty-Eight

Inside the RV, black rain continued to drip like rotten blood onto the air mattress in the back bedroom. Trembling, I couldn't shake a bad case of the creeps, despite nailing a board across the bedroom door.

The ghost of Mullet Daniels was alive and well—and wanted us dead!

Or at least, that was *my* theory.

Grayson had other ideas.

"There has to be some other explanation," he said. He was sitting at the banquette, pulling a wad of bloody cotton from his left nostril.

"Getting punched in the nose by Mullet's skeleton ghost wasn't proof enough for you?" I asked, incredulous.

"Apparitions don't usually engage in physical violence," he said.

"Yes they do!"

He sighed. "Hollywood horror movies don't count, Drex."

"What about *Amityville*?" I argued. "That one was supposed to be true. That poltergeist thing scratched the living daylights out of that guy, didn't it?"

Grayson rubbed his chin. "I said *usually*. Not *never*."

Too nervous to sit still, I paced the floor and took my millionth paranoid glance back at the bedroom door. "So, what are we gonna to do now?"

"Get some sleep," Grayson said, examining the bloody cotton wad in his hand. "We'll survey the damage to the mattress in the morning."

"Mattress damage?" I said. "That stupid mattress is all you think about! What about the damage to *us*?"

"*What* damage?" Grayson asked.

"Your nose!" I yelled.

My psyche!

"I'll live," Grayson said.

I wrung my hands. "But what if it comes back?"

"Doubtful. If the apparition had wanted another round with us, it could've easily engaged us during our original encounter."

I chewed that one over, along with my thumbnail. "I guess you could be right. But what about that huge, white light? Did you see it?"

"Yes."

"*Well?*"

"It could've been ball lightning."

"Ball lightning?" I let out an angry laugh. "Grayson, I'd punch you in the nose right now if Mullet hadn't beaten me to it."

He held up a palm. "Take it easy, Drex. It's *one* theory. I didn't say it was the *only* one. But you have to admit, it's plausible, given there was an active lightning storm building at the time."

I blew out a breath and tried to let go of some of my adrenaline-fueled paranoia. "Okay. But how do you explain my sighting the other night? Or the fact that Doris says she sees lights every night?"

Grayson's brow furrowed. "I'm still working on that."

I stared at Grayson, and realized he looked dead tired. I softened my approach. "Maybe you're right. Maybe we *should* try to get some sleep. You take the sofa bed. I'll take the banquette."

Grayson's eyebrow shot up. "You don't want to join me on the couch?"

"No."

Mullet Daniels might've failed at killing me tonight, but he'd managed to snuff out my libido like a candle in a Cat 4 hurricane.

Chapter Thirty-Nine

When I awoke the next morning, my forehead was on the banquette table and a knife was in my neck.

At least, that's how it felt.

Lured to waking by the smell of coffee brewing, I sat up and rubbed my sore neck.

"Rough night," Grayson said.

"Yeah."

I watched Grayson pour life-giving nectar into two cups and carry them over to the table. The weird energy between us was uncomfortable I could barely breathe. I hadn't felt anything similar to it since I'd caught Carl Blanders cheating on me.

Grayson slid into the booth opposite me, and passed a cup over. As he did, it felt like something important had come to an end. Had we missed our chance at demi-sexual romance and were now forever relegated to the friend zone?

I stared at the steam rising from my coffee mug, unable to take a sip. I really needed it, but its contents reminded me of that black mucky stuff that had dripped on my face last night.

Why had the Universe gone out of its way to conspire with Mother Nature to spoil the best chance I'd had of getting laid in over two years? Were the two unescapable forces a couple of sadists? Or had they actually done me a huge favor?

I pushed the coffee away.

"I've been thinking," Grayson said, tapping a long, tapered finger on his coffee cup. "I'm sorry about last night."

"It wasn't your fault," I said, too heartsick to think of anything sarcastic to say. "Who could've predicted dead-man rain?"

Grayson nodded. "Once the rain clears up, I'll take a look and try to ascertain the origin of the leak."

I smiled weakly. "Well, at least things can't get any worse, right?"

Suddenly, someone rapped on the side door. It flew open. Earl's mangy head poked inside.

I glanced up at Grayson. "Looks like I spoke too soon."

"Hey, you two!" Earl practically yodeled. His cheery tone made me instantly want to kick his rotten head in.

"What are you doing here, Earl?" I grumbled.

"Good morning to you, too, Miss Sunshine." Earl came bounding inside and started fixing a cup of coffee. "That storm last night was a doozy, eh?"

"Yes, it was," Grayson said. "I didn't hear you drive up."

"I came in last night. It was rainin' cats and dogs, so I figured I'd stay in Bessie overnight. Give you two love birds a little privacy."

He wagged his eyebrows at me, then winked at Grayson. "I guess one of us getting soaked to the bone was enough for one night, eh, Mr. G.?"

Grayson cocked his head at Earl. I watched my cousin glance down the hall. He must've seen the board nailed across the bedroom door, because both of his eyebrows shot up.

"Or maybe not," Earl said.

"Why didn't you answer your phone?" I asked. "I called you half a dozen times!"

Earl slid into the booth beside me. "Well, I didn't answer on account a I jumped in a pool with my phone in my pocket."

"A pool?" I glared at him. "Don't tell me you went and checked into a beach motel without me!"

He chortled. "Nope. Guess again."

I stared at his stupid face until it hit me. "You went swimming in Danny's dumpster pool!"

Earl laughed. "Bingo!"

"Gross!" I hissed. "With all that trash inside it? You better go get checked for diseases!"

"What'n no trash. Danny cleaned all the garbage outta that thing before he filled it with water."

I sneered. "That wasn't the trash I was talking about."

Earl let out a sigh and set down his coffee mug. "Look, Bobbie, I know you don't like Danny, but I went over there to make amends. I'm thinkin' about movin' there. And he was cordial enough to let me park Bessie there for the day, free of charge."

"Why?" I asked.

"Why what?" Earl said.

I shook my head. "Just *why*?"

"A man can't let a woman dictate his life, Bobbie." Earl grabbed his coffee and scooted out of the banquette. He laid a hand on Grayson's shoulder. "You ought to take a lesson from that, Mr. G."

Grayson locked eyes with me and said, "Duly noted."

I glared at Earl. "Who died and made you Yoda?"

Earl shook his head, then pulled off his Redman chewing tobacco cap. "Mind if I wash up?" He brushed his bangs away from his face. His forehead was red and blistered.

I gasped. "You!"

Earl rolled his eyes. "What'd I do now?"

"Your head is burned!" I yelled. "You're the flaming skeleton!"

Earl shot Grayson a look. "Doc, is she off her meds?"

"Where'd you get the skeleton outfit?" I yelled. "Walmart?"

Earl held up open palms. "Help me out here, doc. What in tarnation is she talking about?"

"It's a long story," Grayson said.

"How do you explain those blisters on your head?" I asked.

"Uh, I done told you. I got sunburnt swimmin' in the pool. I took off my cap so it wouldn't get wet."

"Right," I said. "You think to save your cap, but not about your phone." Something clicked inside my brain. Actually, that made perfect sense—in Earl World.

I slumped back into the booth and sighed. "I guess there goes *that* theory."

"What theory?" Earl asked.

"I'll explain later," Grayson said. "While you were at Danny's, did he happen to mention anything more about his brother Mullet?"

Earl shrugged. "Like what?"

"I'm not sure," Grayson said, toying with his cup. "I'm trying to figure out when he and Mullet replaced the roof of the RV. It started leaking last night."

"Huh," Earl grunted. "Well, Danny didn't mention nothin' about the roof. But when I was gettin' in the pool, he did say ol' Mullet used to be fat as a hog. His brother lost him a mess a weight on the Keto diet."

"The Keto diet," Grayson repeated thoughtfully.

Earl shrugged. "I ain't never ate a Keto myself. I'm a Frito man."

"That's interesting," Grayson said. "One of the theories proposed for spontaneous human combustion is accidental acetone ignition."

"Huh?" Earl and I said at the same time.

Grayson rubbed his chin. "A few years back, a professor named Brian Ford postulated that most victims of spontaneous human combustion are ill or elderly, thus making them more prone to acetone production. Acetone builds up in fat cells, and can make a person more flammable."

"What's that got to do with eatin' Ketos?" Earl asked.

"Not eating Ketos," Grayson said. "Eating the ketogenic diet. It's a popular weight loss plan that drastically restricts a person's carbohydrate intake and replaces it with fats. The carb reduction puts the body into a metabolic state called ketosis. When that happens, the body becomes a fat-burning machine."

"That'd be rather ironic, wouldn't it?" I said. "You know, if Mullet was trying to burn fat and ending up incinerating himself, instead?"

"I still don't get it," Earl said.

"Think of fat as fuel," Grayson said. "And the liver as an engine."

"Okay," Earl said.

"When someone on the Keto diet reaches ketosis, the fats they release go through the liver, and the liver turns them into ketones," Grayson said.

"Are ketones bad?" Earl asked.

"Not necessarily," Grayson said. "Ketones supply the brain with energy. But another byproduct produced is acetone."

"Isn't that the same as nail polish remover?" I asked.

"Yes," Grayson said. "A highly flammable liquid."

My nose crinkled. "Wouldn't that be poisonous?"

"It can be," Grayson said. "If a body produces more acetone than the liver can break down, it can cause acetone poisoning and liver failure. But for Keto dieters, acetone production mainly results in causing their breath to smell like nail polish remover. This also happens in older people with poor liver function."

"Huh," Earl grunted. "Now that you mention it, when I went to see Aunt Vera at the old folks' home last month, her breath smelled like carburetor cleaning fluid. That stuff'll catch fire if somebody sneezes wrong."

"Exactly," Grayson said. "Acetone evaporates quickly when exposed to air, but remains extremely flammable. So it's theoretically possible Mullet was in ketosis, lit a marijuana cigarette, inhaled, and spontaneously combusted."

"Interesting theory," I said. "But that still doesn't explain why the RV's roof is leaking his body juices into the bedroom."

"Oh. Right." Grayson glanced over at Earl. "Did Danny mention how large Mullet was? Perhaps his weight was enough to crack the RV's chassis?"

"Lawdy," Earl said. "Don't think that's too likely. If 'n ol' Mullet had growed that big, he couldn't a got his carcass though the door to that bedroom."

"Fair enough," Grayson said. "So what do you suppose could be causing the new roof to leak?"

"Only one way to find out," Earl said. "Let's go have us a look."

"Great idea, Captain Obvious," I said.

Earl set his coffee on the counter, then shook his head at me. "You know, I was gonna offer you some a my candy corn, Bobbie. But with that kind a attitude, you done blowed your chances with me."

I let out a sigh.

Get in line, buddy. Get in line.

Chapter Forty

Earl wanted a first-hand look at the leak in the bedroom. But to do that, first he had to pry off the board I'd nailed across the door—the one designed to keep the black, blobby stuff raining from the ceiling from shapeshifting back into Mullet Daniels and killing me while I slept.

Earl grabbed a hammer from his toolbox and walked over to the bedroom door. Suddenly, he burst out laughing. I came over to see what was so funny.

"Good thing this gooey ghost a you'rn don't know how to work a doorknob, Bobbie."

I frowned. "What do you mean?"

Earl turned the handle and pushed on the door. It opened inward. He looked back at me and grinned.

So much for my barricade. I did a mental face-palm.

"What in tarnation was you thinkin'?" Earl asked.

"I was scared. So I took your advice."

Earl stopped chortling. "You did?"

"Yeah," I said. "I did the best I could with the brain cells that were currently at my disposal."

Earl puffed up with pride. "Well, then. There you go." He held the hammer out. "Now hold onto this and stand back."

I took the hammer and took a couple of steps back. Earl ripped the board off with his bare hands.

"Geez," I said.

Earl peered into the bedroom and hollered, "Lord a mighty! What's that black moldy lookin' stuff all over the bed?"

"That's what I was talking about," I said. "I don't know what it is. Maybe Mullet's burned guts?"

Earl put on his pondering face. "Not sure. But from the looks of it, whatever it is was comin outta that there light fixture up there."

I rolled my eyes. "No shit, Sherlock."

Earl walked inside the bedroom and stepped up on the bed. He stood in the middle of it, staring up at the light fixture directly above his head. "Hey Bobbie, come in here and help me while I take this apart."

"Ha!" I said. "Not on your life. I'm not going in that bedroom ever again."

Earl grinned. "So you *was* in here last night, eh?"

"Shut your pie hole," I growled.

Grayson walked up to see what we were doing. Earl winked at him. "Hey Mr. G., you get Bobbie to hold your screwdriver last night?"

Grayson's eyebrows inched closer together. "No. I don't recall that we disassembled anything."

Earl shot me a sly look. "Uh-huh."

I'd had enough. With no coffee to assuage my morning grouchiness, my back molars pressed down at twenty-million pounds of pressure per square inch.

"You're impossible, Earl!" I shouted.

"Impossible to beat," he said. "At least, that's what all the ladies say."

"The ones in the dumpster pool?" I said. "Classy. I bet that isn't sunburn on your stupid head. I bet it's some kind of toxic STD rash!"

Earl looked at me and shook his head. "Now don't you go turnin' into one a them jealousy widows."

"Jealousy widows?" Grayson asked, beating me to it.

"Yeah," Earl said, unscrewing the light fixture, "When I went to see Aunt Vera at the old folks home, she told me she got herself a new boyfriend."

I blew out a sigh. "What has that got to do with anything?"

"Hold your horses," Earl said. "I'm gettin' there. You see, Aunt Vera said all them other women at the home was all red-faced and sour, just like you, Bobbie. She told me it was on account of the place was plum full a jealousy widows."

"Ugh!" I grumbled. "She was probably talking about the heat, Earl. That old nursing home is full of *jalousie windows*, you dingbat!"

"Huh," Earl said. "Well, Aunt Vera *did* have herself a big ol' mouthful of 'naner puddin' when she said it."

I took a long, deep breath to keep from spontaneously combusting, then said, "Are you about done unscrewing that stupid light fixture?"

"Yep." Earl yanked the fixture off the ceiling. A shower of black goo came pouring out.

"Lordy," he said, watching it rain down onto the bed.

"Can you see anything inside the ceiling?" Grayson asked.

Earl shone his flashlight into the hole. "Well, it's a mess up there, all right. But there ain't no body parts up in there to speak of."

"Hmm," Grayson said. "Okay. I think it's time we checked out the roof."

"Oh, goody," I said. "I can't wait."

"Huh," Earl said. "That's just what Aunt Vera said when they started handin' out the 'naner puddin.'"

Chapter Forty-One

As Earl climbed the ladder on the back of the RV, I chewed my lip with worry. My mind couldn't stop replaying the horrific scene from last night—that charred, skeletal hand clawing at me from the middle of the mattress on the roof.

I sat on my hands at the picnic table bench, then said a silent prayer that the horrid hand was gone. Earl was a jerk, but he didn't deserve to end up like Mullet's mattress—gutted from within like that poor guy eating spaghetti next to Sigourney Weaver in *Aliens*.

"Be careful, Earl," I called out.

"Why?" Earl called back. He crawled atop the roof toward the mattress. "Grayson told me all about your silly—"

Suddenly, Earl froze in place like a hound dog pointing out prey. Then he backed up on his knees and let out a strange, garbled, hillbilly holler.

"Aaargg!" he cried out. "Help me, Bobbie! It's done got ahold a me!"

"What?" I screamed.

I jumped up from the bench, nearly spilling my mug of coffee. Stunned, I stared, helpless, as Earl grabbed ahold of the very same charred arm that had tried to kill me last night!

Both of Earl's hands were gripped around the hideous blackened forearm, struggling to hold it at bay as it clawed at his throat!

"Earl!"

I scrambled out of the picnic bench and ran toward the RV.

All the while, Earl flailed about on his knees, wrestling with the horrid, skeletal arm. Then suddenly, he made a choking sound and flopped face down on the roof.

I froze in my tracks. "Earl!" I screeched. "Are you all right?"

Suddenly, his shaggy head lolled down out from the side of the roof. His eyes were rolling. His tongue hung from his mouth.

"Earl!" I screamed again.

In a split second, my cousin's dangling face returned to normal. He sat up, winked, then busted out laughing as he waved the skeleton arm at me.

In the light of day, I realized it was nothing but a small tree branch.

"Watch out, Bobbie!" Earl hollered from the roof. "This here scary monster arm's gonna get you!"

"Aaarggh!" I screeched. "Earl, you're the biggest dumb-head on the planet!"

Grayson came flying out of the RV. "What's going on?"

"Nothing!" I yelled.

"No monsters up here that I can see, chief," Earl said.

I shot Earl a look, and marched back to the picnic table, steeling for a good razzing by my cousin. But to my surprise, he cut me a break. Instead of ratting me out to Grayson, Earl simply went back to investigating the mattress.

"This here memory foam damage looks like the work of varmints," he called down to us. "Prolly a nest a coons got in it."

"Great. There goes eBay," Grayson muttered. He called up to Earl, "Did you find the source of the roof leak?"

"Not yet." Earl lifted up the mattress. "Woo, doggy. I think we just found us a bullet hole."

"Let me have a look at that," Grayson said. He clattered up the ladder, then knelt beside Earl. "Intriguing. The metal around the hole appears to have melted at the edges."

"Fired at close range?" Earl asked.

"Or by some source of intense heat," Grayson said.

Earl nodded. "You thinking what I'm thinking, Mr. G.?"

The two men locked eyes, then spoke simultaneously.

"Alien laser gun!"

Back at the picnic bench, I spewed my sip of coffee all over myself. "*That's* your rational conclusion to this mess?" I yelled back at them. "Mullet was shot with an alien ray gun?"

"*Laser* gun," Grayson corrected. "It fits the facts and observations at hand."

My eyebrows met. "What facts and observations?"

"Well, let's start with the huge white light we saw last night," Grayson said, climbing down off the ladder. "That could be proof of an alien aircraft."

"Pretty flimsy proof," I said.

"I'm not finished," Grayson said, joining me at the picnic table. "This morning, I walked over to the general area we saw the light hovering last night. I found a bald spot."

Earl winced. "It ain't too late, Mr. G. You could get you some a that Rogaine stuff."

Grayson shot Earl a look. "I meant a bald spot on the ground," he said. "It appears as if something large and circular set down in that spot."

"Where was it?" I asked.

"Across the road, between campsites 114 and 118."

"In site 116?" I asked.

"No. That was across the street."

"That's odd," I said.

Grayson gave me half a smile. "Excellent observation."

Earl shook his head. "Sorry, y'all. But number 116 is *even*."

"Ugh!" I groaned. "Earl, what I meant was, why would site 116 be on the same side of the road where only odd-numbered sites are supposed to be?"

"Good question," Grayson said. "I've got another one. When Mullet's trailer burned down, why did he come out here to Fort De Soto Campgrounds, instead of choosing to remain in his own, rent-free trailer park?"

I frowned. "I dunno."

Grayson rubbed his chin. "I postulate that Mullet came out here because he was running away from something."

"Creditors?" I quipped.

"No." Grayson tapped a finger on the table. "I believe he was running from the same entity that had targeted him earlier in his trailer park."

I smirked. "So, creditors."

"No," Grayson said. "*Predators.*"

I picked up my coffee mug. "Ta-may-toe, ta-mah-toe. In my book, they're the same thing."

Earl flopped down in the bench beside me. "You got *that* right, Cuz."

"Listen, you two," Grayson said. "I'm serious. I believe the reason why Mullet had to repair the roof of the RV was due to being the repeat target of alien encounters in the past. He came out here trying to hide, but they found him anyway."

"Aliens and creditors," Earl said. "They'll get ya every time."

Chapter Forty-Two

I picked up my coffee cup from the picnic table. My upper lip snarled. "Aliens were after Mullet? Gimme a break."

Grayson's back stiffened. "Drex, plenty of reports exist of people who claim multiple alien encounters."

"Sure," I said. "But you're telling me these aliens have the technology to travel a billion miles across the galaxy, but they can't manage to figure out how to smoke one trailer-park redneck wearing a cheap mullet wig?"

Grayson set down his coffee cup and rubbed his chin. "You're right, Drex."

I blanched. "I *am*?"

"She *is*?" Earl said, apparently even more stunned than I was at the prospect.

"Yes," Grayson said. "What if *killing* Mullet wasn't the aliens' intention?"

Seriously?

"So, what *was* their intention, Grayson?" I asked. "Galactic collection agency?"

Grayson blew out a breath. "No. And for the last time, this isn't about *money*. Aliens have no use for money."

My eyebrow ticked up a notch. "How do you know that?"

Grayson frowned. "We've already had this discussion. Money holds no perceived value in an alien paradigm."

"I don't get it," Earl said. "How can money have no value *and* be worth a pair of alien dimes?"

"What?" Grayson asked.

I closed my eyes and gave up another tiny fraction of hope. "Look, Earl, I'll explain later. Just let that one go."

My cousin scratched his head. "All right. So if they ain't after Mullet's money and they don't wanna kill him, why'd they bust an alien laser cap in his ass?"

"Good question," Grayson said. "Perhaps this laser weapon wasn't meant to *harm* Mullet, but to *enlighten* him."

"Ignite him?" Earl asked. "Well, it sure done its job."

"No," Grayson said. "*Enlighten* him. Or enhance him. You know, perhaps mend a frayed chromosome."

"Or two," I said. "I could definitely see the logic in that."

Grayson tapped a finger on his mug. "Or perhaps they sought to convey some kind of insight into Mullet with an information download."

I balked. "Information download? Come on, Grayson!"

Grayson's shoulders stiffened. "People throughout the ages have claimed to have received divine messages and information from otherworldly sources. In fact, the term 'inspired' is derived from the words 'in spirit.'"

"You sayin' we human folk get our ideas from spirit aliens?" Earl asked.

Grayson shrugged. "The source of true inspiration has always been up for debate. Some believe every idea and possibility there is lies stored out there in the cosmos, within the universal cosmic consciousness."

"Like one big ol' brain in outer space?" Earl asked.

"In a way, yes. Hindus call it the Akashic Record. They describe it as a holographic library of all knowledge that exists on the astral plane."

"How do you get a ticket on that plane?" Earl asked.

I rolled my eyes. "Earl, in your case, I'm afraid they're all sold out."

"Then again," Grayson said, ignoring us, "some believe inspiration comes from direct telepathy with ancient gods or alien life forms of superior intelligence. Either way, the point is, history records that many huge breakthroughs in science and technology have come to people in great detail, during their dreams or while in meditation."

"Really?" I said, unconvinced. "Name one."

"Sure," Grayson said. "How about Nikola Tesla's free energy concept? Albert Einstein's theory of relativity? Steve Jobs' idea for the iPhone?"

"Uh ... Mr. G., that's *three*," Earl whispered.

"Is that true?" I asked, astounded.

"Absolutely," Grayson said. "Many substantive ideas simply 'come' to people fully formed. For example, a Russian chemist named Dmitri Mendeleev is credited with creating the periodic table of elements. He told his fellow scientists that it came to him in a vision and he simply wrote it down. He even left gaps in the table for elements that had yet to be discovered. The same table Mendeleev created in 1869 is still being used today, virtually unchanged."

"That's amazing," I said. "You know, maybe you're on to something here, Grayson. I keep thinking about that Shroud of Turin you brought up the other day."

Grayson's eyebrow arched. "Yes? What about it?"

"What if the imprint on that cloth *was* created by Jesus's body? What if, while he was wrapped up in it, he received one of these divine messages, or otherworldly downloads you're talking about."

"You sayin' Jesus was an alien?" Earl asked.

I shook my head. "No. Just that maybe he had the same thing happen to him as the other victims of spontaneous human combustion. But that somehow, Jesus was able to survive it unharmed."

"Interesting," Grayson said. "Perhaps a similar event happened to Mullet Daniels. It's possible an information download was supposed to rewire his brain in order to enable him to see the world differently, or impart some hidden knowledge. But for some reason, he wasn't able to handle the process, and it ended up incinerating him instead."

"Exactly," I said. "If Mullet was anything like his brother Danny the dip-wad, I could see where an attempt to increase his IQ could prove deadly. He didn't have the capacity—probably because of that frayed chromosome thingy. Or maybe some altogether missing strands of DNA."

Earl had on his pondering face. "So, you're saying whoever fried ol' Mullet wasn't tryin' to kill him, just make him smarter?"

"Quite possibly," Grayson said.

"Then why'd it kill him?" Earl asked.

I put a hand on my cousin's shoulder. "Maybe some people just can't handle the truth."

"Or perhaps," Grayson said, "like some of the other victims of spontaneous human combustion, Mullet's body was too old or weak to be able to survive the process. So instead of his brain cells incorporating the data as intended, they imploded and incinerated him instead."

"Yes!" I said. "That would explain the shrunken skulls of the victims. And the shattered skull caps. I don't think any of the victims' heads remained intact after spontaneous human combustion, did they?"

"No. I think you're right about that," Grayson said.

Earl took off his Red Man chewing tobacco cap and placed it over his heart. He shook his head and said, "When the laser gun hits, you must be fit."

I took a deep, calming breath to avoid strangling the life out of my poor cousin. I owed him that much for cutting me some slack over the tree branch mummy-arm thing. I turned to Grayson. He was staring up at the sky.

"Yes," he said, nodding to himself. "This theory of downloading gone bad would explain a lot." He glanced over at me and smiled. "Very interesting concept, Cadet. Good work. Now we just need to test your hypothesis."

"Right," I said. "How are we gonna do that?"

Grayson's Spock eyebrow rose half an inch. "With a neutron radiation detector. I thought I already explained that."

Chapter Forty-Three

While the three of us waited for Garth to show up with his neutron radiation detector, Earl got to work repairing the RV with parts he'd collected at a u-pull-it place. I'd smiled to myself when he'd told me about his junkyard adventure. I guess Beth-Ann knew my cousin even better than I did.

Unfortunately, with Earl busy with the RV, that left *me* to assist Grayson in getting rid of Mullet's murderized old mattress. Dreading the task, I'd stalled by semi-feigned interest in seeing the site where Grayson believed an alien craft had touched down.

"Absolutely," Grayson had said, pleased with my interest.

He'd led me down the crushed shell road past a couple of campsites, then crossed to the other side of the lane. There, just as Grayson had described, lay an open, grassy field between sites 114 and 118, exactly where site 116 should have been.

"This is a big space," I said as we wandered around the empty lot. "There's plenty of room for two campsites here. It's awfully weird why they left this empty and put campsite 116 across the street, instead."

"Yes, it is," Grayson said. "There has to be some logical reason for it."

"Good morning!" a slim young man with a buzz cut called out, then began walking toward us. As he approached, I noticed he had on the same uniform as Ranger Provost. His nametag read Randini.

"Can I help you fine folks?" the young ranger asked.

"Yes," Grayson said, high-stepping through the tall grass. "Let me show you something."

"Go right ahead," the man said.

He followed us over to a sandy, circular patch in the grass about twenty feet across. "We noticed this bald patch of ground over here," Grayson said. "Nothing's growing in it."

"Oh," Ranger Randini said. "That's where the old water tower used to be. It was decommissioned in 2016."

"Water tower?" I asked.

"Yes, ma'am. It was built in 1901 as part of the original Army base that used to be here. It was a real work of craftsmanship for its day. The tank held 60,000 gallons and stood on a platform framework 75 feet high. We used to keep it gleaming white with a fresh coat of paint every year or two."

"Interesting," Grayson said. "Tell me. Are there any stories attached to the tower?"

Ranger Randin's brow furrowed. "Stories?"

"Yes. Ghost stories. Like those associated with the Sunshine Skyway Bridge."

The ranger shrugged. "No. Well, not unless you count the one of the ghost tower itself."

My eyebrows inched toward my hairline. "The ghost tower?"

"Yes, ma'am. They say that sometimes at night, especially during storms when lightning lights up the sky, you can catch a brief glimpse of the tower, glowing like a ghost against the dark of the night."

"For real?" I asked, elbowing Grayson in the ribs.

The ranger grinned. "Yes, ma'am. If you believe in such things."

"We do," Grayson said.

"All right, then," the ranger said. "There's another tale if you care to hear it."

"Indeed," Grayson said.

Ranger Randini smiled. "Well, then, legend has it that the spirit of a soldier patrols this area. They say he died defending the water tower during a storm, and that he still haunts this particular campground to this very day."

"Intriguing," Grayson said. "Did he happen to sport a mullet hairstyle?"

The ranger eyed us funny. "No sir, I don't believe he did."

OUR SIDE-TRIP TO THE site of the old water tower had given us yet another possibility about what could be causing the mysterious white lights. Now, besides Mullet Daniels and Daulton Gray, I had to add the ghost of an unknown soldier to the list of potential candidates vying for the 'flaming ghost skeleton of the year' award.

As I sat at the banquette and wrote down Ranger Randini's tale in the *Experiment #5* casefile, I knew I was only delaying the inevitable. Any minute now, Grayson would announce it was time to extricate that disgusting mattress from the roof of the RV.

To prepare myself mentally, I'd eaten a chocolate bar. To prepare myself physically, I'd raided Grayson's cleaning supply cabinet. After absconding with his rubber cleaning gloves, I'd constructed the best hazmat suit I could muster with the supplies on hand.

"You ready?" Grayson called from outside.

"Just a minute," I said, slapping the file closed. I donned my protective armor, comprised of a ball cap, long-sleeved shirt, gloves, jeans, boots, and a ski mask. It covered me from head to toe.

"That's a bit of an overkill," Grayson said as I stomped out of the RV.

"Didn't you say this thing could be radioactive?" I asked. "Not to mention just completely off-the-charts grody."

"Grody?" Grayson asked.

"It's a technical term," I said. "It means totally beyond disgusting."

Grayson smirked as I walked by. "Grody, you say?"

AFTER UNSTRAPPING THE mattress and kicking it off the roof, I helped Grayson haul its mangled carcass over to the picnic table for a thorough post-mortem examination.

"What exactly are we looking for?" I asked.

"Anything unusual," Grayson said.

"There's nothing *usual* about any of this."

"Let's begin the dissection," Grayson said, ignoring me.

"Dissection?" I asked as he handed me a large pair of scissors.

"Yes. We'll begin by removing the cloth covering."

With the skill of a surgeon, Grayson set to work with a scalpel, carefully slicing open the scorched cloth covering of the mattress.

I grimaced as I watched him for a moment. Then, with my rubber-gloved fingers, I clutched the scissors like a kindergarten klutz and began awkwardly cutting away at the fabric.

"Careful," Grayson said.

"Careful?" I said. "This thing's been died on, ravaged by raccoons, and drowned in a thunderstorm. What's the point in being careful?"

"You could be destroying trace evidence," Grayson said. "Plus, I may still be able to sell sections of the cloth on eBay."

My mouth fell open. "You've got to be kidding me."

"Why?" Grayson said. "They did it with chunks of the Berlin Wall."

I sighed, shook my head, and got back to cutting the fabric. Soon, we'd skinned the mattress, leaving only the memory foam core lying on the picnic table like a giant glob of beige whale blubber.

Grayson packed the fabric scraps into a large garbage bag. I breathed a sigh of relief, thinking the disgusting job was over. But then Grayson said, "Now we'll examine the body."

"The body?" I gasped. "*Whose* body?"

"The victim's," Grayson said. "We've skinned the mattress. Now we'll examine the main body."

"Ugh," I grunted. "Aye aye, Captain Creepo."

Grayson handed me a magnifying glass. Following his lead, I stood at one end of the naked mattress foam and began examining it inch by inch.

About a foot from the right corner, I found what appeared to be a scorched linear line about an inch long. I pulled the mattress closer to me for a better look.

When I did, to my surprise, the sides of what I thought had been merely a scorch mark parted. They opened up to form a small hole that could've been caused by a bullet. But the hole was too far from the center scorched area to be connected with Mullet's burned body. If Mullet *had* been shot at, this hole would've had to come from a bullet that missed ...

"Hey, Grayson. Come look at this."

Grayson walked over. "What is it?"

I tugged the hole open again. "Could this be a miss?"

"Hmm," Grayson said. "There's most definitely something amiss all right."

"No, I meant—"

"Intriguing." Grayson rubbed his chin. "What we're looking at here could be evidence that Mullet was indeed targeted, but the first shot failed to hit its target."

I frowned. "That's what I was just about to say!"

Grayson shot me a dubious look. "Drex, I appreciate your efforts, but you can't take credit for *every* idea in the investigation."

Chapter Forty-Four

After an hour of examining naked memory foam, Grayson had collected all the samples he wanted and placed them inside Ziploc baggies. What was left over looked like a giant had leaned over the picnic table and thrown up a fifty-gallon gut's worth of scrambled eggs.

I stared at the mess and shook my head. "Thank god that's over."

Earl poked his head out from under the hood of the RV, then came over to check out our handiwork.

"Would you look at that," he said. "That there's makin' me hungry." He glanced at his watch. "Lordy. No wonder. It's lunchtime, y'all."

"What do we do with this mess?" I asked Grayson.

"We bag it and haul it to a dumpster," he said, zipping up the last baggie. "On the way back, we can get some takeout and bring lunch back here."

Earl elbowed me. "That is, if you can keep Bobbie from goin' dumpster swimmin.'"

I shot him a fake grin. "No, I'll leave that sport to you professionals."

"Yoo hoo!" a woman's voice rang out.

I glanced toward the road. It was Doris.

"I'm here for lunch," she said, toddling toward us.

"Oh, shit!" I said, suddenly remembering I'd invited her last night.

Doris heard me and stuck her nose in the air. "Excuse me, young lady, but I won't have bad language used in my presence."

I winced. "Sorry, Doris. It's just that—"

"Oh my!" Doris exclaimed, noticing the mangled heaps of foam on the picnic table. She grimaced, then stared at me, wide-eyed. "Am I too early?"

"Uh ... just a little," I said. "I lost track of time. Could you give me an hour?"

Her eyes darted unwillingly back for another glance at the scrambled mattress guts. "Oh, don't you worry about it, honey," she said. "You all look really busy. I'll just go back home and have myself a nice Hot Pocket."

I winced. "I'm sorry!"

"It's all right." Doris turned to go, then hesitated. "I hate to ask, but you all didn't happen to see Daulton, did you? That sneaky little rascal got loose again."

"No ma'am," Earl said. "Did you check the dumpsters for him?"

Doris gave Earl an odd look. "Uh, no."

"We'll keep an eye out for him," I said. "If we see him, we'll bring him right to you."

Doris nodded. "If you can catch him. That pipsqueak is quick as lightning."

"Sorry again about lunch," I said. "Time got away from me. How about dinner with us tonight instead?"

Doris took another furtive glance at the pile of foam rubble on the picnic table. "Thanks. Maybe some other time."

As I watched Doris skitter away as fast as her old legs would carry her, I turned to the guys. "That's so weird that her dog's name is Daulton. Just like the ghost."

"What ghost?" Earl asked.

"Daulton Gray," Grayson said. "The spirit of a trout fisherman who likes to flirt with women."

"Even Bobbie?" Earl said. "He must be purty hard up!"

Grayson locked eyes with me. "You know, Drex, the more I think about it, the more convinced I am that the skeletal specter who keeps appearing isn't Mullet Daniels at all, but Daulton Gray."

"I dunno," I said. "If it was Daulton he sure wasn't handsome, like you described him. Maybe it's that soldier ghost Ranger Randini told us about."

"My vote is still for Daulton Gray," Grayson said. "The 'handsome visage' described by other witnesses, could be his daytime image. At night, Daulton may well become a different incorporeal version of himself—such as a flaming skeleton."

Earl's pondering face made another appearance. "Mr. G., you sayin' this feller's a handsome devil one minute and a creepy monster the next? That don't seem too likely to me."

"That's because you've never dated a *guy*," I said.

I turned to Grayson. "Well, the skeleton *did* say, 'Don't do it,' right before he punched you in the nose."

"Exactly," Grayson said. "And unlike Mullet, we know Daulton's spirit is anchored to this area. You said he stopped following you once you left the campground."

"Yeah. He stopped at the back entrance gate." I chewed my lip. "But wait a minute. The ranger said sightings of the soldier's ghost were *also* confined to this specific campground."

Grayson nodded. "True. Specters are often bound to the general location of their trauma. But between the two, I still favor Daulton as the culprit."

"Why?"

"Because he likes the ladies," Grayson said. "In fact, based on our ... uh ... *activities* at the time, he could've seen me as a rival. That would explain his motivation for punching me in the nose."

Earl wagged his eyebrows at me. "Ha ha! Looks like that flaming skeleton wants to jump your bones, Bobbie!"

I shot my cousin a sour face. "I guess you would know, being a giant bonehead yourself."

Chapter Forty-Five

"What'd you bring me?" Earl asked as Grayson and I piled out of Bessie and headed for the picnic table.

Like a pair of remorseless serial killers, Grayson and I'd bagged the dismembered remains of Mullet's mattress and tossed them in a dumpster behind a restaurant called The Island Grille. Then we'd gone in and ordered lunch. Oddly enough, while we waited on the food, I discovered the restaurant had a swimming pool for its customers to enjoy. And it wasn't a dumpster.

Florida. Go figure.

"I got you an oyster po' boy, Earl," I said, shaking a paper sack at him as I sat down at the table. "It seemed appropriate."

Earl winked. "Come on, Bobbie. You know that's my favorite. You love me. Admit it."

I gave him half a smile. "I got myself some lobster sliders—to celebrate the end of being broke."

"What'd you get, Mr. G.?" Earl asked, tearing into the Styrofoam container housing his oyster sandwich.

"Fish tacos, what else?" I answered before Grayson could.

Grayson shrugged. "In my defense, I *did* opt for the mango salsa."

I smirked. "Yeah. You're a regular culinary *Indiana Jones*."

Earl took a huge bite from his oyster po' boy and said, "Well, I think I got her up and runnin.'"

"The RV?" I asked.

"No. Doris," Earl quipped. "A course, the RV."

"Good work," Grayson said. "I'm going to call Garth and have him cancel his trip over. We can drive the RV to Plant City tomorrow morning."

"Excuse me?" I said, nearly choking on my slider. "What about my beach vacation?"

"Four days hasn't been enough for you?" Grayson asked.

My eyebrows hit my hairline. "Are you kidding? I wouldn't exactly call these past few days a *vacation*."

"You're right, Bobbie," Earl said. "They don't even have a dumpster pool here." He took another massive bite of his sandwich and mumbled, "Oh! That reminds me."

"What? That you forgot your table manners?" I asked, watching food tumble around in his open mouth as he talked.

"No." Earl swallowed hard, then said, "When I was over at Danny's, I helped him clear out some of the burned up junk in Mullet's trailer home. I found this. Danny let me keep it."

Earl dug a meaty paw into his shirt pocket. I braced for the worst, figuring it would be some errant body part overlooked by forensics. But it wasn't. At least, not one made of flesh and blood.

"What is that?" I asked, as Earl laid a half-melted blob of plastic on the table. It was about the size of a grape, but shaped more like a tadpole.

"It's Mullet's hearing aid," Earl said. "He needed a Miracle Ear."

"Unlike you," I said, "who just needs a miracle. Geez, Earl. Could you put that away? I'm trying to eat, here."

Earl shrugged and popped the melted blob back into his shirt pocket. I shook my head.

Why on earth would he keep that? No. Just let it go, Bobbie. Erase your memory banks ...

"Hey, Mr. G. You think maybe when Mullet got his alien telegraph message, that it could a short-circuited his hearing aid, and that's why he spontaneously discombobulated?"

"Interesting idea," Grayson said. "Let me see that thing."

Earl fished the blob from his pocket again and handed it to Grayson. He studied it, twirling the melted hearing aid between his thumb and forefinger.

"Theoretically, perhaps overloaded circuits could've provided an ignition source," Grayson said. "But numerous cases of spontaneous human combustion were reported long before such devices were available."

Grayson handed the melted hearing device back to Earl. My cousin twirled it between his thumb and forefinger, mimicking Grayson.

"Hey Bobbie," Earl said. "What'cha call a cougar who needs a hearing aid?"

I sighed. "What?"

"A Def Leopard."

And this, ladies and gentlemen, is my life.

THE SUN WAS HANGING low in the sky, and the hotdogs were burning to a crisp on the grill.

"Hey, you wanna play badminton?" Earl yelled.

My cousin was over by Grayson's wired-up badminton net, swinging both racquets around like a mental patient who'd been driven mad from watching Alfred Hitchock's *The Birds* one too many times.

I hollered at him through the open side door. "You're supposed to be watching the wieners!"

Earl laughed. "You know I don't swing that way."

"The hotdogs!" I yelled. "I can see them from here. They're on fire!"

"Oh, Lawd!" Earl yelled.

He dropped both racquets and made a run for the grill. As he got there, he stopped and smiled. "Hey, scorched and busted open, just the way like I like 'em!"

"That reminds me," Grayson said, pulling condiments from the fridge next to me. "Did I tell you about the case of spontaneous human combustion where the victim was found while she was still on fire?"

Suddenly, the mouthful of potato salad I was sampling didn't taste so good. "Danny Vanzandt, you mean?"

"No. Another one. It's not in the casefile," Grayson said, oblivious to the fact that he was making me a victim of his random facts, yet again. "A woman this time. It happened in Ayer, Massachusetts in May of 1890."

My stomach gurgled.

Grayson set a jar of mayonnaise on the counter. "Interesting case. It seems a doctor by the name of B. H. Hartwell was called to the scene. He arrived to find a deceased woman still engulfed in flames. His report said he witnessed the body in full combustion, emitting bluish flames that were 15 inches high."

"You don't say," I said, then spit my mouthful of potato salad into the trash bin.

"I *do* say. Dr. Hartwell put out the fire, then noticed that leaves and other matter under the woman's body hadn't been touched by the flames. The incident happened right after a rainfall."

"A rainfall?" I asked, grabbing the bowl of salad to take out to the picnic table. "Is that significant?"

Grayson shrugged. "Perhaps atmospheric conditions play a larger role in the phenomenon than we've currently given consideration."

"Consideration?" I scoffed, heading out the door of the RV. "Grayson, if you had any consideration, you wouldn't be talking about dead bodies when we're about to eat dinner."

"I don't see your point," Grayson said.

But I didn't have time to explain. As I marched down the steps of the RV, from the corner of my eye I caught a blur of pink racing toward me.

It was Doris in her bathrobe, sleeping bonnet askew and curlers flying.

"What's the matter?" I asked as she wobbled up to me.

Gasping for breath, Doris stared up at me, wide-eyed, and said, "An alien just stole my pee jar!"

Chapter Forty-Six

I didn't have to worry about extending a dinner invitation to our neighbor anymore. Doris Halafacker was nuts.

"An alien stole your pee jar?" I asked.

"Yes!" Doris said, her bulgy eyes filled with fear. "Just now. As I was coming back from the showers!"

"Intriguing," Grayson said. "What did this alien look like?"

"Gray," Doris said, wobbling on her feet. "With a head shaped like a light bulb."

"Come sit down," I said, grabbing her arm. "You can tell us all about it."

I held the potato salad bowl out and asked Grayson to take it so I could help Doris sit down. When he didn't, I turned to glare at him, only to see him and Earl hot-footing it toward the washrooms.

I shook my head, then set the potato salad on the table. I settled Doris onto a picnic bench and asked, "Are you okay?"

She patted at her curlers. "I think so." She looked up at me with big, liquid eyes. "What would an alien want with my pee jar?"

What would anyone *want with your pee jar?*

"I don't know. Tea?" I asked, holding up a pitcher.

Doris glanced at her watch. "No. I don't take liquids after five. It's five-fifteen."

"Why not?" I asked.

"It'll make me have to pee." She adjusted her sleeping cap and fiddled with a loose curler. "But I'll take a hotdog and some of that potato salad, if you don't mind."

"Uh, sure." I stuck a hotdog in a bun, then began scooping potato salad onto a paper plate. "Could I ask you a question?"

"Go ahead, honey," she said, eyeing my handiwork. "Just a little more potato salad?"

"You got it."

I slapped another spoonful onto her plate and handed it to her. I wondered why Doris was in her bathrobe already, but was kind of afraid to ask. So I settled for a more pressing concern.

"I'm curious," I said. "Why exactly do you keep a pee jar?"

She grimaced. "It's kind of personal. Could we talk about something else?"

"Sure. How about the alien you saw. What did it look like?"

"I already told you," she said. "A gray head as big as a basketball, with big black eyes."

"Right. What about the body?"

Doris frowned. "It didn't have a body."

I blanched. "Then how did it grab your pee jar?"

Doris thought about that while she chewed a mouthful of potato salad. "Hmm. Maybe he teleported it?"

"Uh-huh," I said. "Doris, do you take any medications?"

DORIS WAS ON HER SECOND helping of potato salad when Grayson and Earl came back from their alien-hunting expedition. Since neither appeared to be toting a basketball-sized gray alien head, I figured their mission had been fruitless. Instead, it was *me* who'd found the fruit.

"Any luck?" I asked the guys, mostly to humor crazy-lady Doris.

"Actually, yes," Grayson said.

I gasped. "You actually found the alien?"

"Not exactly," Grayson said. "But we followed Doris' slipper tracks, and found the scene of the scuffle."

Earl winked at Doris. "Looks like you put up a hell of a fight, ma'am."

Doris smiled demurely. "I had to. It was my pee jar, for goodness sakes!"

My jaw dropped. "You mean ... it actually happened?"

Doris turned her bulging-eye gaze my way. "Of course it happened." She scraped her plate and shoved the last bit of potato salad into her mouth. "You put a lot of pickle relish in this."

"Uh, yeah," I said. "It's my Grandma Selma's recipe. You want it?"

Doris shrugged. "Actually, I was wondering if you used up the relish. I need a new pee jar."

WITH DORIS TUCKED SAFELY back in her RV and Earl off to get a shower, I asked Grayson the burning question on my mind.

"What in the world does someone want with a pee jar?"

I should've known Grayson would have some crazy answer.

"Many reasons," he said. "The Romans used to collect urine and use it to whiten their teeth and brighten their clothing."

My nose crinkled. "That was back before they invented Crestius and Cloroximus. No. Somehow, I don't think that's why Doris saves her urine."

"Why not?"

"Because she cringed when I asked her about it. She said it was personal."

"Hmm," Grayson said. "Another possibility is for the ammonia. It makes for an effective household cleanser."

"Et tu, Mr. Clean?" I quipped. "No. Still not personal."

Grayson nodded. "How about this. Some consider urine a health tonic."

My eyebrow shot up. "Yeah, some *crazy* people."

"I beg to differ," Grayson said. "Gandhi drank urine every day to bolster his health. And Madonna claimed that peeing on her athletes' foot cured it."

I cringed. "Seriously?"

"Seriously. Or, it could be that Doris is into urotherapy."

"Urotherpy?"

"Yes. Using urine to make a 'pee facial', if you will."

"I *won't*!" I grimaced in disgust. "Why would anyone willingly put pee on their face?"

"Urine is high in urea, a natural exfoliant. It's purported to soften skin and help resolve skin issues like acne, psoriasis and patches of dark pigmentation."

"Okay, fine," I said, not wanting to know anymore. "Let's go with that. I suppose if I was putting pee on my face, I wouldn't want anyone to know about it, either. But that still doesn't answer the real question."

"Which is?" Grayson asked.

"What would an *alien* want with Doris Halafacker's pee?"

"Yes, that is a bit more complex," Grayson said. "We may not know the answer yet. Humans are just now discovering more uses for urine, including urine-eating bacteria that can create electric power."

My eyebrow twitched. "You're saying some space alien out there may be going around snatching pee jars to fuel his spacecraft?"

Grayson shrugged. "It's possible. Perhaps his craft malfunctioned, leaving him to have to McGyver his way home."

"Well, if stealing pee is his solution, I hope he's got a long lifespan. He's gonna need it to find enough people out there toting around their own urine."

Chapter Forty-Seven

"You're not going to sleep in the RV?" Grayson asked, watching me gather up my things for the night. "I mopped up the black goo and cleaned the air mattress with disinfectant."

"Tempting, but no," I said, grabbing my Walmart bag full of toiletries hanging from the bathroom doorknob. "Especially not with Earl here. He tortures me bad enough about you as it is. I'm gonna sleep in the truck tonight."

"Fair enough," Grayson said, following me down the hall into the main cabin. "But you're still going to assist me in trying to capture the spectral light again tonight, aren't you?"

My mouth fell open. I turned around to face Grayson. "You really want to try that again?"

"Of course. I thought that went without saying."

"So, of course, you didn't say it."

Grayson cocked his head. "Exactly. I don't see your point—"

"Grayson, you saw the size of that light last night. It was as big as a house! How do you think you're going to capture it with that flimsy badminton net?"

His brow furrowed. "Drex, the field net is insufficient for the task."

"Ya think?"

"By capture, I meant with *our cameras*. This could be our last opportunity to gather evidentiary proof of the ghost tower or spectral orbs."

"Spectral orbs?" I asked.

"Yes. Small, spherical lights that can't be seen with the naked eye, but show up quite often in photographs taken by ghost hunters."

I sighed. "Say you capture some of these orb thingies on your camera. What does that actually prove?"

Grayson's back stiffened. "It proves that something is happening that we're unable to explain at this time. But perhaps we can in the future, once we've acquired the higher intelligence required."

I smirked. "How? By alien download?"

Grayson frowned. "I'm serious."

"So am I. I don't see what chasing spectral orbs has to do with trying to figure out if Mullet's death was caused by spontaneous human combustion, or proving what causes the phenomenon."

"Don't you see?" Grayson asked. "Sometimes collecting the evidence at hand is all one can do for the moment. As investigators, we catalogue what we find, then hope future scientific advancements will make the evidence useful in solving the mystery."

"Oh."

Grayson locked eyes with me. "Think of all the old cases being solved by DNA matching. If the original investigators hadn't bothered to collect and catalogue evidence, no matter how unfruitful it seemed at the time, these cases would have remained forever unsolved."

I chewed my lip.

Dammit. That makes sense.

"Okay," I said. "So what we're doing is gathering evidence that could be used by others in the future?"

"Precisely."

Grayson picked up the file folder labeled *Experiment #5*.

"Drex, you and I are adding to the growing body of evidence to help determine the cause of spontaneous human combustion. We're following in the footsteps of those who investigated the cases in this file. We may solve this ourselves, or we may not. But either way, we can be a part of the solution."

"Okay, fine." I set my bag of toiletries on the banquette table. "Hey, can I name the mission this time?"

Grayson smiled. "Sure."

"I'm calling it Operation Orb-It-All. Get it?"

Grayson winced. "Yes."

I grinned. "And one other thing. Can we keep Earl's role in this to a minimum, please?"

Grayson shrugged. "Well, that may be a moot point. I've already given him the position of lookout."

I sighed. "Great. Then I guess we'd better prepare to look out."

Chapter Forty-Eight

"Let Operation Orb-It-All commence," I deadpanned as I walked past Earl. "Doris has left the building."

It was quarter to seven in the evening. Earl was at his post, keeping watch at the spot where our campsite bordered the main road. As for me, I was heading back from the washroom slightly ahead Doris, my spy mission on the old lady completed.

"Roger dodger," Earl said, then crossed his arms and struck a redneck bar-bouncer stance.

I rolled my eyes and headed for the picnic table, where I planned to park my butt until it was absolutely necessary for me to get up again.

"Ev'nin', Miss Doris," I heard Earl say behind me.

I turned and watched from the corner of my eye as the old woman tottered up to him in her pink bathrobe and curlers.

"Good evening," she answered. "What are you doing out here?"

"Uh ... I'm keeping an eye out, ma'am," Earl said.

"For what?"

"Well ...."

"Never mind," she said, shaking her head. "I'm just an old crazy woman who sees aliens. You have fun, young man."

"I'll do my best," Earl said.

"Goodnight." Doris took a step, then stopped again. "Son, could you do me a favor and keep an eye out for Daulton? He's gotten out again. He always comes home before too long. But I worry about him, you know?"

"Yes, ma'am," Earl said, saluting. "If I see him, I'll grab him by the collar and bring him right over to you."

Doris smiled. "Thank you."

"Yore welcome."

Suddenly, Doris gasped. Her arm shot up and she glanced at her watch.

"Oh, my word! It's 6:59!" she squealed. "What am I doing dawdling around out here? I can't miss Sajak sashaying in. He's such a hottie!"

"I'm a Wheel fan myself," Earl said.

But, except for me, his words went unheard. Doris had already hightailed it out of there, her pink robe disappearing into the dusky shadows.

AFTER TWO HOURS OF complaining and swatting mosquitos, I declared Operation Orb-It-All a flop, and officially called it.

"Not even a single dadburned lightning bug," Earl said, shaking his head. "Gaul dang it. I wanted to see me this flamin' skeleton critter."

"I second your disappointment," Grayson said, taking random snapshots of the dark campsite. "I was hoping for at least some kind of action."

I sighed.

You and me both, buddy.

"I'm going to bed," I said, hauling myself up from the picnic bench. "Or should I say, 'I'm going to the truck.'"

"Don't let the ghosties get you, Cuz," Earl teased.

"Ha ha." Ungrateful for the reminder, I tried to calm my sudden case of the willies by blowing it off. "Ghosts aren't real."

"Sure they are," Earl said.

"No they're not," I argued. "And even if they were, they couldn't 'get me'. They're nothing but mist."

"Tell that to Mr. Dale Earnardt," Earl said. "When he wrecked his Corvette in Sonoma and it caught fire, he says he felt somebody put their hands under his armpits and pull him outta his car."

I groaned. "Earl, how in the world is that relevant?"

Earl straightened his shoulders. "Well, my boy Dale said when he got to the hospital, he asked the folks who come to see him about who saved him, on account he wanted to thank the feller."

I frowned. "So?"

"Dale swore he felt somebody pull him out. But when he asked, nobody seen anybody do it. Folks on the scene of the accident got a picture of Dale layin' on the ground by the car. But they wasn't nobody else anywhere near him."

"So he was saved by a ghost?" I said dryly.

"That or an angel," Earl said.

"Awesome. I hope angels like monster trucks as much as they do race cars."

"Me, too," Earl said. "Sleep tight."

"You too." I turned and headed for Bessie. Grayson left his reconnaissance position in the bushes and followed me over.

"You sure you'll be okay in there alone tonight?" he asked.

I shrugged. "Yeah. I think so."

"If anything happens, don't drive off this time," he said. "Blast the horn. I'll be out here in under five seconds. Okay?"

I nodded. "Okay."

We stood there for an awkward couple of seconds. I thought maybe I'd get a goodnight kiss. But apparently that wasn't on any ghost's or angel's agenda, either.

"Goodnight," I said, then began climbing up into the truck.

"Goodnight," Grayson said.

Suddenly, I felt his hands push my bottom, propelling me up into the six-foot high cab.

Grayson closed the door and turned to go. As I watched him walk back toward the RV, a big smile crept across my face.

This time, I was sure.

He had most *definitely* been copping a feel.

Chapter Forty-Nine

The smile lingered on my lips as I sprawled out across the monster truck's bench seat and prepared for sleep. I recalled the feeling of his warm hands on my butt cheeks.

Maybe there's hope for me and Grayson yet.

I pulled the sheet up to my neck and was drifting off to sleep when I heard a familiar noise.

The spirit drums were sounding again.

Instantly, I was wide awake. My eyes flew open. An image flashed in my mind of a flaming skeleton beating on a fiery drum set.

The thought sent my heart thumping in my throat. Was Mullet or Daulton or that soldier ghost coming to get me?

No, Bobbie. Forget about it!

I squeezed my eyes tight. If that blasted skeleton *was* out there loitering around in the dark, I didn't want to know about it.

But what if the sound wasn't spirit drums at all, but Doris' poor little dog, Daulton? Maybe he was out there, lost in the dark, thumping his ratty little tail against a cooler or something.

Cautiously, I cracked open an eye. What I saw made me nearly swallow my tongue.

Staring at me through the driver's window was Daulton, all right. Not the dog, but the fiery-headed skeleton creep!

I opened my mouth to scream. But then the skeletal specter did something altogether unexpected. It cocked its flaming skull at me and waved a boney hand.

Are you kidding me?

I returned its friendly greeting by belting out a scream that could've curdled a steel-belted radial. Then I raised both feet up and stomped on Bessie's horn for all I was worth.

"Hoooonnnnkkkk!"

Through the windshield, I saw a light flick on in the old RV. A second later, Earl and Grayson came tumbling out, making a beeline for me.

But as quick as those two were, that damned skeleton was quicker.

When I turned back for another glance out the driver's window, the spectral being had vanished into the night.

Chapter Fifty

After surviving another round with the flaming skeleton, Earl had teased me unmercifully about my 'invisible boney boyfriend'. Unlike Grayson and me, my cousin had yet to face head on the frightening, fiery bag of bones.

Secretly, I hoped Earl would get his chance, and that it scared the bejeezus out of him. It certainly had *me*.

After a third run-in with the skeleton scumbag, I swallowed my pride and slept on the air mattress beside Grayson. I was too traumatized to give a crap anymore about what my cousin thought of it.

As I lay there beside Grayson, breathing in the smell of the industrial disinfectant he'd used to clean the air mattress, adrenaline pulsed through me. But not in a good way.

Instead of feeling amorous, I was wired stiff with fright.

I rolled over, turned my back to Grayson, and lay curled up at the edge of the bed, sure I'd never sleep again.

SOMEHOW, DURING THE night I'd managed to doze off. And when I was awakened this time, it wasn't by a skeleton with a flaming mullet. It was by a way-too-handsome private eye holding a steaming mug of fresh-brewed coffee.

"How are you?" Grayson asked, handing me the mug as I sat up in bed.

"I'm not sure. But this will definitely help. Thanks."

Grayson nodded. "The specter. Was it the same one we saw by the badminton net the other night?"

"Yeah. Unless there's more than one of those jerks running around."

Grayson's eyebrow twitched. "Hmm. I hadn't considered *that* possibility. Perhaps we should stay another—"

My eyes narrowed. "Look, Grayson. I know you want to stay and investigate this apparition thing, but I've had enough. I've seen all the flaming ghost mullets I want to in this lifetime. I'm sorry, but I won't be hanging around here for another round. Not unless the stupid thing just happens to drop by for breakfast this morning."

A knock sounded at the door.

Grayson smirked. "Huh. There he is now."

I sneered. "Not funny."

"I'll get it," Earl hollered from down the hall.

I started to say something, but was interrupted by a strange, unearthly screech.

It was Earl—screaming as if he was being attacked by a swarm of seven-year cicadas.

Chapter Fifty-One

Earl was screaming like a little girl with a bug on her nose.

"Stay here," Grayson said. He handed me his coffee mug, then turned and ran out of the bedroom.

Still sitting in bed with a cups of coffee in each hand, I turned to the left, then right, looking for a place to set them down. Meanwhile, the hollering down the hallway ceased. It had been replaced by the sound of grunting—and thumping and crashing.

It sounded as if a barroom brawl had broken out in the living room!

I plunked both mugs onto the nightstand, then leapt out of bed and ran down the hall. What I discovered there left me wondering whether to laugh or scream.

Over by the stove, Earl and Grayson were rolling around on the floor—with that freaking skeleton!

"What the?" I gasped.

I grabbed a skillet off the stove and held it over my head with both hands. But trying to crack the right nut over the head was harder than playing a high-speed game of whack a mole.

"Pin it down!" I hollered.

Earl shot me a *Gee, why didn't I think of that?* Look, then dove back into the wrestling match.

I stood there, helpless, and watched as he and Grayson tag-teamed the squirming bag of bones. Finally, they flipped the thing onto its stomach. Earl grabbed ahold of its leg bones. Grayson pinned its arm bones behind its spine.

The skeleton subdued, Earl and Grayson both looked up at me—as if I was supposed to know what to do next.

"What?" I said. "Should we call *Ghostbusters*?"

"No. That won't be necessary," Grayson said, hitching the skeleton's arms up higher.

"Ow!" the skeleton grunted in protest. "Take it easy. I was only joking!"

My mouth fell open. "It's a guy in a costume," I said.

"You think?" Grayson said.

He reached over and yanked the rubber mask head off of the prankster. A tangle of sweaty blond hair came tumbling out. The face of the man was so beet red, I almost didn't recognize it.

But I'd have known that set of buck teeth anywhere.

"Garth!" I yelled. "What are you doing here?"

"I came to bring the neutron detector," he grunted, his face still pinned to the floor.

"Garth?" Grayson said, releasing his arms from behind his back. "Why are you here? I told your brother Jimmy we had a change of plans."

"He must not a gave him the message," Earl said, letting go of Garth's legs.

"Would you two forget about that?" I yelled. "What I want to know is, what the hell's up with the skeleton suit, bro?"

"IT'S SKULLET OF SKULLETON," Garth said, as if that should've explained everything.

No longer pretzel-pinned to the floor, Garth had peeled off the rubberized skeleton suit and was now perched in the banquette with Earl and Grayson, happily sipping a cup of coffee and munching on a donut from the boxful he'd brought with him.

I walked over to the table and picked up the rubber mask head. "Skullet of Skulleton?"

"Yeah," Garth said. "The Legend of Skulleton. You've never heard of it?"

"No," the three of us said simultaneously.

Garth's blond eyebrows rose an inch. "It's the latest online video game craze. Skullet is master of Skulleton." He nodded at the mask in my hand. "Somebody laid down some large for that bad boy."

"Huh?" I grunted.

"That mask is top of the line," Garth said. "The whole Cosplay suit is. Too bad it's missing its fiery mullet. See the hole on the top?"

I examined the rubber skull. There was a ragged hole in it, as if something had been ripped from the top of its cranium.

"Yeah," I said, tossing the mask back onto the banquette table. "But you still haven't answered my question. Why have you been terrorizing me in this thing? You think it's funny?"

Garth blanched. "What?"

"This whole week," I hissed. "You've been sneaking up on us in the dark in that skeleton getup!"

Garth's eyes grew wide behind his black nerd glasses. "It wasn't me, I swear! I just found the suit in the bushes this morning—when I walked over here from the parking lot."

Garth shot a skeptical glance at Earl and Grayson. "Sorry, Pandora, but I think it was one of *these* guys who's been pranking you."

I glared at Grayson.

"Hey, it wasn't me," he said. "I was with you the night we *both* saw it. Remember?"

Oh yeah.

My death stare moved over to Earl.

"Uh, it wasn't me, Bobbie. I swear." Earl picked up the suit's rubber leggings. "I couldn't fit in these here thangs even if I wanted to. Face it, Bobbie. If the suit don't fit, you must acquit."

Garth snorted.

I shot the bucktoothed nerd a look that could shrivel grapes to raisins in five milliseconds.

Garth winced. "Sorry, Pandora."

I crossed my arms and flopped down onto the sofa opposite the banquette, still staring at all the three guys. "What jerk would get his jollies from scaring the bejeebers out of someone? Besides *us*, I mean."

"No thoughts come to mind," Garth said.

I shook my head. "Geez. A costume. This whole trip had been nothing but a wild ghost chase!"

"Not completely," Grayson said. "We still need to check for neutron radiation."

Aargh!

"You and that stupid neutron radiation!" I hissed.

Earl picked up the rubber skull mask. "Mr. G., what'll that neutron stuff tell us about ol' Mulleton here?"

"Not Mulleton," Garth corrected, grabbing the mask from Earl. "This is mighty Skullet. Of Skulleton!"

Earl saluted the mask in Garth's hands. "'Scuse me, Mr. Skullet."

Grayson cleared his throat. "To answer your question, Earl, neutron radiation won't shed any insight into our prankster. But it could help us determine whether or not Mullet Daniels spontaneously combusted by terrestrial means, or if he was zapped by an alien laser gun."

I sighed. "Are those our only two options?"

Chapter Fifty-Two

Armed with Garth's Geiger counter, Grayson headed to the RV's back bedroom to check it for neutron radiation.

"Remind me how this neutron radiation stuff works," I said, watching him wave the gizmo's wand over the wooden bedframe where the memory foam mattress had once lain.

"If neutron radiation is present, it would provide compelling evidence of a nuclear fusion or fission event," Grayson explained.

"And that would mean?"

"That would depend on the levels of radiation detected. Low levels could offer evidence pointing to an internal nuclear event as the ignition source that caused Mullet to spontaneously combust. If higher levels of neutron radiation are detected, it could provide proof of a more powerful external force as the source of his unfortunate combustion."

I nodded. "And if none is detected?"

Grayson stopped waving the wand. "It would rule out the possibility of nuclear fusion or fission as the ignition source."

"So what's the verdict?" I asked.

"Nothing detected," Grayson said, setting the detector down. "But do you remember me telling you that if Mullet spontaneously combusted due to an internal nuclear event, the plastic in his memory foam mattress could actually 'remember' the neutron radiation blast by recording it?"

"Uh ... sort of, yeah," I said. "But we threw the mattress out."

"Not *all* of it. I kept a small section of the 'epicenter' for testing."

Oh, goody.

"Hold on," he said.

I watched as Grayson pulled a garbage bag out of a drawer in the closet and dug around in it. He pulled out a foot-square piece of gnarly foam that looked like a giant blob of burnt chicken fat.

"Ah! Here it is," he said. He laid the hunk of mattress foam on the bed and passed the Geiger counter over it. It crackled.

"It's radioactive?" I asked, visualizing my ovaries shriveling into prunes.

"No," Grayson said. "The meter indicates it's still within the parameters of normal background radiation."

"So we're done here?" I asked hopefully.

"In the bedroom, yes. Disappointing, but there's one other place I want to test."

"Where?" I asked.

"That bald patch of ground where the old water tower used to stand."

"You think the spot could be radioactive?"

Grayson rubbed his chin. "From my calculations, the bare spot is directly below where we sighted the huge white light the other night. If the light isn't a ghost, but a nuclear-powered alien craft, then there could be residual traces of neutron radiation in the surrounding area."

"Uh, okay," I said. "And these aliens would have come camping in Fort De Soto for what reason?"

Grayson clicked off the Geiger counter and shot me an annoyed look. "I don't have all the answers, Drex. That's why what we do is called an *investigation*."

GARTH, EARL, GRAYSON and I wandered down the road to the open space between campsites 114 and 118, where the old water tower once stood. But after twenty minutes of waving around the Geiger counter, Grayson didn't find squat.

"There's no evidence of neutron radiation," Grayson said, sounding disappointed.

"But Mr. Gray," Garth said, "If an alien craft lit down here, its neutron trail could've been blocked by the tower itself. Water is one of the best shields against neutron radiation."

"Yes, you're right," Grayson said, nodding. "The tower itself could've provided a physical hiding place as well."

I raised an index finger. "Uh, one little problem, guys. The tower isn't here anymore."

"Perhaps not in this dimension," Garth said.

Grayson smiled. "Exactly."

"Hello?" I said. "Earth to Garth and Grayson."

"If there can be a spectral Greyhound bus, why not a spectral water tower?" Grayson said. "Ranger Randini offered anecdotal evidence to support it. It's been theorized that spectral sightings are glimpses into other dimensions in time and space."

"Or," Garth said, pushing his glasses up on his button nose, "the old tower could be existing in a parallel universe."

"You know what?" I said. "So could *I*. In fact, I'm calling a cab to come take me to a parallel universe right now."

"You can do that?" Earl asked.

"I sure can," I said. "It's called a beach motel, and it's about as far from this nonsense as Alpha Centauri. You guys go to Plant City and have fun nerdifying that stupid old RV. In the meantime, I'm going on vacation. For *real* this time."

I turned and began stomping my way back toward our campsite. Then a thought made me stop short. I turned around and crossed my arms like Wonder Woman.

"Oh," I said. "And for your information, gentlemen? That stupid ghost tower light is probably nothing more than a cumulonimbus cloud backlit by refracted heat lightning."

My piece said, I hitched myself up, turned back around, and marched toward the old RV.

Chapter Fifty-Three

"Wait, Drex!" Grayson said, racing to catch up with me as I made my way back toward our campsite. "That was actually a plausible argument you gave back there."

"What was?" I grumbled. "The reason I don't want to go to Plant City and waste my life rehabbing that old RV?"

"No," he said, grabbing my arm. "I'm talking about your explanation for the ghost tower. Light refracting within a cumulonimbus cloud. It was impressive."

"Oh," I said, softening a little. "Well, I can Google search stuff, too, you know. In fact, I have another theory if you want to hear it."

Grayson's shoulders straightened. "Of *course* I do."

"Okay. How about this? The huge ghost light could've been car lights. Specifically, they could've been Bessie's rooftop high beams reflecting off a disc-shaped lenticular cloud. Earl said he arrived at the campgrounds just as the storm was about to hit, remember?"

"Yeah, blame it on me," Earl said, jogging up to join us.

"Well, it usually *is* your fault," I said. "But you don't even know what we're talking about."

"Could you two stop your constant bickering?" Grayson said. "You remind me of—" He stopped cold. "That's it!"

"What's it?" I asked.

"The water tower. You two constantly arguing. It's like the Tower of Babel."

"Huh?" Earl and I grunted at the same time.

233

"It's a Bible story," Garth said, walking up to us. "After the big flood, these people began building a tower that was supposed to reach to the heavens, but God wasn't too happy about it and—"

"We know the story, Garth," I said, shutting him down. I turned to Grayson. "What's your point?"

Grayson locked eyes with me. "Do you know how God was purported to have stopped the construction of the tower?"

"By confusing people," I said. "Making them speak other languages."

"And how could that have been possible?" Grayson asked.

I shrugged. "I dunno."

Earl folded his hands prayerfully. "The Lord works in mysterious ways."

"Indeed," Grayson said. "Ancient accounts of the event reported that 'the people's minds were touched' by some otherworldly source. And that the strange contact caused the people's brains to rewire."

"Rewire?" Earl asked.

Grayson nodded. "Yes. After the tower went down, not only did the people speak different languages, but *strife* was also introduced to what was once a peaceful, unified society. Suddenly, people could no longer work together in harmony. Instead, they began bickering and fighting amongst each other."

"Kinda' like this?" Earl asked, grabbing me in a headlock.

"Let me go, you overgrown ape!" I hissed, struggling to free myself.

"So, what's your point about Babel, Mr. Gray?" Garth asked as Earl and I wrestled.

"My point is, perhaps the same mind-altering process that was used at the Tower of Babel is still going on right now, and *has* been throughout the ages."

"Don't be ridiculous!" I said, grappling to poke my finger in Earl's eye. "Why would some otherworldly source want to zap people's brains just to turn them into jerks?"

Jerks ... jerks ... jerks ...
The word echoed oddly in my head.
Then a flaming bolt of fire shot across my vision.
My knees buckled.
I felt the jar as they hit the ground.
Then my world went black.

Chapter Fifty-Four

I awoke with my head throbbing, unable to move.

Lying spread eagle, my spine pressed painfully against a hard, cold surface. I cracked open an eye. A blinding light stabbed my retina.

Hovering over me was a pasty-faced, alien creature. Its elongated head had a huge gaping mouth and no chin. To my horror, two rows of beady, insectoid eyes ran vertically up and down its narrow face.

Suddenly, a pair of spindly arms reached toward me...

"Breathe," the alien said, then put its open mouth over my own mouth and nose. I didn't know if it was performing CPR or trying to suck out my soul.

Unable to hold my breath, I breathed in. In an instant, my gut curdled from the foul, otherworldly odor emanating from its dry, squishy mouth.

I gotta get out of here!

"Unk," I grunted, willing my frozen body to move.

"She's coming to," I heard a familiar voice say.

Grayson!

I blinked. My vision sharpened. But the reality facing me was almost worse than my nightmarish vision.

I lay sprawled out on the Army-green picnic table like Mullet's dead mattress. And that hideous, alien being French-kissing me? It was actually one of Earl's ginormous, nasty tennis shoes!

"Ack!" I cried out. "Get that thing away from me!"

"Sorry," Grayson said, pulling the shoe from my face. "It was the closest thing we could find to smelling salts."

"Smelling salts?" I asked. "What happened?"

"Earl and you were wrestling, and you suddenly passed out," Grayson said. "Earl tried to stop your fall, and ended up snatching your wig off."

I reached for my bald head. Nothing but skin. "Oh, crap!"

"Oh, crap is right," Grayson said. "That wig was cutting off circulation to your scalp, Drex. Earl saved your life."

"What?" I said, sitting up.

Grayson handed me a mirror. "Take a look."

I studied my bizarre reflection. In addition to the six-inch surgical scar running from the center of my cranium, a deep red ring now lined my entire head. The combination made my head look strikingly like ... a certain feature of the male anatomy that shall remain unnamed.

"Oh. My. God," I said.

"You should have seen it a few minutes ago," Grayson said. "It was purple. Thankfully, circulation is returning. Earl caught this just in time."

"Just in time for what?" I asked. "My public humiliation? Come on, give me my wig back!"

Grayson appeared shocked. "You'd risk death for beauty?"

"Uh, are you totally out of touch with human society?" I said, grabbing at the wig in his hand. "Of course I would!"

"Not on my watch, you won't." Grayson turned the wig inside out and showed me the label. "See that?"

"Hestia?" I read aloud.

"Yes. Drex, Hestia is the name of the Greek goddess of fire. I don't know if it has any correlation to why you've been so crabby lately, but I'm not taking any chances. When was the last time you took this wig off?"

I winced. "Uh ... not since I put it on in the Walmart parking lot three days ago."

"What?" Grayson gasped. "Not even while you were sleeping?"

I winced. "Sorry. I just didn't think about it."

That was a lie. I'd thought about it plenty. But the truth was, every night I'd been hoping Grayson would sneak into the truck with me for a little nookie. I didn't want him to catch me all bald and unattractive.

I glanced at myself in the mirror again.

No worries about that now.

Not only had I been acting like a complete dickhead—I now looked like one, too. I grabbed for the wig again. "Quick, Grayson! Help me cover my head before Earl sees me."

"I'm afraid he already has," he replied. "In fact, he and Garth walked to the camp store to see if they could find something to revive you."

"Great. Just great."

Grayson locked eyes with me. "Can you describe to me what happened?"

I shrugged. "I was just talking—then I saw a flame shoot before my eyes!" I gasped. "Do you think I might've gotten one of those alien Tower of Babel downloads?"

"Unlikely," Grayson said. "This was probably caused by a lack of oxygen to your brain."

"Oh. What about the flame I saw?"

"That would've been you catching a glimpse of your wig as Earl snatched it from your head."

"Oh. Okay."

"I found some ammonia!" Doris said, racing up in her pink golf cart. She spied me and smiled. "She's up! Thank goodness! Honey that was a close call."

"It sure was," Earl said, walking up with Garth.

I cringed. "Does the whole campground know about this?"

Grayson shrugged. "I'd say about half."

Doris hopped out of her cart for a closer inspection. "That's some weird-looking noggin you got there."

Garth laughed. "Pandora, you look like Pat Sajak without his wig."

Doris drew herself up to her full five-feet-nothing. "Pat Sajak is not bald!" she shouted.

Garth blanched. "Oh, no ma'am, I know. I'm referring to the 2008 episode of *Wheel of Fortune*. The one where he pulled that April Fools' Day prank on Vanna."

"Oh. Yes, I remember that," Doris said, chortling.

"What the?" I asked, trying to hide my bald head with my hands.

"You see," Garth said. "There was this rumor going around that Pat wore a rug, because he had a full head of hair back then, even though he was in his sixties. So he had the makeup team put him in a skin head and top it with a toupee. Then Vanna yanked the toupee off Pat for an April Fools' joke."

"It was more than a joke, young man," Doris said. "It was to prove a point. Pat's not only super sexy—he's got a great sense of humor, too."

"Yes, ma'am," Garth said. "He sure does."

"Uh, hello?" I said, still mortified by my phallic noggin. "Does anybody have a hat? A cap? A plastic grocery bag, perhaps?"

Doris smiled up at Garth. "You know, young man, you remind me a lot of Daulton."

I glanced at the little rat dog in the crook of Doris' arm and snickered. Mostly because Doris was dead right.

"You think Garth looks like your dog?" Grayson said. "I fail to see the resemblance."

"What?" Doris said. "Heavens no."

Grayson's eyebrow shot up. "Then you mean the ghost of Daulton Gray? You've seen it?"

Doris' eyes grew wide. She took a step back, holding out her bottle of ammonia like a weapon. "I don't know what kind of drugs you people are on, but I'm referring to Daulton, my grandson."

"Your grandson?" I asked.

"Yes," the old woman said. "You know. The one I keep telling you about. The one who's always getting loose?" She shook her head. "Every time I take my Xanax and watch the *Wheel*, the little jerk sneaks out of the RV. A couple of days ago, he even sawed off his ankle leash!"

"You have a grandson named Daulton staying with you?" I asked. "And you keep him on a leash?"

"Are you high?" Doris said. "Of *course* he's staying with me. I had to take the little runt off my daughter's hands for a few weeks. The pothead got sentenced to house arrest as a juvenile offender."

"Huh," Earl grunted. "Which juvenile did he offend?"

"Uh ... hey, Gramma Doris," a voice sounded behind us.

We all turned to see a skinny, blond, pimple-faced teenager peeking out from behind the border hedge.

"Daulton! There you are!" Doris growled. "Where have you been?"

"Just out," Daulton said.

"Come here!"

Daulton stepped out from the hedge. He was clad in nothing but a pair of black boxer shorts dotted with green alien heads.

"You were prancing around here in your underwear?" Doris gasped. "Are you stoned?"

"No," Daulton said. He shrugged sheepishly. "I just went for a swim last night and somebody stole my Skullet suit."

Chapter Fifty-Five

"You!" I hissed at the knobby-kneed teenager. "You're the guy who's been scaring the crap out of me at night!"

"Hey," the pimply-faced punk said. "At least *my* outfit was fake. Who're you supposed to be? Wiener Woman?"

I blanched. Then my eyes narrowed like a queen cobra about to strike.

Oh no you didn't*!*

I launched myself off the picnic table, penis-head be damned, and made a beeline toward the juvenile pipsqueak. Suddenly, something snagged my arm. It was Grayson, pulling me back.

"Let me handle this," he said.

"But you heard that little shi—"

Grayson tugged my elbow. "Let it go. Do so and I promise I'll make it worth your while."

"Worth my while?" I said, taking another step toward Daulton. "You better make it a Wilshire wig, or I'm gonna pop that kid's pimples with a cast-iron skillet!"

"It is," Grayson said, yanking me back.

I stopped in my tracks. "Seriously?"

"Seriously," Grayson said.

I folded my arms and said, "Fine, then. Proceed."

DORIS' GRANDSON SAT perched in a lawn chair, dressed in the bodysuit of Skullet of Skulleton. The matching rubber skull mask lay in his lap.

Earl, Doris, Garth and I were seated at the Army-green juror's bench beside the charcoal grill, watching like hungry vultures as Grayson interrogated the skeletal perpetrator like a younger, better-looking Perry Mason.

"Get him, Grayson!" I shouted.

Earl stood up and yelled, "If the suit fit, you in the shi—"

"No comments from the jury," Grayson yelled over us. He folded his hands in prayer position. "I request everyone please ignore those outbursts."

Doris swatted Earl on the arm. "Hush! We all know he's guilty, but I want to hear this."

Grayson circled his lawn-chair prey. "Daulton, what motivated you to put on that suit and terrorize my colleague, Ms. Drex?"

Daulton shrugged. "Boredom, I guess. What motivated her to turn her head into a frankfurter?"

"Erase that remark," Grayson said to us, then turned back to Daulton. "Was it not your intention to make Ms. Drex believe you were the ghost of Daulton Gray?"

The kid's face puckered. "Who's that?"

Grayson's eyebrow formed its familiar pyramid shape. "Are you saying that when you remarked to me, 'Don't do it,' then punched me in the nose, that you had no idea about the legend of Daulton Gray?"

"Uh ... yeah," Daulton said. "Look, I just didn't want you to hit me with that stupid badminton racquet."

"You hit him with a badminton racquet?" Doris exclaimed.

"No," Grayson said. "He punched me in the nose, first."

"Daulton!" Doris said. "I'm telling your mother!"

"It was self-defense!" Daulton yelled.

"Aha!" Grayson said. "So you don't deny terrorizing me and my colleague?"

Daulton shrugged. "I guess. Look, mister. It was just a joke."

Grayson's green eyes narrowed. "A joke you played on your grandmother, as well, I suspect."

Doris stood up. "What are you talking about?"

Grayson grabbed the rubber mask from Daulton's hands. "I believe your grandson also owns an alien mask of similar quality. I propose that it was *he* who stole your pee jar."

Doris gasped. "You little shitbird!"

My nose crinkled. "Why would Daulton steal your pee jar?"

Doris ground her dentures. "It wasn't *my* pee. It was *his*. I was taking it to the washroom to test it for drugs, like I do every day."

"Ah," Grayson said. "And Daulton stole it because he knew his urine wasn't going to pass the litmus test."

"I don't know about litmus," Doris said. "I only test for pot and amphetamines."

Earl poked me on the arm. "So, all this time, that flaming skeleton was just a costume?"

I shook my head. "Boy, Earl, you catch on fast."

"No," Earl said. "I mean, I get the skeleton part, but what about the flames?"

I frowned. "I don't know—"

Suddenly, the little rat dog leapt out of Doris' arms.

"Killer! Get back here!" Doris yelled.

"Killer?" I snickered, watching the two-pound, arthritic dog hobble over to a palmetto hedge.

Killer growled, clamped his tiny jaws on something and tugged it free. He pranced back to us, proudly toting a sparkly red clump of fake hair. He dropped it at Doris' feet.

Earl reached down, picked up the mangled wig, and turned to me. "You done lost another one, Bobbie?"

"Gimme that," I said, snatching it from him.

I turned the wig inside out and read the label inside. A smile curled my lips. I stood up and announced, "I think I know how the flames worked."

"How?" Grayson asked.

I smiled smugly. "This is a Diamonette wig."

"So?" Grayson said, coming over for a look.

"The flames we saw were nothing more than a trick of the light," I said, holding the wig up to the sunlight.

"A trick of the light?" Grayson pursed his lips. "That seems implausible."

"Not with a Diamonette wig," I said. "All it took was a good shot of moonlight—and the latest in polyester technology."

Chapter Fifty-Six

With Daulton the juvenile delinquent found guilty on all charges, our makeshift picnic-table jury was officially dismissed.

"I was wondering," I said, helping Doris up from the bench. "Why didn't you take Daulton with you anywhere?"

"Survival," she said, hobbling over to her pink golf cart. "I need my breaks from his constant online gaming. It sounds like a blasted penny arcade inside my RV! Plus, Daulton's under house arrest, remember? He's not exactly a huge source of family pride, if you catch my drift."

Daulton shuffled over in his skeleton outfit. "Come on, Gramma. Let's go. I want to get out of my Skullet suit and have a Hot Pocket."

"No Hot Pockets for you," Doris said, shaking a finger at him. "All you're doing is packing your crap, kid. I've had it. I'm taking you back to your mother's."

WITH DORIS AND DAULTON riding off into the sunset in her deluxe RV, one mystery was solved. But a few others still lingered. Like what really killed Mullet Daniels? Were spirit drums real? And what was the source of those strange white lights?

But I had something else on my mind that needed to be solved first.

"Well, it's disappointing the flaming skeleton wasn't a true spectral phenomenon," Grayson said, waving to Doris as her RV passed by us and disappeared down the road. "But at least we know you weren't hallucinating due to brain damage."

"Yeah, yeah," I said. "Now where's my Wilshire?"

Grayson smirked. "Drex, I must say, you've got a one-track mind."

Yeah. I sorta wish you did, too.

"No I don't," I argued. "But tell me. If your head looked like a dildo, what would be *your* top priority?"

Grayson looked me over. "I kind of like it."

My eyebrows hit what should've been my hairline. "Seriously? Now I *know* you're a pervert!"

Grayson laughed. "Okay. Fine. Follow me."

We went inside the RV. I thought he was going to get the keys for Bessie to take me into town. Instead he began rummaging through a cabinet in the hallway.

"It's *here*?" I asked, surprised. "What are you doing with a Wilshire wig?"

Grayson shuffled things around in the cabinet. "Given your track record with wigs, I figured it wouldn't be long before you'd be needing a backup."

Well, I couldn't argue with that.

"Here it is," Grayson said, pulling out a small box. "You can try it on in the bath—"

"Gimme that!" I said, snatching it from his hands.

I sprinted the three steps to the bathroom and slammed the door. Alone with the box, I opened it and nearly burst into tears. It was the most beautiful wig I'd ever seen.

I slipped the auburn pixie-cut Wilshire wig over my dildo dome and instantly went from Wiener Woman to Bobbie Drex, Goddess of the Universe.

Oh, yeah. That'll work.

Chapter Fifty-Seven

"I feel like a million bucks," I said, emerging from the bathroom sporting my gorgeous, new Wilshire wig.

"Good," Grayson said. "You were in there so long I was beginning to worry."

"Yeah," Earl said. "That new bathroom fan must be exhausted." He winked and nodded. "Exhausted. Get it?"

"Unfortunately, yes," I said.

"Well, you look great," Grayson said.

I should. I just spent half an hour primping.

"You really think so?" I asked coyly.

"Yep," Earl said, shoving a Pop-Tart halfway into his mouth. "I gotta say, you look bettern' a new puppy on Christmas Day."

Coming from Earl, that was really saying something.

I blushed. "Thanks. You know, I feel like going out. Where are you two taking me to dinner?"

"How about that stone crab place you mentioned?" Grayson said.

"It's on!" I grabbed my purse and headed for the door before they could change their minds.

"Too bad we didn't get to see a real ghost," Earl said as we locked up the RV and headed over to Bessie.

"There's still the ghost tower," Grayson said. "And I'm not finished with my investigation into spontaneous human combustion."

"Speaking of human discombobulation, Garth said he had to go to the community outhouse," Earl said. "I think that fourth Hot Pocket at lunch was too much for him."

"Go find him so we can go," I said.

"Yes, ma'am."

Earl walked over to the road, then sprinted back to us. "Uh, look out, I think the Boy Scouts are after you."

Grayson and I turned to see a man in a khaki shirt and olive-green cargo pants approach. "Excuse me," he said. "Could I see your camping permit?"

"Oh. Hello, Ranger Provost," I said. "Uh ... we lost our papers. But we're paid up for the week."

He shot me a dubious look. "Bessie and Frank, I presume?"

I smiled sheepishly. "Uh ... yes."

"Your permit expired at eleven this morning. I'm afraid you're going to have to vacate the site."

"I guess the weed-heads lied to us," Grayson said to me under his breath.

"What was that?" Ranger Provost asked.

"Nothing," I said. "Sorry about the misunderstanding. We'll leave right after we get back from dinner."

"You'll leave right away," Ranger Provost said. "Look, I wouldn't be so hardnosed about it, but the new campers are here, and they're not too happy about finding you still loitering in their spot."

"Loitering?" I said, my ire rising.

"We'll be out of here in ten minutes," Grayson said.

The ranger nodded sharply. "Good."

Grabbing the chance to solve the mystery of the white lights so we didn't have to come back here, I posed a question to Ranger Provost. "Excuse me, but is what Ranger Randini told us about the ghost tower true?"

Ranger Provost's brow furrowed. "Randini? There's no ranger working here by that name."

"Yes there is," I said. "We saw him yesterday. Over where the old water tower used to be."

He shook his head. "You must be mistaken."

"I saw him, too," Grayson said.

"He's a bit younger than you," I said to Ranger Provost. "He had on a uniform like yours. A khaki button-down shirt, with big brass buttons on the lapels and tight boots that came up to his knees."

"Ma'am, my buttons are brown. And knee-boots aren't part of our standard-issue kit. What you're describing sounds to me like a pre-WWII Army uniform."

"Oh. Sorry."

"Now let's move it on out of here, okay?"

"Yes, sir," I said.

Ranger Provost turned back toward the road, shaking his head. As he walked away, I heard him mutter to himself, "And *that's* why we don't allow alcohol on the premises."

Chapter Fifty-Eight

"What did I miss?" Garth asked as he arrived back from his emergency stint in the community washroom. "That ranger I just passed looked pretty pissed."

"Long story," Grayson said. "We'll explain later. But right now, we need to exit the premises, pronto."

Garth showed us his buck-toothed grin. "Evac! This is not a drill!" He laughed. "You got it, Mr. Gray! I'll run get in my Pinto and wait for you all at the main gate."

Garth took off toward the road. Just as he disappeared around the hedge, I heard him yell, "Whoa! Take it easy, man!"

I walked over to the road to make sure Garth was all right. I blanched. Roaring up the lane was an RV as big as a blue whale. It stopped in a whoosh of hydraulic brakes, then idled menacingly at the edge of our campsite entrance.

A horn tooted, and two pairs of angry eyes glared at me from the cockpit. The couple inside looked like a pair of albino manatees clad in the latest in polyester tourist wear.

As I stared at them, the man said something to his wife. Then he raised a giant, ham-hock arm gave me the one-finger salute.

Oh no you didn't, dirtbag!

I grinned, pulled off my wig, then ran my hands up and down the sides of my dildo dome.

The look on their faces was priceless.

WITH EARL THE MOST adept at making the jiggly Popeye face, Grayson and I let him command the RV. I rode shotgun with Grayson in command of the monster truck.

The big jerks in the giant motorhome barely left us enough room to back Bessie out. Instead of reversing to help out, the manatee couple stood their ground, revving their engine and giving us the evil eye.

"What a couple of dipwads," I said. "I don't understand why you left them the badminton net and racquets."

"They gave us no time to recover them."

Grayson glanced over at me and smirked. "With any luck, there's still a little charge left in the battery bank."

I grinned. Then a thought struck me.

"Oh, crap! What'd you do about that hotdog stick booby trap thing?"

Grayson shrugged. "Like I said, they left us no time to fill it in."

Just then, the giant RV's horn blared. The man inside yelled, "Get a move on, you deadbeats!"

Grayson glanced at me. "Should we go back and—"

"No," I said. "Hit the gas. Who are we to mess with universal laws?"

"Universal laws?" Grayson asked, shifting into drive.

"Yeah," I said. "Karma. She's a bitch."

Chapter Fifty-Nine

I guess karma wasn't through with *me*, yet, either. I never got my stone crab dinner. Instead, once again I found myself camping in an old RV in a Walmart parking lot.

Karma really was *a bitch.*

"It's not my fault it's high season," Grayson said, closing his laptop. "I found a motel that had a room for the night, but it didn't meet your standards."

"The pictures online made me long for Mullet's bedroom," I said, sliding into the burnt orange banquette opposite him. "Not the one in the RV, but the roofless one in his burned-up trailer home."

"Well, I hope dinner made up for it," he said, tapping away at his laptop keyboard.

"Yeah, nothing tells a woman she's special quite like a Filet O'Fish sandwich."

Grayson glanced up, his eyebrow arched. "What? I supersized your fries."

My fingers curled into a fist, ready to supersize Grayson's lip. With Earl and Garth away making a run to a u-pull-it junkyard for emergency parts, there would be no witnesses.

"Take a look at this," Grayson said, turning his laptop around to give me a view of the screen. On it, a video was playing. It was of a man in a harness welding off a hunk of metal.

"What is it?" I asked.

"A YouTube video of the old water tower at Fort De Soto being torn down. According to an article I read, the tower was no longer being used, and was costing the taxpayers a fortune in upkeep. So it was dismantled and removed."

"Riveting," I said, pushing the laptop back over to Grayson.

"Or in this case, un-riveting," he said.

I shook my head. Grayson never could tell a joke.

"This is interesting," he said, reading from his laptop. "The water tower was built as part of an Army outpost in 1901, just like Ranger Randini told us. It actually did hold 60,000 gallons of water and was elevated 75 feet up in the air."

"Whoa," I said. "That would put it right about where we sighted that huge white light."

"Indeed."

Grayson glanced down at his laptop. "The Army closed the station in May of 1923, leaving only one caretaker behind. Nine years later, a huge storm called the Florida-Alabama hurricane devastated coastal areas across the western coast of Florida."

"Is there a point to this random barrage of facts?" I asked.

"Always," Grayson said. "Haven't you figured that out yet?"

I sighed and rolled my eyes. "Proceed."

"It says one person died in that storm. Let's see, that would've been 1932. Right between WWI and WWII." Grayson tapped on a few keys. "Here. Look at this."

I glanced at the screen. On it was the photo of a squadron of guys wearing Ranger Randini's exact outfit.

"They look just like Randini," I said.

"This photo was taken in 1931," Grayson said. "Ranger Randini was dressed in period fatigues."

My breath caught in my throat. "Grayson, you don't think Ranger Randini was actually a ghost, do you? That guy who died in the storm?"

Grayson's eyebrow arched. "Quite possibly. Either that, or a retired veteran reliving his glory days in Florida."

"God knows that happens enough," I said. "But no. Randini was too young."

"Or he had an excellent plastic surgeon."

I shot Grayson half a smile for that one, and grabbed the computer away from him.

"Oh my word!" I said. "You're not going to believe this!"

"What?"

I read from the article on the screen. "It says here that in September of 1938, Pinellas County bought the land from the Army for $12,500."

Grayson nodded. "That was a bargain, indeed. But not beyond the scope of believability."

"That's not the unbelievable part."

"What is, then?" he asked.

"You know the land the campground and fort are on?"

"Yes."

"It's called *Mullet* Key."

Grayson's mouth fell open. "You're joking."

"Nope."

A thought hit me. I smiled. "But you know what? Maybe someone else *is*."

Grayson cocked his head. "I'm not following you."

I grinned. "What if Ranger Randini was actually The Amazing Randi, giving us a nod from the other side?"

Grayson smiled. "Interesting theory, Cadet. Interesting indeed."

Chapter Sixty

As the sun set over the steaming asphalt of the Walmart parking lot, I grabbed a Tootsie Pop and opened the case file labeled *Experiment #5*. I'd yet to actually read through Grayson's notes. But given what my life choices had been whittled down to at the moment, reading about charred remains had finally risen to the top like scorched cream.

While Grayson showered, I sifted through the case files. First off was Mary Reeser, aka The Cinder Woman. She'd been the case that had initiated our trip to St. Petersburg in the first place. Next up was Dr. Bentley's case—the old man who'd been reduced to half a leg and a metal walker.

They'd both been elderly, infirm, and alone. But case number three was different. Danny Vanzandt. His was the most recent case on record, and he'd still been on fire when firefighters found him on his kitchen floor. They'd put out his remains, mistaking him for burning trash.

What a weird way to go.

Case number four was new to me. It involved a woman named Countess Cornelia de Bandi. In 1731, her remains were found in her bedroom by her chambermaid.

According to Grayson's notes, the Countess' demise had been investigated by that Rolli guy. He'd blamed her death on "effluvia"—a combination of gases and waste within the stomach and intestines. Coupled with vapors and liquors and body fat, the whole mess had congealed to form a highly flammable substance. If that wasn't unbelievable enough, Rolli had suggested that the ignition source had been the "friction" of the Countess' own breathing!

"That's nuts," I said aloud.

Then I spotted something at the bottom of the page that Grayson had circled with red pen. It seemed even crazier still.

> *The Countess had been reduced to two lower legs and a skull fragment, which had been found between the severed legs. It was as if whatever had happened to her had come upon her all of a sudden, vaporizing her as she stood—leaving the top of her skull to fall to the ground between the remains of her legs.*

"Sheesh," I said, "That's unbelievable!"

I flipped to case number five, wondering how Grayson was going to top case number four. Oddly, the page was blank.

"Finally getting around to it, eh?" Grayson asked.

I looked up from the file and gawked. Grayson had emerged from the bathroom clad in a pink, fuzzy bathrobe. And I'll be damned. He still managed to look good.

"What are you doing in that getup?" I asked.

Grayson shrugged. "I liked the feel of it. So I got it when we went in Walmart this afternoon. I hope you don't mind, but I put it on my expense report."

I laughed. "No worries."

Then I spotted something that made my mouth dry up like a sand sandwich with a side of sand.

It was a bulge.

A giant bulge.

And it was poking from the middle of Grayson's bathrobe.

My ears grew hot.

Was this finally going to be our moment? With me sitting here in dirty sweatpants with a blue Tootsie Pop tongue? Arrgh!

"I've got something for you," Grayson said, sauntering up to me. He reached for the bulge—and pulled a jar from a pocket in the robe.

"A pee jar?" I gasped. "Oh, Grayson! No. Just ... no!"

"It's not a pee jar," he said. "Though I do find the idea rather practical. Don't you recognize it? It's the container holding our vestigial parts."

Grayson scooted into the booth opposite me and set the jar on the table. Inside the amber fluid, two odd globs of flesh floated symbiotically together. One was Grayson's nubbin, removed from just above his naval. The other was the gonad twin removed from my brain.

"Thank god," I said. "For a moment there, I thought we were over."

"Over what?" Grayson asked.

I winced. "Uh ... never mind. On another note, I just finished reading the case files. Why is case number five blank?"

Grayson studied me carefully. "Because it's unfinished," he said. "I have yet to—"

Suddenly, the door to the RV burst open. Earl and Garth came tromping inside.

"We got the parts," Earl said, holding up a greasy carburetor like he was *The Lion King* and that was part was his baby.

"Nice robe, Mr. Gray," Garth said, grinning and pushing up his black nerd glasses. "I've got one just like it. Love that cushy, soft feel!"

Geez. Maybe I should get one ...

"Excellent work, operatives," Grayson said. "Based on new information Drex and I discussed earlier, I believe another trip out to Fort De Soto is warranted. I want to execute one more attempt to witness the white lights reported out there. Who's up for one last stakeout?"

"I am!" Earl said.

"Me, too!" Garth said.

All eyes fell on me.

I sighed. "How could I possibly say no to an offer like that?"

Chapter Sixty-One

The four of us crammed into Bessie's front seat, hipbone to hipbone like human sardines. Mercifully, it was nearly 9 p.m. and dark as soot outside. That meant the only witnesses to our current stupidity were the Walmart parking lot lamps and the bugs flying around the yellow haze of their glowing bulbs.

Grayson shut the door and said, "Let's roll."

Earl cranked the monster truck's engine, then flipped on the headlights.

We all gasped.

Standing thirty feet in front of us was Danny Daniels. Dressed in a sleeveless wife-beater T-shirt and cutoff-jeans shorts, he was caught in Earl's high-beams like an old gopher tortoise toting twin grocery bags.

"Huh," Earl grunted. "Danny must a gone to get him some more cleanin' stuff for the dumpster pool."

I snorted. "There's not enough Mr. Clean in the world to remove *that* human stain."

"Be nice," Earl said, then honked Bessie's truck horn and waved at the guy.

Danny dropped his bags and stared straight at us, his eyes as big as boiled eggs.

"Get your headlights out of his eyes," Grayson said. "You're blinding him."

Earl reached for the switch, then said, "My high-beams ain't on. And the engine done cut out on us."

Earl reached for the keys in the ignition. Despite making his best jiggle face, Bessie wouldn't crank. But my cousin's lunatic Popeye impression wasn't the best show in town.

Not even close.

Ten yards in front of us, a beam of light shone down from the heavens, capturing Danny Daniels in its spotlight.

As we all stared, open mouthed, slowly Danny's bare feet lifted off the ground. Suspended in air, the withered old redneck began to writhe around inside the beam of light like a cockroach caught in a Mason jar full of Mountain Dew.

"It's true! It's true!" Earl hollered.

He laid on Bessie's horn again, then elbowed me in the ribs.

"It's true, Bobbie! Every time a monster-truck horn sings, a Walmartian gets its wings!"

Chapter Sixty-Two

I couldn't believe it. Hovering above the Walmart parking lot was a huge, white orb, just like the one we'd seen at Fort De Soto Campgrounds.

But this one sure as Shinola wasn't lightning refracting inside a cumulonimbus cloud.

As I stared at the glowing oval in the sky, I heard the passenger side door open. Before I could react, Grayson and Garth had jumped out of Bessie and were racing toward Danny, who was still caught in the strange beam of light.

Earl and I turned and stared at each other for a moment. Then we bailed out and hightailed it after them.

We were only a few yards behind Grayson and Garth when the beam of light suddenly cut out. A second later, the glowing orb shot across the sky like a lightning bolt.

"Whoa!" Earl hollered. "I think we done seen us a gen-u-wine alien rocket-ship!"

Suddenly, the lights in the parking lot came back on. I hadn't even noticed they'd gone off.

Too stunned to move any faster than a stunted shuffle, by the time we reached the place where Danny had been hovering above the parking lot, there was nothing left of him but two bags full of Dingdongs and a left foot with the name D-A-N-N-Y-D spelled out—a letter on each toe.

"That was totally freaking awesome!" Garth yelled, jumping around like an idiot, shaking his fist in the air.

As for Grayson, he stood still as a statue, silently surveying the sky.

"I thought you ruled out alien involvement with that neutron detector thing," I said to him.

Grayson glanced over at me. "Not *all* alien craft," he said. "Only those powered by nuclear fusion or fission."

"Hey! Anybody want a Dingdong?" Earl asked. Then he shoved a whole one into his big, dumb mouth.

Chapter Sixty-Three

When we got back to the RV, the door was wide open. I glanced over at the banquette. The jar containing Grayson's and my vestigial body parts was gone.

"Oh my lord," I said. "Somebody took our jar!"

Earl shook his head. "Them alien critters sure do take them a shine to people's pee jars. What's up with that?"

I locked eyes with Grayson. "What does this mean?"

Grayson rubbed his chin. "Either we've been robbed by a human pervert, or Earl's right."

AFTER CHECKING THE RV to make sure no robbers remained in the camper—whichever planet they originated from—the four of us sat around the banquette, still in shock from Danny's unexpected, yet spectacular demise.

"I guess that solves the mystery of spontaneous human combustion," Garth said.

"It does in my book," Grayson said.

The three men exchanged glances, then simultaneously shouted, "Alien laser gun!"

I shook my head. "Shouldn't we notify somebody about Danny?"

"And say what?" Grayson asked.

"Yeah," Garth said, adjusting his *Dungeons & Dragons* ball cap and unwrapping a Dingdong. "You don't want people thinking we're some kind of weirdos!"

My nose crinkled. "What if some wild animal carries away his foot before somebody finds him?"

Garth laughed. "How's a wild animal gonna get into your refrigerator?"

I shot a wide-eyed glance at the mini-fridge.

"I wouldn't open the Dingdong box inside there," Garth said.

"You know that's right," Earl said. "I done learned my lesson with them mystery meatballs."

"Grayson!" I yelled. "How could you?"

Grayson shrugged. "What purpose would it serve to leave Danny's foot lying around for scavengers to get it? Or have it burned as biohazard waste? His death should be put it to good use."

"By selling his foot on eBay?" I said.

"Don't be ridiculous," Grayson said. "They don't allow trading in human body parts anymore."

"We've got other buyers for things like that," Garth said.

"But ... what about his family?" I asked.

"Danny ain't got none, now that Mullet's gone," Earl said. "He done tole me hisself."

"Come on, Drex," Grayson said. "Danny's foot could end up in an incinerator, or it could live on, preserved for posterity."

"What about the cops?" I asked.

"They'd never believe our story in a million years," Garth said.

Grayson nodded. "Garth's right. There's no point in getting tangled up in a no-win investigation."

"So, what happens to Danny then?" I asked.

Grayson shrugged. "I'm afraid Danny Daniels will become another one of the tens of thousands of people who go missing every year without a trace."

"Geez," I said. The thought sent a shiver down my spine.

"You cold, Bobbie?" Earl asked, elbowing me. "Or you just got the honeymoon jitters?"

"Ha ha," I said, then scooted out of the booth.

"Where you goin'?" Earl asked.

"If you must know," I said, glaring at my cousin, "I'm going to brush my teeth and go to bed."

Earl grinned at Grayson. "Gonna be some hot springs in the ol' Walmart parkin' lot tonight!"

"Arrggh!" I growled, then stomped down the hallway to the bathroom.

I WAS PUTTING TOOTHPASTE on my brush when Earl popped his shaggy head in the doorframe. "Night, Bobbie. Sleep tight."

I scowled. "Earl, I wish you wouldn't tease me about Grayson. I don't know where it's going with him, and your stupid comments aren't helping."

Earl's eyebrows rose an inch. "Gosh, Bobbie. I didn't mean no harm. I was just trying to lighten up things. You get so wadded up when you're around him."

I let out a big sigh. "I know. I'm hopeless."

Earl wrapped a big, bear arm over my shoulders. "No you ain't. You're my Cuz, and I love you."

"Yeah, right." I sucker punched him in the gut—but gently. "I love you, too, Earl."

"I know," he said. "Now, take my advice, would you?"

I eyed him with suspicion. "What advice?"

He smiled and said, "If two hearts fit, the love is legit."

I grinned despite myself. "Thank you, and goodnight, Johnnie."

Chapter Sixty-Four

Earl and Garth had gone, leaving me alone in the RV with Grayson. Freshly showered, I donned my best pair of sweatpants PJs and loosened the adjustable band on my fabulous Wilshire wig.

It was now or never.

Nervously, I made my way toward the bedroom. As I did, I thought I heard those damned spirit drums start up again.

Seriously, Karma? Mess this up for me tonight, and I'm gonna rip you a new one!

I opened the bedroom door. Grayson was standing by the window, the air mattress pump in his hand.

"What's going on?" I asked.

"Watch."

He plugged the pump in and set it back on the ground. A familiar thumping sound began to play.

I smirked. "So much for the spirit of Mullet paradiddling away with Titanic in another dimension."

Grayson nodded. "Perhaps Titanic really *did* go down with the trailer."

I laughed, then my nerves got the best of me.

"Grayson, are we ever going to, you know, do it?"

"Solve the mystery of spontaneous human combustion?" he asked. "I thought we just did."

An angry flame of frustration set my ears on fire. "You know, as a comic, you have terrible timing, Grayson. Goodnight. I'm going to go sleep on the sofa."

I turned to go. Grayson caught me by the arm. He pulled me to him and whispered in my ear, "Don't go."

"I'm so confused," I said. "One minute, I think you're into me. The next, I feel like one of your lab experiments!"

"You *are*," Grayson said. "Drex, *you're* experiment number five."

"*What?*"

I beat my fists on his chest. "I knew it! I don't mean anything to you, do I?"

"Let me explain," he said.

"What's to explain?" I yelled. "I'm your lab rat! I get it!" I turned to go, then whipped back around. "Correction. I *was* your lab rat! I quit!"

"Please," Grayson said. "Give me five minutes. Then do whatever you want. I'll understand. And I'll sign off on your private eye training certificate so you can get your license."

My jaw flexed. "You think I'm upset about that lousy P.I. certificate?"

"No, I'm not *that* big a blockhead. But at the moment, it's all I can offer you."

Grayson sat down on the edge of the bed. "Please? Just five minutes. That's all I ask."

Chapter Sixty-Five

"I was on the run when I met you," Grayson said as I stood, arms crossed, and glared at him as he sat perched on the edge of the bed.

"I knew it!" I hissed. "You're a criminal!"

"No. I'm not," Grayson said. "I was running, but I wasn't sure what I was running from. If you recall, I hit my head in the accident, right before I met you in Point Paradise."

"Yeah," I said. "You cracked the windshield."

"Right. I woke up from the accident not knowing who I was or how I got there. I searched my wallet. That's when I found a driver's license and a credit card for Nick Grayson. I figured that was me. The only other thing in there was a business card for a man named Warren Engles."

"The FBI chief?" I asked.

"Yes. I called him, thinking he must've been a friend. But as my memory began to slowly return over these past nine months, I began to question everything."

"Don't tell my you're not really Nick Grayson!" I said.

"No, that part's true. When I figured out all that, I contacted my adoptive parents. You met them. They helped fill in some blanks. After that, gaps in my memory came flooding back."

"Why didn't you tell me any of this?" I asked.

"What could I tell you? I didn't know anything myself until the memories returned. But the odd thing is, I have no recollection of knowing Warren Engles. It's the only gap I have left to fill."

"He must be some bigshot," I said. "I remember when you mentioned his name to the FBI guy who was busting our chops about Mothman, we went from zeroes to heroes in his eyes in no seconds flat."

"Yes," Grayson said. "Apparently Engles pulls significant weight at the FBI. That's why I continued to call him whenever we ran across cryptids we couldn't handle. I figured it was better to assume he was a friend rather than a foe. But the more I've thought about it, the less sure I am about his true intentions."

"What do you mean?" I asked.

Grayson locked eyes with me. "I think Warren Engles is a fisherman—and I'm the bait.

My jaw dropped. "The bait? What are you talking about?"

"I think Engles may be using me. Dangling me here in Florida, hoping for a bite."

I shot a worried look at Grayson. Was he insane?

"A bite from who?" I asked.

"Alien life forms."

I gulped. Before tonight, I'd have run out of here like a madwoman and called 9-1-1 to have Grayson Baker Acted. But since seeing it for myself just an hour ago ...

Hold on. Maybe that's it. That's why he's waited so long to tell me!

"Go on," I said, sitting down on the bed beside him. "How could Engles use you like that?"

Grayson shook his head. "I don't know. Perhaps Engles implanted an alien biological beacon inside me, then erased my memory of it."

"Maybe your first idea was right. Maybe Engles is a good guy and he's just trying to help you out."

"It's a possibility."

"*Or*," I said, "maybe Engles has a whole other scheme in mind altogether."

Chapter Sixty-Six

"What do you mean, Engles might have a different plan going on?" Grayson asked.

"What if he wants to cash in on cryptid artifacts himself?"

Grayson blanched. "What?"

"Remember Occam's Razor," I said, taking Grayson's hand. "Do you really think what we witnessed tonight was the work of aliens from some distant galaxy? Or could it have been an elaborate hoax orchestrated right here, by our fellow Earthlings?"

Grayson's brow furrowed. "A hoax? But to what end?"

"What if whatever happened to Danny was just a decoy designed to lure us away from the *real* cryptid prize?"

The lines in Grayson's brow smoothed. "Our vestigial body parts. Stealing them was the *real* goal."

"Exactly."

Grayson shook his head. "Drex, you could be right."

"If I am, what does that mean about us?"

"I don't know." Grayson squeezed my hand. "All I know is that, for now, the unexplained remains unexplained for a reason. And that in and of itself intrigues me."

"I'm not sure I follow you, Grayson."

He locked eyes with me. "Drex, I don't know if I was born with the desire to chase down the unknown or it was implanted in me. But either way, it's a passion I can't explain. It's like a fire burning deep down inside me."

I nodded. "I know that, Grayson."

"I know you do. But what I'm trying to say is, I'm not like other people."

I laughed. "I know *that*, too."

"I guess I need to be more direct. I believe I possess an inalienable drive to seek out the unexplained. It may very well be a genetic characteristic of my species."

"Your species?" I blanched. "Hold on a minute. Are you saying you're a space alien?"

Grayson's green eyes glowed with a fervor I'd never seen before. "I don't know, Drex. Are *you*?"

My eyebrows shot up. "I don't think so. I mean, my mother was Southern Baptist, for crying out loud!"

"And your father?" Grayson asked.

My gut dropped. "I don't know. All I know about Mr. Applewhite is that he used to be a postman."

Grayson cocked his head. "What more perfect way to surveil humankind unnoticed, than to deliver the mail door to door?"

I grimaced. "That actually makes sense. But then, how do you explain why they sometimes go postal?"

"Easy," Grayson said. "It's not unreasonable to assume aliens would find human life on this planet too perplexing to comprehend. I know *I* do. And no matter how deep I delve into 'the facts' for answers, human behavior remains elusively inexplicable."

Boy, I can relate to that.

"Well, you got me there," I said softly. "But Grayson, you still haven't explained what you meant when you said that *I* was experiment number five."

"Right."

Grayson chewed his lip for a moment. "Drex, I have a confession to make. You're not my first potential mate. There have been four others before you."

Thank god!

"Okay," I said.

"When I met you, I started a folder on you and labeled it *Experiment #5*. But when I needed a folder for spontaneous human combustion cases, I realized I'd used the last one. So I repurposed your file."

"Oh."

Grayson smiled. "I guess, in a way, that makes you the *original* 'hot body.'"

I laughed. "So, you *do* like Earth women, then?"

He shrugged. "That remains to be seen."

Say what?

"What do you mean?" I asked.

Grayson shifted uncomfortably. "I've always thought I was a demisexual because its definition offered the best fit for how I relate to the opposite sex. You see, up to now, I never met a woman who interested me enough to be attracted to her physically."

"So you've never ...?"

Grayson shook his head. "No."

"Hey, so you're no James Kirk," I said. "That's nothing to be ashamed of."

"That's a good analogy," Grayson said. "Because he, too was driven to explore new worlds and new civilizations. But unlike Captain Kirk, I believe in the prime directive."

I stifled a smirk. "Come on, Grayson. Do you think making love to a woman is going to change Earth's course of history?"

He shrugged. "It might. If I'm an alien and I don't know it."

I smiled. "What if I'm an alien, too, and don't know it? Would that still be breaking the prime directive?"

He thought about it for a moment. "No. If we were of the same species, I suppose that would be all right."

I smirked. "Excellent deduction, Cadet."

Prime directive? Amygdala anomaly? Who the hell cares?

I leaned in and laid a giant, wet kiss on Grayson's lips. He didn't resist.

"Shall we proceed?" I asked.

Grayson nodded. "Yes."

I pushed my handsome partner back onto the bed and said, "Come on, Captain Grayson. Let's boldly go where this nerd has never gone before."

The End

I hope you enjoyed Smoked Mullet! If you did, it would be freaking fantastic if you would post a review on Amazon, Goodreads and/or BookBub. You'll be helping me keep the series going! Thanks in advance for being so awesome!

https://www.amazon.com/dp/B09BG5JPL1#customerReviews

Ready for More *Freaky Florida Adventures?*
Find out where Bobbie and Grayson go from here. Check out episode 8, **Half Crocked!**
https://www.amazon.com/dp/B09JCKDPCR

Get a Free Gift!

INTERESTED IN MORE Florida-based mysteries? Sign up for my newsletter and be the first to learn about sales, sneak previews, and new releases! I'll send you a free copy of the *Welcome to Florida, Now Go Home as a* welcome gift!

https://dl.bookfunnel.com/ikfes8er75

For more laughs and discussions with fellow fans, follow me on Facebook, Amazon and BookBub:

Facebook:

https://www.facebook.com/valandpalspage/
Amazon: https://www.amazon.com/-/e/B06XKJ3YD8
BookBub: https://www.bookbub.com/search/authors?search=margaret%20lashley
Thank you!

Excerpt of Half Crocked

Chapter One

I stared at my buzzing cellphone as if it were a humongous rattlesnake about to strike. Uncertainty and anticipation fist-fought in my gut as I watched the phone vibrate and shimmy until it teetered on the edge of the wobbly table beside my rusty lounge chair.

"Come on, Bobbie," I whispered to myself. "You're ready for this."

Before I could lose my nerve, I snatched up the phone. Sending the rickety table and empty margarita glass tumbling over onto the stained pool deck.

"Crap!" I said, then took a deep breath.

You can do this, Roberta Drex.

Just. Stay. Calm.

I clicked the *answer* button, then tried to sound breezy. "Oh. Hi, Grayson."

"Drex," he said. "How are you?"

Tipsy. Tanned. Ten pounds heavier...

"I'm good," I said. "You?"

"Good."

I desperately wanted to say something charming and clever, but a sudden bout of awkwardness blocked my brain and tied my tongue. "Well, uh ... that's good."

"You sound good," Grayson said.

"Uh ... you sound good, too."

"Good."

We listened to each other breathe for a moment. After what seemed like an eternity, mercifully Grayson said, "Are you ready to see our new company vehicle?"

I nearly blanched. "Oh. Uh ... yes. Sure! So you're done with the retrofit?"

"Of course. Otherwise, I wouldn't be calling. That *was* our agreement, wasn't it?"

Grayson's matter-of-fact tone made my heart sink.

So that's it. We're back to strictly business partners.

"Right," I said, hiding my disappointment. "That was our agreement."

"I'd like to give you a test drive," he said, then cleared his throat. "Uh ... I mean in the *vehicle*, of course."

I winced. Apparently, I wasn't the only one feeling completely weirded out by this.

"Okay," I said. "Sure. When—"

"Excellent. I'll be by in five minutes."

"What?" I yelped. "You don't even know where I am!"

I waited for a reply, then realized Grayson had already hung up.

What the?

"You ready for another one?" a voice asked, interrupting my panic attack.

I glanced up from my phone to see a young man in shorts and an unbuttoned Hawaiian shirt. The blonde cutie's name was Ariel. He ran the budget motel's shabby little tiki bar.

"Uh, no thanks," I said, scrambling to my feet and frantically grabbing up my towel and sunscreen.

"Okay. No problemo."

He picked up my empty margarita glass and glanced around, no doubt searching for the five-dollar tip I usually handed him whenever he served me a drink. I peeled one out of my sweaty bathing-suit bra and handed it to him.

"See you this afternoon?" he asked, smiling hopefully.

"Uh ... I'm not sure," I said, hastily inching into my flip flops. "I think I may be checking out today."

The smile on Ariel's boyish face disappeared. "What? You can't leave, Miss Bobbie!"

"Why? Don't tell me you're actually going to *miss* me."

"I sure will." Ariel hung his head and stared at me with puppy-dog eyes. "How am I ever gonna pay for college *now*?"

FIVE LOUSY MINUTES.

My mind raced like a squirrel trapped in a room full of acorns. After three months apart, Grayson had given me just five lousy minutes to prepare for seeing him again.

Typical man!

Sweaty, tipsy, and bloated like a pufferfish, I raced from the shabby pool area, my towel trailing in my wake. Halfway to my motel room, I stubbed my toe on a crack in the sidewalk and blew out my left flip-flop.

"Seriously?" I growled as I hobbled up to my door.

After fiddling the lock open, I tumbled inside, kicked off my other flip-flop, peeled off my sticky bathing suit, and made a beeline for the plastic shower stall for a quick rinse. Sixty seconds later, sweat removed, I dried off with a threadbare towel, then rifled through the pile of semi-dirty clothes heaped atop a rickety bamboo chair wedged in the corner of the room.

After fishing through the crumpled pile for a shirt and shorts with less noticeable strawberry margarita stains, I'd barely managed to button my shirt when a knock sounded at the door.

Crap!

A quick glance through the peephole told me it was Grayson, looking as fit and professional as ever in his black shirt and jeans.

Double crap! No makeup. Not even time to brush my teeth! I bet my tongue is as red as a midlife-crisis Corvette...

Thankfully, at least my hair was passable. Three months apart had given it time to grow out—albeit only to the length of a man's military cut.

But as I ran my hand through my short, damp locks, I wondered why I even cared. Through the peephole, I'd seen that Grayson had regrown that horrible bushy moustache I hated. And his business-like tone on the phone had said what his words hadn't.

Face it, Bobbie. Your budding romance with Grayson is over. Nada. Zilch. Dumpster fodder.

Grayson knocked again. I straightened my shoulders and reached for the doorknob.

Here goes nothing.

I slapped on a smile and flung open the door. "Grayson! How did you know where to find me?"

His handsome head cocked to one side. "Good to see you, too."

I winced. "Sorry. It's just ... well, you caught me by surprise."

"Understandable." His green eyes glanced around the room. "Nice place you have here."

I put a hand to my heart—mainly to hide the large, red, strawberry margarita stain covering half my left boob. "I was trying to be budget conscious."

"Hmm," he said, noting the dated decor. "If I had picked this place, you'd have never ceased complaining about it."

He was right. I wouldn't have. Was I that big a hypocrite?

Grayson's eagle eyes turned to study me. His left eyebrow rose. "Are those blood stains on your blouse?"

My free hand rose to cover a blotch on my belly. "Uh ... no. Hey! You never answered my question. How did you know how to find me?"

"GPS," he said, walking past me into the room.

"GPS?" I asked. I whipped around to follow him, hoping against hope I'd picked up all my dirty underwear. "Is that one of the new gizmos you installed in the RV?"

"No. GPS is a common cellphone app, Drex."

"Oh. Yeah, of course."

Grayson shot a furtive glance at a pair of underpants on the floor, but kept whatever he was thinking to himself. "So, are you ready to see what Garth and I have done to Gabbie?"

"Gabbie?" I asked, kicking the panties under the bed.

"The RV," he said. "I named it. I hope you don't mind."

"Oh. No. That's fine. But why Gabbie?"

"Pack your things and I'll explain on the way."

I snatched my purse from the nightstand and tossed my room key on the bed. "I'm ready. Let's go."

Grayson eyed the mound of dirty shorts and shirts lying in a heap in the corner. "What about your clothes and whatnot?"

"I'll get new ones," I said, shoving Grayson outside.

"Good. I'd like to get going as soon as possible," he said.

As the door closed behind me, he eyed my blouse again. "Are you sure you're okay?"

I nodded.

"Yeah. I don't know what they put in the strawberry margaritas around here, but even Mr. Clean doesn't have the muscle to get the stains out."

Keep reading! Click here to order **Half Crocked now!**
https://www.amazon.com/dp/B09JCKDPCR

More Freaky Florida Mysteries

by Margaret Lashley
Moth Busters
Dr. Prepper
Oral Robbers
Ape Shift
Weevil Spirits
Scatman Dues
Smoked Mullet
Half Crocked

"The things a girl's gotta do to get a lousy PI license. Geez!"

Bobbie Drex

About the Author

Why do I love underdogs? Well, it takes one to know one. Like the main characters in my novels, I haven't lead a life of wealth or luxury. In fact, as it stands now, I'm set to inherit a half-eaten jar of Cheez Whiz...if my siblings don't beat me to it.

During my illustrious career, I've been a roller-skating waitress, an actuarial assistant, an advertising copywriter, a real estate agent, a house flipper, an organic farmer, and a traveling vagabond/truth seeker. But no matter where I've gone or what I've done, I've always felt like a weirdo.

I've learned a heck of a lot in my life. But getting to know myself has been my greatest journey. Today, I know I'm smart. I'm direct. I'm jaded. I'm hopeful. I'm funny. I'm fierce. I'm a pushover. And I have a laugh that lures strangers over, wanting to join in the fun.

In other words, I'm a jumble of opposing talents and flaws and emotions. And it's all good.

I enjoy underdogs because we've got spunk. And hope. And secrets that drive us to be different from the rest.

So dare to be different. It's the only way to be!

Happy reading!

Printed in Poland
by Amazon Fulfillment
Poland Sp. z o.o., Wrocław

86947481R00169